Death in a Cold Climate

A Guide to Scandinavian Crime Fiction

Barry Forshaw

palgrave
macmillan

First published 2012 by
PALGRAVE MACMILLAN

Palgrave Macmillan in the UK is an imprint of Macmillan Publishers Limited, registered in England, company number 785998, of Houndmills, Basingstoke, Hampshire RG21 6XS.

Palgrave Macmillan in the US is a division of St Martin's Press LLC, 175 Fifth Avenue, New York, NY 10010.

Palgrave Macmillan is the global academic imprint of the above companies and has companies and representatives throughout the world.

Palgrave® and Macmillan® are registered trademarks in the United States, the United Kingdom, Europe and other countries.

ISBN 978–0–230–30369–0   hardback
ISBN 978–0–230–36144–7   paperback

This book is printed on paper suitable for recycling and made from fully managed and sustained forest sources. Logging, pulping and manufacturing processes are expected to conform to the environmental regulations of the country of origin.

A catalogue record for this book is available from the British Library.

A catalog record for this book is available from the Library of Congress.

10   9   8   7   6   5   4   3
21 20 19 18 17 16 15 14 13 12

Printed and bound in Great Britain by
CPI Antony Rowe, Chippenham and Eastbourne

Crime Files Series

General Editor: **Clive Bloom**

Since its invention in the nineteenth century, detective fiction has never been more popular. In novels, short stories, films, radio, television and now in computer games, private detectives and psychopaths, prim poisoners and overworked cops, tommy gun gangsters and cocaine criminals are the very stuff of modern imagination, and their creators one mainstay of popular consciousness. Crime Files is a ground-breaking series offering scholars, students and discerning readers a comprehensive set of guides to the world of crime and detective fiction. Every aspect of crime writing, detective fiction, gangster movie, true-crime exposé, police procedural and post-colonial investigation is explored through clear and informative texts offering comprehensive coverage and theoretical sophistication.

Published titles include:

Maurizio Ascari
A COUNTER-HISTORY OF CRIME FICTION
Supernatural, Gothic, Sensational

Hans Bertens and Theo D'haen
CONTEMPORARY AMERICAN CRIME FICTION

Anita Biressi
CRIME, FEAR AND THE LAW IN TRUE CRIME STORIES

Ed Christian (*editor*)
THE POST-COLONIAL DETECTIVE

Paul Cobley
THE AMERICAN THRILLER
Generic Innovation and Social Change in the 1970s

Michael Cook
NARRATIVES OF ENCLOSURE IN DETECTIVE FICTION
The Locked Room Mystery

Barry Forshaw
DEATH IN A COLD CLIMATE
A Guide to Scandinavian Crime Fiction

Emelyne Godfrey
MASCULINITY, CRIME AND SELF-DEFENCE IN VICTORIAN LITERATURE

Christiana Gregoriou
DEVIANCE IN CONTEMPORARY CRIME FICTION

Lee Horsley
THE NOIR THRILLER

Merja Makinen
AGATHA CHRISTIE
Investigating Femininity

Crime Files
Series Standing Order ISBN 978–0–333–71471–3 (hardback)
978–0–333–93064–9 (paperback)
(*outside North America only*)

You can receive future titles in this series as they are published by placing a standing order. Please contact your bookseller or, in case of difficulty, write to us at the address below with your name and address, the title of the series and the ISBN quoted above.

Customer Services Department, Macmillan Distribution Ltd, Houndmills, Basingstoke, Hampshire RG21 6XS, England

'With customary depth and precision, Forshaw gets under the skin of this celebrated genre, uncovering many of its secrets and riches. Like its subjects, this book is hard to put down, and will undoubtedly be returned to time and again.'

– Dr Steven Peacock, University of Hertfordshire, UK

'Not a stone is left unturned in Barry Forshaw's witty, encyclopedic investigation into the fictional crimes that have made Scandinavia the most talked about region in the world of books. *Death in a Cold Climate* is a unique and admirable personal testament to the writers, translators and publishers who have dedicated themselves to introducing Scandinavian crime fiction, its many languages and cultures, to the English speaking world. If upon turning the last page of Forshaw's book you are not immediately heading for the nearest bookstore to buy up every Scandinavian crime novel on its shelves, you were probably not meant to read this book in the first place.'

– Jakob Stougaard-Nielsen, University College London, UK

Barry Forshaw is a writer and journalist specialising in crime fiction and cinema. His books include *The Man Who Left Too Soon: The Life and Works of Stieg Larsson* (2010), *British Crime Writing: An Encyclopedia* (2008), *The Rough Guide to Crime Fiction* (2007), *Italian Cinema: Arthouse to Exploitation* (2006) and the forthcoming *British Crime Film* (2012), and he has contributed to the *Directory of World Cinema*. He has also written for a variety of national newspapers as well as for *Movie Mail*, Waterstone's *Books Quarterly* and *Good Book Guide* and is editor of the online *Crime Time* magazine. He is also a talking head for the ITV Crime Thriller author profiles and BBC TV documentaries, and has been Vice Chair of the Crime Writers' Association.

Contents

Acknowledgements

When writing *Death in a Cold Climate*, I decided that it was important to call on more than my own resources. Writing about, reviewing and interviewing many Scandinavian authors for both print and broadcast media over the years has brought me into contact with most of the principal writers, publishers and translators of this astonishingly rich genre, but it was important for me to ensure that my impressions were as up-to-date as I could possibly manage. To that end, I contacted again every author I could with whom I had previously spoken, along with many with whom I had not been in touch before. In the entire field of Nordic crime fiction I found a welcome readiness (almost without exception) among novelists to discuss their own writing, and to answer the many questions I had about their individual countries and societies. Similarly, all of the doughty translators of my acquaintance (along with several I had not met) proved equally ready to give me their impressions – this was particularly important to me, as it is an open secret to all cognoscenti of fiction in translation how crucial is the role of these talented people. I also called upon one of the key crime fiction journalists in Britain, Bob Cornwell, whose research work on international crime fiction for *Tangled Web* is prodigious (when editing *Crime Time*, I found his 'crime scene' articles on a variety of countries invaluable in the sheer depth of their organisation), and he has made a great deal of material available for me for this book. Rather than thanking the many individual authors who have been helpful, I would simply direct the reader to the variety of entries that follow. But I would like to register a special mention for three of the most important translators in Britain: Sarah Death (who also edits *Swedish Book Review*, the files of which she generously opened for me); the immensely well-informed Tom Geddes; and the man who bids fair to be the doyen of Scandinavian translators in this country, Laurie Thompson (a man who avoids the Metropolis like the plague). A woman who doesn't mince her words, Sofia Odsberg of the Nordin Agency, has been an early warning system for me regarding new talent (and helpfully – and patiently – corrected my Swedish pronunciation, when we both worked for *Publishing News*). Several obliging people at London's various Scandinavian embassies have also been a highly useful resource, such as the cosmopolitan Stein Iversen of the Norwegian Embassy, as has Jakob Stougaard-Nielsen of University College London. And being invited to a Saint Lucia evening at the Swedish Ambassador's residence by Carl Otto Werkelid and Ann Nilsen helped put me in the right Nordic mindset. Without these individuals on my side, my task would have been considerably more difficult.

Although not strictly accurate, the words 'Scandinavian' and 'Nordic' are used throughout this book to refer to the countries of Sweden, Norway, Iceland, Finland and Denmark.

Where two dates are listed for novels, parentheses indicate the English-language publication date and square brackets the year of publication in the original language.

Introduction

The Scandinavian literary invasion is complete – at least in terms of crime fiction produced in the Nordic countries: now, in sympathetic translations, that fiction is jostling for pole position with (often resentful) British and American practitioners in the field. The Vikings made bloody sorties against Britain in the era when storytelling was largely an oral form. Thirteen centuries later, however, the descendants of those ruthless pillagers now make their mark not with axes but with computer keyboards, dispensing bleak and atmospheric (but strangely exhilarating) genre fiction. Long after their ancestors left their mark on hapless Britishers, more and more British readers are coming to the realisation that crime fiction from the Scandinavian countries affords subtle pleasures often more rich and atmospheric than those provided by the standard British or American variety with which we are so familiar. But just why has the field of Nordic crime fiction in translation – for so long caviar to the general – become such a hot ticket in recent years? The desire for novelty in an exhausted, over-visited field? That is one factor, certainly, but there are a variety of reasons – and the study of this phenomenon makes for some fascinating conclusions, relating as much to the insights into Scandinavian society provided by this fiction as much as to any intrinsic literary merit (and regarding the latter, it is undoubtedly true that Nordic crime fiction carries a more respectable cachet – justifiably or otherwise – than similar genre fiction produced in Britain or the US). Novelty and perceived 'quality' are both factors in the astonishing success in Britain of the lengthy, slow-burning Danish TV series *The Killing*, which refracted and reinvented police procedural clichés through an intriguing Danish prism; the actress Sofie Gråbøl, as the tenacious, unsmiling copper Sarah Lund with a dysfunctional personal

1

life (in unvarying black-and-white Faroe Island jumper), is now a cult figure, and has even generated leader columns in *The Times*.

Despite the proximity to each other of the various Scandinavian countries, their individual identities are remarkably pronounced, and the patience generally shown by the inhabitants when the British and the Americans lazily lump all the Scandinavian nations together is admirable – it is a laziness that this study will do its best to avoid. However, if there is anglocentric bias here, it lies in the concentration on authors available in translation, for ease of general reader accessibility – though I have made an attempt to include key names from the past not available in English, and promising authors yet to be (or on the point of being) translated. The eternal publishers' question: 'Who is the Next Big Name in Scandinavian crime fiction?' is answered – somewhere in this book.

But the commercial exigencies are only one consideration here (albeit a persuasive one in making a mass of unfamiliar material available in translated form): any intelligent reader of the genre will quickly become aware of the sociopolitical insights afforded by the novels, building up a complex picture of Scandinavian society – in particular, the cracks that have appeared in the social democratic ideal, an ideal which has been cherished for so long by observers in America, Britain and the rest of Europe.

But these insights, it should be stressed, are not conveyed by any po-faced editorialising on the part of the various Nordic authors: such notions have appeared, *inter alia*, within the context of reader-friendly popular fiction, in which the pleasures of narrative remain paramount. In this context, the analysis of society freighted into the novels is more forensic and detailed than in the crime fiction of virtually any other country, even within the orbit of such mordant social critics as the writers James Lee Burke (in America) and Val McDermid (in Britain). The political narrative of this cold wind from the North was clearly worth both anatomising and expanding – and those are two of the imperatives of this volume (along with a celebration of the crucial role of translation). *Death in a Cold Climate* attempts to place all the key authors and their work in the context of social changes in their respective countries, and illustrates the radical revision (via the novels) of fondly held British and American images of Nordic society.

While writing the first biography of Stieg Larsson (and covering and interviewing Nordic writers for a variety of newspapers and magazines), along with recording television and radio programmes on Scandinavian crime fiction, it became clear to me that there had not been a definitive book on what is now a key arena of the crime fiction field: writing from Sweden, Denmark and the other Scandinavian countries, already highly successful in its native countries and Germany. But by the first decade of the twenty-first century, the books were beginning to break through in Britain and America. The fact that there is an ever-growing market is clearly evidenced by the TV, radio and newspaper articles now appearing on the subject – and the current initiatives by many publishers to sign up new Scandinavian authors to (hopefully) match the sales of Mankell, Larsson *et al.* (a marked change from several years ago, when Scandinavian literary agencies trying to sell the rights to their hard-to-pronounce authors in Britain were met with an unenthusiastic response).

Many authors are content to relate their narratives in carefully organised, linear fashion without attempting to test the elasticity of the medium. The result: work which is weighted with precisely those elements required to produce a Pavlovian response in the reader, with all the customary elements (suspense, obfuscation, resolution) employed in a straightforward contract between author and reader. Scandinavian crime fiction, however, is more prepared to toy with notions of improvisation and destabilisation of the generic form, producing writing which may sketch in the rough parameters of the crime novel but also attempts to expand the possibilities of the medium – those possibilities which so often remained unexplored. The publishing industry, of course, survives (and thrives) by creating a production-line product without any individual signature (or, to put it another way, with an anonymous but reliable series of signifiers that will satisfy the undemanding crime reader). In fact, the great majority of product coasts by with this kind of anonymity, and to some degree this is a consequence of the dictates and expectations of the reading audience. There is often an initial resistance to unfamiliar, convention-stretching innovation which is why so much anodyne product is available. Even the least ambitious Nordic fiction, however, is often prepared to take some audacious steps into the unknown, producing fiction which can function as both popular product and personal statement from the author.

This is not to say that the elements of innovation (or improvisation) are incorporated into the majority of Nordic crime novels – the field has more than its fair share of workaday writers. But the very best novelists are well aware that it is almost always necessary to resist lazy, warmed-over conclusions delivered by rote about both society and human psychology within the context of a crime novel. Such writers – the most ambitious practitioners of the form – are temperamentally unable to merely recycle and reheat clichés and various second-hand aspects of the genre. These writers are obliged to dig more assiduously beneath the engaging surface of popular fiction and discover the hidden striations of meaning and significance that are often under-exploited in the crime fiction genre. With a newly forged technical and psychological armoury in place, the writer with this approach has a capacity to elevate the genre above its most basic entertainment status. Again, this level of ambition appears to be more readily employed in the Nordic countries.

Denmark remains a country that can lay claim to the most European of identities, with its residents defining themselves by their cosmopolitan nature and the easygoing attitude exemplified by life in the capital Copenhagen. By contrast, the forbidding landscapes of Norway (with its storm-blown northern coast and massive fjords) belong to a region that can seem exotic and challenging to metropolitan outsiders. The inhabitants are proud of the fact that they are not living cheek-by-jowl with their neighbours – residents of Norway are widely spread throughout the region. It is, undoubtedly, a country in which it is possible to breathe. Isolated communities are spread along the line of the coast which reaches to the borders of Russia.

It is sometimes frustrating for many residents of Scandinavia that Sweden is often considered a sort of catch-all generic term for the four countries. The reasons are not hard to see: the massive Swedish successes in terms of exports, both cultural and commercial, and the long-held view that the country's enlightened politics represent a perfect exemplar (although that is a view challenged by the work and publicly expressed opinions of many of the authors examined in this book). Certainly, in strictly numerical terms, Sweden's crime fiction practitioners outnumber those from other Nordic countries, although this situation is in a state of flux. Regarding the striking physical qualities of Sweden, its worldwide reputation is impossible to contest: the exquisite lakes and wooded areas stretching for many miles create a landscape almost without equal in the world.

Which is not to deny the immense, bracing appeal of neighbouring Finland. To some degree, this is a country that is still (even today) coming to terms with its own independence; for centuries it was Swedish territory, before the Russian invasion established a new domination, and the historical scars remain deep. The resistance to Russian occupation is something celebrated in the music of the country's greatest composer, Jean Sibelius, whose settings of nationalistic texts were immensely influential (though the true genius of the composer resides in his abstract, European 'absolute' music – in the latter respect, Sibelius is something of a harbinger of the writers discussed in this book who eschew an uncomplicated nationalism in favour of more nuanced views of their country). The Finns, more than most Scandinavians, are fiercely proud of their sometimes breathtaking natural environment – and, similarly, are proud of their linguistic difference from their Nordic neighbours (the Finnish language is utterly different from that of its neighbours, with strikingly distinct – and ancient – etymological roots).

The geographical relocation of the crime genre northwards was initiated by the unprecedented success – both critical and commercial – of one book. The fulsome acclaim granted to Peter Høeg's *Miss Smilla's Feeling for Snow* (published in Britain by Christopher MacLehose at Harvill in 1993) was a clarion call to British readers that there was (in the words of Shakespeare's Coriolanus) 'a world elsewhere'. Here was intelligent, exquisitely honed crime fiction infused with all the textural complexity of more overtly literary fare, spreading before us an intriguing new topography for the crime fiction genre. That book's stamping ground, vividly evoked, was Copenhagen and Denmark. But Høeg's *Miss Smilla* was merely the visible tip of the iceberg: the Scandinavian territories (readers were to learn) afforded an impressive new panoply, with the Swedish maestro Henning Mankell as the standard bearer, chronicling the darkly mesmerising narratives of Kurt Wallander. Stockholm is the haunt of another talented writer, Liza Marklund, with her tenacious investigative journalist heroine, not to mention Jens Lapidus's lacerating and uncompromising *Stockholm Noir* sequence, offering a more cosmopolitan canvas than those of the other writers. Not far away on the map can be found the very different writing of the coolly observant Mari Jungstedt, transporting the reader to the windblown island of Gotland, where bloody murder is dispassionately done. Other possibilities in this striking new literary landscape might include a trip to Åke Edwardson's menacing Gothenburg, or the Reykjavík of Arnaldur Indriðason (whose *Jar City* – also known as *Tainted Blood* – written in pared-down existential prose, was one of several Trojan horses for the new Nordic writing), or Karin Fossum's bleak and emotionally frigid Norway. As for the Sweden of the all-flattening juggernaut that was the *Millennium* trilogy of the late Stieg Larsson, sales records were broken – and continue to be broken – on an almost daily basis by readers eager for a journey into Larsson's dark world; the 2009 film of his first book, *The Girl with the Dragon Tattoo*, is now comfortably the most successful Swedish movie of all time. No other writer from outside the Anglo-Saxon orbit has matched the astonishing success of the late investigative journalist, a specialist in tackling extremists and far right organisations (not to mention arguing for the rights of women in fundamentalist Middle Eastern countries) before his untimely death at the age of fifty. The headlong rush by publishers' marketing departments to sign up still-productive successors to the creator of tattooed and pierced Goth anti-heroine Lisbeth Salander is having a truly seismic effect on the book trade, with talented fellow Scandinavian Jo Nesbø now (it would appear) having snatched the Larsson crown (even though his books – highly impressive after their own fashion – are not greatly like those of his late confrère). I am probably obliged to enter a personal *mea culpa* here, as one of my comparisons between the two writers now appears, slightly finessed, on Nesbø's book jackets.

If this book is an examination of why the field of Nordic crime fiction in translation – for so long a minority taste – has become so commercially successful, it is necessary to stress both literary factors and the genre's foregrounding of political and socioeconomic observations. And there is another key factor: the language in which non-Nordic readers can access this material, facilitated by the skill of translators both highly adept and more workaday. The translations via which English readers encounter the novels of Johan Theorin, Camilla Läckberg and their compatriots are not quite the books that their authors created – and the rendering of Scandinavian literature into English offers problems to their translators that are subtly different to those encountered in other languages – one of the issues keenly examined here. It is perhaps worth investigating the subtle shift in emphasis between the work of various translators and whether or not any degree of finessing the original author's intentions may be discerned: an example of this shift may be noted in comparisons (in another medium) between the Swedish and British television adaptations of the Kurt Wallander novels (and the various non-Mankell-derived extrapolations of the character). The original series shoots its Swedish locales in a flat, naturalistic fashion with absolutely no attempt at importing extra aesthetic appeal, while the British series (admirable in its own fashion) repeatedly foregrounds the intense beauty of the country, presenting it as waving fields of wheat, russet-coloured sunsets and so forth. It might be argued that (in similar fashion) certain translators incorporate a discreet element of editorialising by their very choice of adjectives and nouns.

Sarah Death is one of the most respected translators of Scandinavian books in Britain (a recent assignment is Kristina Ohlsson's *Unwanted* (2011) for the British arm of the publisher Simon & Schuster). She also edits the influential *Swedish Book Review*.

She sees the particular challenges of translating Scandinavian crime fiction as specifically relating to writing characteristics of the individual authors – the problems will be much the same as they are with a non-crime writer: to convey another culture, and an author's distinctive style if they have one, but fluently in the translator's own mother tongue.

'A novel set in a remote northern wasteland will have some challenges of geographical terminology,' she suggests. 'Getting the right equivalent for, say, Scandinavian police ranks can be a little tricky, and there might be technical vocabulary involved. A historical novel needs the right vocabulary for the period. The social differences will not be as vast as those between Britain and some other language areas, but there are always the quirks of another culture to get across. Gruesome plots can be rather stressful to translate of course, but the most gut-churning content I have had to grapple with on occasions has in fact not been in books of the crime fiction genre.

'It does, of course, help if you can visualise the settings. There is never time or funding to go to visit a specific place for the purpose, so it is just luck if one has been there or can arrange a relevant holiday round one's work.'

Asking Sarah Death whether or not it is necessary to be familiar with the mores of a country for translation purposes produces a thoughtful response.

' "Cultural competence" is, of course, crucial to a good translation. But this is something literary translators should have acquired gradually over their many years of apprenticeship, while trying to get a first foot in the publishing door, and then as practitioners. They will have it securely there in the background when they get down to the linguistic nitty-gritty. I make an effort to keep abreast of politics in the countries represented in the books I am translating, by talking to acquaintances in Sweden, colleagues at University College London, and reading newspapers online.

'I might learn something about a country when doing the initial read-through of a novel before I start translating, or when I am reporting on other books in the genre for publishers. But once I am in the grip of the text I am not thinking about mores, politics or the bigger picture. I am operating at a more micro level: thinking about characters and point of view, register, weighing words, keeping my vocabulary wide, recreating natural dialogue, trying to emulate the style of the original if it has a distinct one, and so on.

'British and American readers are getting the sort of picture that one can imagine getting of any country from only reading its crime fiction. Readers are getting some reasonable social insights, but are not getting a representative sample of what is on offer in modern Swedish literature. But this isn't a new phenomenon: translation has always been market-oriented. Icelandic-saga translator Keneva Kunz's line "No one but a blockhead ever translated except for money" is à propos (it can be found in Peter Bush and Kirsten Malmkjaer (eds), *Rimbaud's Rainbow: Literary Translation in Higher Education* (John Benjamins, 1998)).

'There are also distortions going on as a result of the translated crime boom: some Swedish writers almost seem to be writing to order. Agents are over-selling, as is their wont, and one fears British publishers scrambling for Swedish crime fiction are on occasion acquiring some rather third-rate stuff nowadays. But the appeal remains the same: we are shown a country which is different from Britain – but not too different. The lure of the (slightly) exotic, plus a vague sense of schadenfreude that the wheels are coming off the utopian welfare-state bus. There is an unquenchable thirst for a steady supply of plot-driven material among general readers. The avid readers in the reading group at my local library look rather blank when I ask them what they thought of the style, or the translation, of a crime novel from another country, and say they were just carried along by the story.

'Having said that, the only book I have ever in my life stayed up all night to read was Kerstin Ekman's *Händelser vid vatten* (1993) in the original Swedish. This is so much more than a crime novel and is written in Ekman's inimitably rich style, but I have to admit that on that occasion it was the remote upland setting and narrative tension as much as the poetry of language and the insights into environmental vandalism and rural depopulation that kept me from bed. The late Joan Tate's workmanlike English rendering (published as *Blackwater* in 1995) is absolutely fine for plot-hungry readers.

'For anyone wanting to read up on translation theory (which the majority of currently practising fiction translators, including me, have never studied, by the way), anything by Susan Bassnett is pretty approachable for the layman. The classic text is Lawrence Venuti's *The Translator's Invisibility* (1994). Everyone quotes his theory about 'domestication' versus 'foreignisation' in translation.'

The image of Scandinavia cherished in Britain and the rest of Europe is sometimes a lazy one, evoking as it does a variety of contradictory notions: initially, of course, the unspoilt vastness of the fjords, gambolling reindeer and modern, well-designed towns inhabited by blonde-haired, healthy types with virtually no subcutaneous fat. These lotus eaters benefit from a perfectly functioning welfare state. (It is an image that bears some tangential relationship to reality, but begs a host of questions; questions that are trenchantly addressed by the often anti-establishment probings of Scandinavian crime fiction.)

The other clichéd image, of course, involves long nights in the land of the midnight sun – long nights that (in contrast to the idyllic images detailed above) present the perfect stage for simmering familial resentments and the violent dispatch of inconvenient spouses or business associates. It is interesting to note that the shop-worn imagery with its picturesque vistas of unspoilt terrain is less utilised by Nordic novelists today than the urban landscapes of the south (where the greatest concentration of population is found). The nightlife, businesses, urban sprawl and cultural upheavals caused by mass immigration are, it seems, far more fertile territory for those dealing in the darker aspects of human behaviour than the picture-postcard landscapes that fuel most non-Scandinavian imaginations. However, rural traditions still hold sway within much of the land inside the Arctic Circle, and the region's indigenous population maintain their centuries-old trades of hunting and fishing. Fertile territory, one might have thought, for crime writers – but used less than the more familiar urban landscapes (and possibly, therefore, allowing for a more straightforward recognition of the parallels between English, American and Scandinavian society). It is notable, for instance, that following the original Swedish television adaptations referred to above of Henning Mankell's Wallander novels from the production company Yellow Bird (also responsible for the films based on the *Millennium* trilogy of Stieg Larsson), the same company was involved in the production of the British series starring Kenneth Branagh. English audiences were massively enthusiastic towards the latter, having no problems with a largely English cast, speaking English but set down in a genuine Swedish milieu. The alienated detective's name was now pronounced (for the benefit of the language-challenged British and Americans who could not have coped) with a 'W' rather than a fricative 'V', with the stress now comfortably on the first syllable rather than the second. With the concept thus anglicised, British television audiences began to see Swedish locations such as Ystad as slightly more picturesque versions of, say, London and Manchester – it might be argued that the success of the show is down to this piquant synthesis of familiarity and novelty.

The classical literature of the Scandinavian countries is insanguin-ated (the *locus classicus* is, of course, the Icelandic saga); bloody death has long been a principal concern of many of the region's great writers, right up to their current heirs. The earliest examples of Scandinavian literature are from the era of the Vikings, a legacy that precedes the separate literary traditions of individual countries in the region. And the development of this literature notably (and famously) followed fatalistic and gloomy lines; the perfect breeding ground, in fact, for the criminal pursuits of modern Scandinavian literature. The Norwegian master Henrik Ibsen and his equally celebrated Swedish colleague August Strindberg dealt in a particularly scabrous view of human relationships, and although the fates of their protagonists are not tied to criminal-ity, the slow, painful uncovering of dark secrets (as in Ibsen's *Ghosts*) is the *lingua franca* of crime fiction. Similarly, the most acclaimed of Scandinavian directors – and the film-maker who many would consider to be the greatest artist to have worked in the cinema – Ingmar Bergman, moves in a universe in which the interaction between his characters, violent, extreme and confrontational, suggests parallels with the darker recesses of the human soul customarily accessed in crime fiction. (The look of Bergman's films, too, is often redolent of the crime genre – the director was an admirer of the American film noir genre, and the moody black-and-white cinematography of his films frequently bears echoes of the highly influential work of John Alton, director of photography for the crime films of director Anthony Mann.) All of these antecedents, of course, are part of the woof and weave of Scandinavian culture, and (more than in most countries) these high culture antecedents have left a pronounced mark on popular genres such as the crime field – in fact, Henning Mankell's father-in-law was no less than Ingmar Bergman, and both men joked about the fact that the world perceived them as the principal spokesmen for the dark, astringent view of the world that was generally identified as Scandinavian.

Any serious consideration of Scandinavian crime fiction must be finessed by a consideration of the influence – direct or otherwise – of all the characters and narratives of the great Nordic myths, notably the highly influential *Volsung* saga. The mythology surrounding Scandinavian heroes and gods is, of course, not simply a part of the cultural inherit-ance of Icelanders and the further reaches of northern Europe. Many of the great artists of Britain and Germany, for instance, were heavily influenced (and their successors continue to be) by the myths that inform the cultural consciousness of the region. Richard Wagner trans-muted these myths into his massive operatic tone poem *Der Ring des*

Nibelungen, and cinema audiences enthusiastically followed generations of readers in a willing immersion in J.R.R. Tolkien's rewriting of similar myths in his *Lord of the Rings* cycle. The whole colourful mythological *dramatis personae* of the literature of myth has proved ripe for reinterpretation and reimagining, both directly and by their use as metaphor: the powerful gods and resilient heroes, but also the unspeakable monsters and demons which often provide the most entertaining facets of the myths (the latter have more than a few modern incarnations in Nordic crime fiction, even occasionally bearing characteristics of the preternatural). The quest of legend, of course, may be seen to have been transmogrified into the solving-of-a-mystery journey undertaken by the modern detective protagonist. More intriguingly, sociological aspects of modern crime writing also channel this compendious literature of myth: sacrificial rituals, burial rites and etymology are all treated to intelligent reworkings (even to the extent that several characters in mythology perish via curiously 'passive' deaths).

To some degree, the picture of Scandinavian society conveyed through its crime literature is an accurate one, though inevitably tendentious. British crime writers such as Colin Dexter frequently make sardonic comments about the necessary massaging of reality to produce their murderous crime scenarios; and in the same way that Dexter's Oxford has a considerably higher body count than the actual geographical location, it would be rash to extrapolate from Scandinavian crime fiction any concrete conclusions about the society depicted (interestingly, while Scandinavian readers are proud of the worldwide success of such books as *The Girl with the Dragon Tattoo*, they are a little uneasy with the devastatingly negative picture of virtually all the important institutions in Sweden presented by Stieg Larsson – while acknowledging the author's strategy in throwing up a labyrinthine network of conspiracy and corruption for his protagonists to become enmeshed in).

Finland, Norway and Sweden can boast some of the lowest crime rates in Europe (even though that admirable record has faltered recently, notably with the tragic killings in Norway in July 2011), while Denmark hews more closely to European norms, with an unenviable record for robbery, car theft and racially aggravated crime. Sweden can claim the lowest rate of burglary in the European Union. Denmark's record may be contrasted with the admirably low crime rate in Finland. Attitudes to the forces of law and order vary from country to country, with the Danes demonstrating a largely unalloyed confidence in their police force – an attitude also found in Sweden (it is instructive to compare these facts with the grim picture of endemic police corruption presented in the work of many of the country's most successful writers). One area that has seen a notable increase in the reporting of criminal incidents is that of sexual offences against women (perhaps due to the postwar adjustment of the relative status of men and women), and this incendiary area has become much utilised territory for Scandinavian crime writers.

A constant source of annoyance – or wry acceptance – among Swedes visiting Great Britain is the fondly held, slightly envious British notion (also nurtured by Americans) of Sweden as a fount of sexual liberation and erotic adventure; a land without inhibitions where all forms of erotic behaviour are tolerated, and saunas are used more creatively than simply to open the pores of the skin. Much of this perception stems from the sexual revolution of the 1960s, which was by no means a solely Swedish phenomenon. The writer Håkan Nesser is fond of nailing one particular culprit in this identification of unbuttoned sexuality with the Swedes: the great international success of the 1967 film *I Am Curious Yellow* (directed by Vilgot Sjöman), which, though largely a dispiriting (and would-be humorous) left-wing political tract, famously featured a good deal of nudity and one groundbreaking scene in which the plump actress Lena Nyman fondled the penis of actor Börje Ahlstedt. According to Nesser, the massive international success and censorship furore surrounding this film (largely because of its relatively minimal erotic content) established a template in the minds of non-Swedes for the country; a template, what's more, which hardly told the whole story. Swedes, according to Nesser, have been living with this lazy cliché ever since. But other, more prestigious, Swedish film-makers might have been said to have contributed to this perception of Nordic carnality, notably the man many cinéastes consider to be nonpareil, Ingmar Bergman. His mid-period masterpiece *Summer with Monika* (1952) enjoyed a great deal of attention not only for its undeniably impressive cinematic qualities, but for a scene in which a nubile Harriet Anderson removed her sweater – at a time when actresses kept their bodies largely covered. Later Bergman films such as *The Silence* (1963) further expanded the sexual parameters with actress (and then-Bergman muse) Ingrid Thulin in a particularly joyless masturbation scene, while a young couple have sex in a cinema in a sequence that was considered very graphic at that time (despite the impeccable reputation of the director, *The Silence* encountered much crass tampering by censors at the time – and, as with most such storms-in-teacups occasioned by moral guardians, the film's sexual candour is mainstream today).

Interestingly, this perception of Scandinavia as a land of erotic lotus eaters has not been explored in Nordic crime fiction to any great extent (no doubt because native writers know the truth behind such erroneous perceptions), although Karin Alvtegen – while utilising the form of the traditional 'cosy' mystery – incorporates audacious sexual elements into her narrative. The Icelandic Yrsa Sigurðardóttir, a woman not afraid to confront the shibboleths of her society, utilises asphyxiation for sexual ends in *Last Rituals*. The author, of course, who most fully explored the sexual arena was the late Stieg Larsson, whose unblushing and graphic descriptions of sexual acts have caused much controversy (not least inspiring debates over whether or not the author's unflinching – and repeated – descriptions of sexual abuse are exploitative or feminist). Interestingly, the duo who are the inspiration behind much current Scandinavian crime fiction, Maj Sjöwall and Per Wahlöö, are notably chaste and discreet in their treatment of sex. Regarding other areas of sexual politics (including homosexuality), certain Scandinavian writers have been much more upfront – notably Anne Holt with her lesbian protagonist Hanne Wilhelmsen – although the character's sexuality is utilised as a means of creating her personality rather than introducing any erotic elements. If the Nordic noir novel may be considered as a sub-versive sub-genre of a generic form (which is ostensibly concerned with the restoration of the status quo), it is not so in the sexual arena (despite occasionally addressing gender issues) but in the political field.

Regarding gender issues, there is one area markedly unlike the British and American fields: the contrast between urban settings and bucolic backdrops in the Nordic field frequently serves more complex functions than simple evocation of place. The genre's burgeoning army of female detectives are sometimes shown to be more in sympathy with the natural canvas that is presented by the Scandinavian countryside, and feminist points are sometimes made about the male detectives' identification with the less intuitive, more impersonalised city environment as opposed to the more natural elements that their female counterparts are able to forge a synchronicity with. To some degree, such notions are a reversal/antinomy of what were previously conceived as sexist assumptions, demonstrating something akin to Plato's concept of the fixed essence of human beings. It might be argued that one set of assumptions about gender determinants are simply replaced by another. But such criticisms have less force in the face of the fact that even in the twenty-first century, police forces throughout the world are hardly exemplars of flexibility in terms of gender roles.

It might be argued that the incidental function of such novelists as Henning Mankell as social historians (leaving aside their primary personae as literary entertainers) is due to the fact that these writers address issues explored less forensically by their non-genre-writing colleagues; an example might be the view that the collapse of communism and the succeeding increase in immigration into the Nordic countries has been an engine for the conflicts that power much of the region's crime fiction. But any consideration of the puncturing of the social democratic ideal has to take into account the death of Olof Palme. The murder of the Swedish prime minister in 1986 remains an unsolved crime, and as an indicator of the country's increasingly bleak view of its society, the impact of the incident is not to be underestimated. Certainly, most Scandinavian crime fiction writers in conversation will inevitably refer to this murder as the moment when the scales fell from the eyes of many who considered that the Scandinavian countries were somehow above the maelstrom of conflict and division in the rest of the world. Similarly, the subsequent killing of Swedish minister for foreign affairs Anna Lindh had a seismic effect, offering further proof that the region had been jolted painfully into the same world in which the rest of us live. These incidents, more than any similar assassinations in other countries (such as, for instance, that of John F. Kennedy), became emblematic in Scandinavian fiction, and inspired a Nordic feeling along the lines of John Buchan's observation in *The Power-House* (1916) noting how thin the veneer of civilisation is.

Scandinavian crime fiction has long extrapolated elements of social critique into literary form and as an index to the society it reflects is most cogent, from Sjöwahl and Wahlöö's influential hard-left ideology in the Martin Beck series through Henning Mankell's concerns for the third world to Stieg Larsson's ruthless demolition of the image of the Swedish social democratic ideal (creating for outsiders a new, astringent vision of modern Sweden). At the same time, it provides an illustration of Nordic cultural differences from Iceland to Norway, as seen through such novelists as Karin Fossum and Jo Nesbø (the latter has remarked that 'the writer of fiction has traditionally been regarded as an opinion former in questions of politics, ethics and society').

As Shakespeare's Denmark held a mirror up to the English society of its day, a case might be made for Scandinavian crime fiction as being similarly universal in its application. The writer Håkan Nesser has pointed out that the differences between British and Scandinavian society are less marked than either nation considers them to be – and in the twenty-first century, the parallels and congruencies between these cold north European countries become ever more pronounced. The traveller's guide to this territory is popular Nordic crime fiction. And this particular cornucopia is self-replenishing: hopes are high (for instance) for three new crime authors – the Icelandic Stefán Máni (who writes in a markedly noir, atmospheric idiom), the Danish Susanne Staun (whose speciality consists of dark, psychologically oriented forensic thrillers) and the Norwegian Unni Lindell (who favours solid, traditional detective novels).

1
Crime and the Left

Two writers from the left – a crime-writing team with a markedly Marxist perspective – might (without too much argument) be said to have started it all in terms of important Scandinavian crime fiction: the spectacularly talented Maj Sjöwall and Per Wahlöö. Their continuing influence (since the death of Per Wahlöö) remains prodigious.

It was something of a scandal that for some considerable time the complete oeuvre of this most influential team of crime writers was not available in translation (certain books – such as *The Laughing Policeman* (1971 [1968]) – haunted various publishers' lists, and then would inexorably melt away). This relative invisibility (until recent – and welcome – reissue programmes remedied this egregious blot on the reputation of publishing) was particularly odd, as the almost viral penetration of the duo's literary reach was total, with many crime fiction writers citing them as the *ne plus ultra* of the socially committed crime novel. What's more, the team has been – in many cases – a source of personal inspiration for the work of contemporary crime writers. The sequence of books featuring their tenacious policeman Martin Beck are shot through with the ideological rigour of his creators; that's to say: as well as being lean and compelling crime novels, they simultaneously function as an unforgiving left-wing critique of Swedish society (and, *inter alia*, of Western society in general). But this shouldn't put off those readers conscious of Marxism's fall from favour since it first inspired Maj Sjöwall and Per Wahlöö in a very different era; like the elements of Catholicism in Graham Greene's work (which does not interfere with an appreciation of his peerless skills as novelist), the Marxist underpinnings of Sjöwall and Wahlöö's Martin Beck books may be considered to be less important than the edgy, pared-down prose in which these finely honed police procedurals trade. A prime example is *The Man Who Went Up in*

Smoke (1970 [1966]), with Beck holidaying on an island with his family but obliged to track down a missing journalist. Sjöwall and Wahlöö took the relatively conservative format of the detective novel and shook it until many of the more retrograde elements fell out like loose nails. By introducing genuinely radical elements into what was at the time an unthreatening form (with, they felt, distinctly bourgeois values), the duo were able to both enrich and re-energise what had become something of a moribund field, with the realism of their work married to its political attitudes. To this end, the characterising of certain elements in the police force as corrupt or totalitarian was part and parcel of the radical political agenda underlying the books. But at no point in any of the Martin Beck novels (thankfully) are such notions allowed to be transformed into simple agitprop. The marked quotidian quality of the duo's approach and the rigorous presentation of social realities identified the sequence as material much more radical and realistic than the Christie-inspired cosiness of an earlier generation of Swedish writers such as Maria Lang.

Their sequence of ten books (all of which originally bore the subtitle 'a novel about a crime') were published in the decades of the 1950s and the 1960s, and the setting is (for the most part) Stockholm, although there is a notable involvement of Martin Beck's associates from Malmö. In rather the same fashion that Luis Buñuel used his film *Viridiana* as something of a time bomb to expose the hypocrisies of Spain and the Catholic Church, Sjöwall and Wahlöö regarded the crime fiction genre as an instrument for transforming society and, to some degree, for the proselytising of radical views. By the very nature of the crimes and criminals that Martin Beck came into contact with, a variety of insights and observations were permissible for the writers, and the social critiques were considerably more incendiary than anything the genre had known before. What's more, the team's reinvention and politicisation of the form was, despite its confrontational nature, able to travel widely throughout the world, with their books being published in over twenty-five countries.

The fact that Sweden has the largest market share in terms of Scandinavian crime fiction is echoed by the fact that the country is the largest in the Nordic quintet; twice the size, in fact, of Great Britain. As with the other Nordic countries, the image that foreigners cherish of Sweden is an idyllic one: the awe-inspiring lakes, the massive, sweeping forests and a host of breathtaking locales. In stark contrast to this picture postcard image, of course, are the social realities of the country – thorny problems, for instance, with immigration, that have led in some ways to the strengthening of the influence of the far right (a syndrome which is, ironically, grist to the mill of most of the crime writers considered in this study). The stamping ground of any of the Swedish genre novelists is the south of the country, with the greatest concentration of population but also boasting massive swathes of the country barely troubled by human presence. This region is part of the warp and woof of the country's soul.

The Swedes famously have two things in common with what used to be considered an English trait: a certain reined-in, reserved quality in conversation that is put aside when a decision has been made as to the suitability of the person addressed; and (something which is a continuing source of surprise to the British) most Swedes' impressive command of the English language. This, of course, facilitates the involvement of Nordic writers with the English translators of their books – unlike non-English crime writers of the past such as Georges Simenon (who rarely troubled himself with the translations of his work), a more fruitful interaction is possible between Swedish writers and their literary conduits. It's a syndrome that may account for the notably high standard of most English translations of Scandinavian novelists.

The coastal regions of Sweden are of course celebrated for their highly individual topography but Stockholm remains, quite rightly, the focus of both national pride and international attention. Striking historical architecture was built across the islands as a repository for the country's celebrated art collections, and the leisure activities of the city are most vibrant at night (and much utilised by crime novelists). The Swedish winters, of course, are lengthy and punishing, and are well known for their frigid temperatures – and are as much a part of the national psyche as anything else. The long dark nights, as has been repeatedly observed, are perfect for the commission of crime – as grimly and unsparingly celebrated in many novels by Swedish writers.

There has always been, of course, a conflict between the demands of commerce and writers' desire to produce the most truthful work they can within the form of the popular novel. Publisher fine-tuning based on the economics of marketing a book (as à propos as any notions of literary merit) is inevitably part of the editing process, and it is by no means always the case that editors will insist on overtly commercial elements (a greater infusion of violence or sexuality, for instance). A selling point of much of the best crime fiction to the more sophisticated reader – and certainly that of the Scandinavian variety – is the guarantee of a certain degree of literary quality folded into the exigencies of the crime/thriller genre. This extra level of quality is something of a door of opportunity for more ambitious writers who (left to their own devices) produce work that conspicuously stretches the parameters of the genre.

Those parameters often take on board an ambiguous attitude to the past; not exactly Proustian (Swedes live in the present more than the narrator of *A la Recherche du Temps Perdu*), but picking at unhealed wounds; such as, for instance, the legacy of the Cold War. The ambiguity felt in this country towards such organisations as the CIA – now regarded with suspicion, if not quite with the same distaste as the KGB and its successors – is almost conciliatory compared to the Swedish attitude to the American spooks; Swedes have something of a tendency to bracket the two security services together in an ideological line of fire.

But the antecedents of the current, complex strain of writing were relatively straightforward. To say that the original Swedish Queen of Crime Maria Lang is somewhat less well known than the writer who bears that soubriquet for England, Agatha Christie, would be a monumental understatement. But among Nordic writers, Lang's achievement is celebrated to this day – and there are several current Nordic novelists who regard her as an exemplar who remains genuinely inspirational. Maria Lang was, in actual fact, Dagmar Lange (who was born in Västerås in 1914 and who died in 1991), and to some degree, she was the writer who spearheaded the great wave of popularity for the crime fiction genre in Sweden in the 1950s. Her predecessor, both in terms of sales and reputation, was the highly capable writer Stieg Trenter, but Lang demonstrated new possibilities for the field with her innovative series of novels. Her first book, *Mördaren ljuger inte ensam/The Murderer Does Not Tell Lies Alone* (1949), achieved instant acclaim, and established Lang as a bestseller – a position she was to maintain throughout her career. Her literary blueprint would appear to have been the novels of Christie, along with other golden age writers such as Dorothy Sayers, and – like Christie – she was keen to maintain as much of her own privacy as she could, despite the growing demands of celebrity. Her prose style was unadorned, and she appeared to take from her English colleague – the creator of Miss Marple – a concentration on clearly drawn, relatively unnuanced characters fitted into plotting of great precision and rigour. Although her books were translated and made available in the United Kingdom, she never achieved the success of other translated crime writers such as Georges Simenon with his long-running series of Maigret books, although British crime fiction cognoscenti were well aware of her achievements. If Lang is more remembered than read these days, her legacy still has a solid basis – and many current Nordic crime writers of the baby boomer generation are happy to acknowledge that they avidly consumed her books in their youth.

Inevitably, an author has to come to terms with the requirements of his editor and publisher whose schedules demand a particular number of novels in given genres aimed at specific markets, but a new dimension is added when Nordic crime fiction is translated and sold in the American and British markets. The sales strategy demands that the generic categorisation becomes very much about the perception of the book and author as discrete elements; publishers will take on one or two Scandinavian writers in order to ensure that such writing is represented in their lists alongside more straightforward blockbusters, celebrity memoirs and so on. (It would be churlish to describe such commercial strategies as publishers feeling the need for a 'token' Nordic author or two – such publishers are generally more rigorous in their planning.)

But neither is this the result of simple commercial imperatives; British publishers in particular are now well aware that translated fiction can showcase some of the best writing available at present – and if sufficiently enthusiastic notices are gleaned in the broadsheets, then more-than-respectable sales will follow – perhaps not in the prodigious quantities of Stieg Larsson and Henning Mankell, but in quantities sufficient to keep the accountants happy. Unlike film-making, where the egos of stars and directors must be massaged even as the end product is stage-managed and finessed towards completion, publishers (in these more straitened times) are unable to indulge in the luxury of commercial missteps; each new Scandinavian acquisition for a publisher's list has to be heavily presold, not least to the colleagues of the editor who has risked the company's money in purchasing a given book (the feeling in publishing circles is that any bubble, however buoyant, is always on the point of bursting – and that destabilising feeling is as pressing as ever with this latest trend). With unchallenging commercial novels (aimed at the lowest common denominator) biting at the tail of a trend, the imperative is to operate quickly and efficiently, ensuring that the product is available in a serviceable form before a given fashion has petered out. But much more time is taken over Scandinavian acquisition. Apart from anything else, there is the translation process, but as more Nordic fiction is made available, a reliable list of translators may be guaranteed to deliver a polished product which not only does justice to the concept of the original writer, but functions as an independent work of fiction within its own right, with its own distinct literary character.

In the area of translated fiction, it might be said that power has been displaced from the heads of companies (no longer given these days to quixotic or despotic decisions after lengthy liquid luncheons) to the editors and agents whose ears must be always close to the ground, forensically examining ever-shifting popular opinion and developing trends.

2
The Cracks Appear: Henning Mankell

Kurt Wallander's Sweden is not a good advertisement for the success of the welfare state – the cracks in the consensus of Scandinavian society widening, Swedish family life riven by deep psychological traumas. An examination of Wallander's creator Mankell and his work demonstrates how the keen social conscience that illuminates Mankell's books chimes with his own commitment to make disadvantaged people's lives better (as is evidenced by his theatre work in Africa), plus the cool and unsparing examination of nationalism and intolerance in the novels.

In the past, various non-English-speaking crime writers have achieved classic status, but if there's one modern writer who is the market leader for foreign crime in translation, it is Sweden's Henning Mankell. Not very long ago, Mankell was a clandestine pleasure, savoured by a privileged few outside his homeland, but slowly his reputation grew. Rather in the way that the band Dire Straits was the blunt instrument that kickstarted the CD industry, Mankell's novels became the standard bearer for foreign crime in translation (and he's been very lucky in his translators, usually graced with excellent translations by Laurie Thompson).

His dyspeptic detective Kurt Wallander (something of an alter ego for Mankell, despite the author's distancing himself from his creation), is one of the signal creations of contemporary crime fiction: out of condition, diabetes-suffering and with all the headaches of modern society leaving scars on his soul (and currently the subject of two TV series – one British, one Swedish). Wallander is as rounded a character as any in more literary fiction. In such books as *Sidetracked* (2000 [1995]) and *Firewall* (2004 [1998]), non-Swedish readers were taken into pungently realised Scandinavian settings that were subtly similar to Britain, but also fascinatingly different. But like the late film director Ingmar Bergman (who, as mentioned earlier, was Mankell's father-in-law), the writer frequently confounds all stereotypical expectations of Nordic gloom and produces books crammed with humanity and guarded optimism (plus the bloodshed and murder that are prerequisites of the crime genre). The keen social conscience that illuminates Mankell's books chimes with his own commitment to make disadvantaged people's lives better: he has done a great deal of theatre work in Africa, and his reach as a writer extends beyond the crime genre, with such books as the ambitious *Kennedy's Brain* (2007), *Depths* (2006 [2004]) and *Eye of the Leopard* (2008 [1990]). The latter, straddling the 1970s and 1980s, is a vigorous examination of the relationship between white farmers and their native workers in Africa, with a protagonist battling a hostile land and descending into his own mental firestorm.

For quite some time, European readers were cognisant of the fact that some of the most provocative modern crime novels were being written by this Swedish master, in many aspects reflecting his celebrated father-in-law, Sweden's most illustrious film director, not least the total seriousness and rigour of his work (within the context, in Mankell's case, of a popular genre). *Firewall* (2004) is one of the writer's most challenging (and unvarnished) portraits of modern life, in which society and all its institutions (not least the family) are put under the microscope. In this book, Mankell's long-term protagonist finds himself propelled into a new area of crime: cyberspace. Several deaths have occurred: the victims include the user of a cash dispenser, and a taxi driver murdered by two young girls. The country is plunged into blackout by an electricity failure, and a grim find is made at a power station. What is the connection? Wallander finds himself tracking down cyber terrorists, with shady anarchic aims. But can his own malfunctioning team of coppers pull together to help catch them – or is there a fifth columnist in the police? Plotting here is as impeccable as ever, though *Firewall* is not quite vintage Mankell. Nevertheless, the forensically acute exploration of diverse influences on modern society is impressive (notably the more sinister capacities of the internet and political movements devoted to the destruction of what they perceive to be corrupt institutions; Sweden, as usual, standing in for the whole of Western society). Perhaps some boxes are merely ticked, while others are ransacked for significance, but Mankell never spoon-feeds the reader a ready-made set of the correct attitudes.

Depths (2006) is a darkly compelling tale set in 1914 Sweden, with a naval commander dispatched on a clandestine mission who becomes obsessed with a woman he meets on a desolate island. But whatever genre Mankell chooses to write in nowadays, he has an impatient audience ready for each new book – though the Wallander books remain his calling card. *Firewall*, for instance, was received by readers in many countries with much fanfare, which is as it should be; Mankell is something special. Some of the initial resistance to Mankell's work might be understandable; like Bergman, Mankell is from a country noted for Nordic gloom, and the lazy-minded are not always prepared to go beyond stereotypes. Their loss: like his late father-in-law, Mankell is an artist of rare achievement.

For a while, it looked as if the post-Kurt Wallander trajectory sought for by his creator might involve the detective's daughter, Linda – until the suicide of the actress Johanna Sällström (who played Linda in the Swedish TV series with Krister Henriksson, and who suffered from depression) affected the author so profoundly that he found himself unable to continue writing about the character. *Before the Frost* (2004) was the book in which Mankell opted to put Wallander's daughter centre stage, perhaps an indicator of the author's desire to freshen the literary brew for himself. After a maladroit start, it is soon clear that Linda Wallander shares many of the bloody-minded, anti-authoritarian characteristics of her father, and (after a certain amount of adjustment on the reader's part) it appeared that a utilitarian solution had been found to the author's desire to move on – though it was, sadly, not to be. *Before the Frost* begins in the shadowy forest near Wallander's stamping ground of Ystad, where a grim discovery is made: severed human hands and a head, disposed in a macabre parody of the act of prayer. A bible, apparently annotated by the murderer, is also discovered. But this is not the only grotesque incident plaguing Kurt Wallander: there have been cruel attacks on domestic animals. A fraught time, in fact, for the detective's daughter Linda to begin working as another detective on the force – which she does. But (it goes without saying) Linda is quickly demonstrating her father's crime-solving acumen in nailing the criminals – a malign group with a penchant for biblical punishments on their unflinching agenda. Linda's moment in the sun, however, was to be short-lived, when Mankell found it too painful to continue writing about the character.

Those dismayed by Kurt Wallander being put on the shelf by his creator were pleased by the appearance of *The Man Who Smiled* in 2005, something of a comeback novel. Crime aficionados had long taken the Scandinavian investigator to their hearts, and the news that Wallander's daughter was to take centre stage didn't exactly whet the appetite. When the initial outing of Wallander *fille* didn't match the panache of the earlier books, Mankell fans wore expressions as bleak as the Scandinavian winters.

But even as British readers became aware that some of the finest modern crime novels were being produced by this Swedish master (with such books as *Sidetracked* and *Firewall*), Mankell's work still encountered some resistance. In *The Man Who Smiled*, Wallander is having a tough time. He has been responsible for the death of a man, and has decided to quit the force. Drink doesn't help to relieve his depression – the reverse, in fact – and when a solicitor friend asks for Wallander's aid to look into the death of the former's father, he declines – and then the solicitor himself is murdered. With deep reluctance, Wallander returns to work, and finds that on this double murder case he's obliged to shepherd a novice female detective. The investigation points in the direction of a mysterious captain of industry – and Wallander is soon in immediate danger.

Plotting here is as impeccable as ever, though this isn't quite Mankell with all the cylinders firing. Still, those fearing that regular doses of Wallander had been abruptly curtailed were grateful for this surprise reappearance of the reliable protagonist.

The ongoing analysis of society (in terms of the strictures – both personal and political) imposed on its complaisant citizens was now an integral aspect of Mankell's novels, but the exposé of endemic corruption (the author's principal concern for some considerable time) was perhaps becoming over-familiar, as were the problems and foibles of the troubled character. So the time was propitious for the fresh approach of *The Pyramid* (2008), a foray (or series of forays) into the personal and professional past of the character. Wallander had first appeared in *Faceless Killers* in 1991, when he was a senior police officer just out of his 30s and with his private life in chaos. The stories in *The Pyramid* chronicle his early years: the events, the people and the crimes that forged the man we first met in that debut appearance. The analysis of the milieu in which the detective moved is here, but (inevitably) in more fragmented – and less rigorous – form, but there are aperçus aplenty. We encounter Wallander as a young beat cop attempting to crack a murder in his spare time; we follow him in his tentative first steps with Mona, the woman he has decided to marry (his wife, of course, had left him by the time of the events in that first book), and we are shown why his relationship with his father is quite so fractious. The elements that make the full-length Wallander novels so successful are all here in microcosm: a cool, dispassionate treatment of crime and its deleterious effects, the understated evocation of the Scandinavian locales and insights into the mores of the society; and (best of all) the puzzling, fascinating character of the complex man at the centre of the narrative. Mankell admirers may prefer the full-length novels (and not every story here has fully engaged the author's creative juices), but the insights provided by these striking stories are intriguing and variegated.

As with most ambitious crime writers, some of the author's most challenging work was to be found in his non-series novels – such as *Italian Shoes* (2009). A naked man stands in the freezing cold of the Swedish archipelago, an axe in his hand. He chops a hole in the ice of the lake outside his house, and immerses himself in the sub-zero water. It is a ritual – a way of reminding himself he is still alive. Then, one morning he sees a figure struggling across the ice towards him. Her name is Harriet. She is the only woman he ever loved – and whom he cruelly abandoned. To say that the opening of *Italian Shoes* instantly grabs the attention is hardly a surprise – Mankell's ironclad storytelling skills are what have made his books featuring Wallander such an international publishing success. But *Italian Shoes* is something very different. The naked man on the ice is Frederick Welin, who has enjoyed a successful career as a surgeon, until a cover-up for a lethal mistake on the operating table ended his career. For twelve years, he has buried himself in frigid isolation. But (as in Mankell's Wallander books), the past never leaves people alone for long. Frederick's ex-lover, Harriet, has searched him out to make good on a promise he made forty years ago, before he left her to study in America; she wants him to take her to a small, secluded lake in northern Sweden, a beautiful black pool he has talked about, hidden deep in a forest. Frederick is reluctantly persuaded, and the duo begin a strange odyssey through a cold landscape, full of subtle menace and even the erotic charge of the couple's earlier affair (Frederick takes another icy plunge – this time, an unwelcome one – and Harriet takes off their clothes to warm him with an embrace). Fredrick searches Harriet's handbag, and discovers that she has a terminal illness. And when they reach the almost mystic destination, she has another devastating surprise for him. Mankell's narrative here sports his customary marriage of authoritative plotting and well-defined characterisation. But *Italian Shoes* is also a trenchant examination of the boundless human capacity for making the wrong decisions (along with the difficulty of meeting the challenges the ageing process sets for us). Not, perhaps, for those who seek the more straightforward detective plots of a Wallander novel, but it is definitely a book for those of us who might feel we could have handled the trajectory of our lives with more skill.

By this stage of his writing career, Mankell had decided that he had bigger fish to fry than crime novels dealing with the ills of Swedish society (however universal the application of these books). And the canvas in *The Man from Beijing* (2010) is painted on a global scale – though, admittedly, with controversially received results; the book encountered something of a mixed reception. The novel begins with a scene of unspeakable horror. In the small Swedish village of Hesjövallen, a grim discovery is made: nineteen people have been slaughtered with the most appalling savagery (they had been dismembered with a sword). The local police, keen to make a swift arrest, decide (without too much deliberation) that the killer is a solitary psychopath. However, Judge Birgitta Roslin reads about the crime and comes to very different conclusions. She has a personal interest: the Andréns, adoptive parents of her mother, are among the victims. Birgitta rejects the too-facile solution, but the police have little time for her queries. She begins her own dangerous search for the truth – and a journey that will take her from liberal Sweden to repressive Beijing, taking in Robert Mugabe's Zimbabwe. There is a final confrontation in London's Chinatown.

When Mankell wrote *finis* to Wallander's career in 2010, it wasn't quite the end for the character. Uniquely, the two separate TV series had kept him alive; the handsome-looking British version with Branagh, while the Swedish series (the preferred option for those who know about such things) infuses more of the books' atmosphere. Wallander on the page, however, has been obliged, as we will see, to hang up his revolver and is drinking in the same retired detective's saloon as Ian Rankin's DI Jack Rebus. But for a writer of Mankell's accomplishments, there is clearly life after Wallander; the writer has demonstrated his skills with female protagonists before, and the tenacious Birgitta in *The Man from Beijing* proves to be a sterling substitute for her male predecessor – though she has fewer character facets than her predecessor. In an ambitious narrative arc that covers 100 years, from the USA and China of the nineteenth century to today's Beijing and Africa, Birgitta Roslin's investigation throws up some disturbing coincidences – such as a nineteenth-century document that talks about the murder of a family called Andrén, cut to pieces (as with her modern relatives of that name) with a sword. And Mankell – via Birgitta – addresses some serious issues in the context of an investigative thriller.

There will, inevitably, be readers who will yearn for those comfortingly gloomy mysteries in the familiar company of the author's signature character, but Mankell's skills at orchestrating all the elements of his globe-spanning narrative are as surefooted as ever here. But there were those who disagreed with the none-too-understated political messages of *The Man from Beijing* (such as the apparent special pleading for Robert Mugabe), and tackling a globe-trotting narrative a tad reminiscent of Dan Brown and co. had its risks: the picaresque qualities help with the nailing of Mankell's global targets, but there is an inevitable diffusion of focus compared to the earlier books.

In a recent major international news story, one key element went curiously under-reported. While the world watched as Israeli soldiers captured ships attempting to break the Gaza strip blockade, few people were aware that among the prisoners of the Israelis was one of the world's most successful and acclaimed writers: Henning Mankell. Mankell has long been known as much for his keen commitment to social and political issues, and the author had spent a great deal of time working with HIV-infected children in Africa, so his personal involvement with a hot-button issue such as the Gaza flotilla raid should have come as no surprise.

Since sidelining Wallander, Mankell's social concerns had assumed centre stage in his fiction; his books and his conscience are now, it seems, working in tandem. *The Man from Beijing* had taken on board global worries involving China and Zimbabwe. And with its successor, *Daniel* (2010), a winsome dark-skinned boy in a blanket on the jacket tells the reader that Mankell is once again moving out of standard crime fiction territory – though the too-pretty image (not, presumably, Mankell's choice) suggested a less than hard-edged approach might be on the cards. Fortunately, this was not to be the case, as the concerns of the novel were not a million miles away from the actions that resulted in Mankell's imprisonment as part of the sanctions-busting flotilla.

The time is 1875. Young Swedish entomologist Hans Bengler is full of ambition as he undertakes an odyssey to the Kalahari Desert to find an undiscovered insect which will bear his name. What he finds, however, is the survivor of a tribe wiped out by marauding Europeans. The survivor is a little boy, and Hans – perceiving him, perhaps, as another specimen – adopts the boy and christens him Daniel. Back in Sweden, the 'wild child' finds it impossible to adjust to civilisation and a new cold climate. His family is still with him – in dreams – and his one real companion is not Hans, but another alienated youngster, Sanna. What follows is both moving and disturbing, and the book's ending is a sobering one.

Many a crime writer has been cast adrift after retiring a signature character, but there was never any danger of that with Mankell, post-Wallander. He has always been, above all, a consummate novelist; even when his subject matter (as in *Daniel*) is something as serious as the destructive effects of colonialism, the storytelling ethos is always primary with him. And despite the sentimental image of a photogenic native child on the jacket, this is a powerfully involving, uncompromising novel about the loss of childhood and innocence.

To say that British readers had been impatient for the (sadly) final outing for Mankell's gloomy Swedish detective is something of an understatement – not least because the Kurt Wallander franchise has been
kept in rude health by the appearance of not one but *three* TV incarnations of the detective: two Swedish series and the Branagh version. But
Mankell fans know that what really counts is what Wallander's creator
put on the page – everything else is a gloss. Does the final book add a
suitable full stop to the series?

With *The Troubled Man* (2011), Mankell must have known that he
had to deliver something really special – and that is (to a great extent)
what he has done, though the Nordic gloom is applied at industrial
strength; this is the right kind of valedictory novel (and for how we last
see Wallander here, 'valedictory' is *le mot juste*). The Ystad copper has,
as usual, personal problems, not least trying to come to terms with his
daughter Linda's pregnancy by a man he finds unsympathetic. (Linda's
new lover, Hans, is a highly paid banker, and Mankell fans will know
precisely what to make of that – though, against the odds, Hans turns
out to be a likeable man.) The detective's professional life is as fraught
as ever. A body is found (suicide or murder?), and Wallander learns of
several enigmatic disappearances, somehow connected with a series of
incidents in the 1980s when Russian submarines were found in Swedish
territorial waters. There are also rumours of a high-level spy infiltrated
by the Soviets in a position of power in the Swedish military. What is the
involvement of the parents of Linda's new inamorato? (Hans' father is a
retired submarine officer.) None of this skulduggery is really Wallander's
territory, but he bludgeons his way in, behaving in customary cavalier
fashion. Standard procedure is jettisoned and his health ignored, even
as he frets about encroaching age. And something is to happen to
Wallander that is – soberingly and unexpectedly – new to him.

The good news is that *The Troubled Man* is Henning Mankell (almost)
on good form (ably translated, as ever, by Laurie Thompson); fears that
the final appearance of a beloved character would be something of
an anti-climax were quickly banished, and it appears that Mankell has
worked very hard to ensure that his customary storytelling engines
are suitably oiled, delivering one of the most plangent experiences in
the Wallander canon. He was never easy company, but we'll miss this
depressive, rule-breaking policeman.

Henning Mankell, like all Scandinavian writers, needed a facilitator to
deliver his books in English. The translator Laurie Thompson – considered
by many to be the doyen of the profession – points out that he only
translates from Swedish; and doesn't profess to know much about crime

fiction apart from the books he's translated. But as the crime writers whose books he's translated are Henning Mankell, Håkan Nesser, Åke Edwardson and (most recently) Åsa Larsson, this might seem to be a modest claim (in the late 1980s Thompson translated three books by Kjell-Olof Bornemark).

Thompson sees the principal problems in translating Scandinavian crime fiction as issues involving the differences in legal proceedings and police organisation – for instance, there are no sergeants in the Swedish police force. Nesser, of course, sets his novels in a fictional country and so procedures and police ranks are not 'authentic'; accordingly, it is fair to 'invent' titles if necessary, or use 'real' ones without bothering too much about strict accuracy. Thompson regularly visits several of the locales of the novels he is translating.

'Regarding a sense of place, Håkan Nesser is a special case, of course,' said Thompson. 'Åke Edwardson's Inspector Winter novels are set in Gothenburg, and all the background is meticulously authentic, even down to the names of shops in particular streets, and the routes of local trams, so it is important to know the facts. Luckily I have been a frequent visitor to Gothenburg, and generally know about such details.

'I am not familiar with Wallander's Ystad, but I don't think that is a problem as the references are not as meticulous as Edwardson's to Gothenburg, and Mankell includes an afterword admitting that he plays fast and loose with geographical accuracy. I'm reasonably familiar with the geography of Skåne, and have plenty of maps that I can check. In Mankell's non-Wallander novels he often has his characters travel to Norrland, even if they don't actually live there. I am quite familiar with Norrland and the vast forests and mountainous areas, and have been to Sveg where Mankell grew up; his descriptions of Norrland are often of the countryside within reach of Sveg, which I often visited. I found this helpful both with regard to geography and the attitudes and lifestyles of locals.

'Åsa Larsson's novels are set mainly in the far north of Sweden – further north than where we lived in Umeå. I don't know details of her Kiruna references, but can usually find them in reference books. But the Norrland atmosphere, landscape and attitudes (not least the trilingualism – Swedish, Tornedalen Finnish and Lappish) are things I am familiar with, and I have been to several of the places a bit further south than Kiruna, which she refers to. It's important to have intimate knowledge of the locales – but it depends on the writer and the novel. Not so crucial in most Mankell novels, very important in Edwardson novels, irrelevant to Nesser's geographically non-specific novels. To be frank, I don't think a translator should attempt to translate realistic novels set in specific locations without making an effort to familiarise him/herself with the locations.'

But does Thompson regard familiarity with the mores of a country as on a par with knowing the geography?

'Oh yes, I'd have thought this was essential in order to produce an "authentic" translation. Having lived in Sweden for four years, being married to a Swede, and being a frequent visitor, as well as having taught "Swedish life and institutions", I'd like to think I was pretty much au fait with the mores. I'd have thought that not being so would be a handicap. I'm not sure if it counts as "mores", but an example of one thing I think it is essential for a translator to know about is the connotations of the word "skog" for Swedes: it translates as "forest", possibly "woods". But the word has spiritual, almost magical connotations for Swedes. There is nothing of the "If you go down to the woods today" teddy bear implications, the nearest thing to that is connotations of trolls who live in mountain forests, but those references are Romantic rather than kiddies' stuff. The further north you go in Sweden, the more the word "forest" implies something that uplifts the soul and brings man closer to nature, to God, if you like. Southerners tend to be more urban, more linked with modern "sophisticated" life, and so they often regard the northern forests as depressing, remote – although since Sweden is more recently urbanised than England, quite a few have a nostalgic, Romantic yearning for the past. It is nicely summarised in Mankell's *The Troubled Man* when the pathologist Nyberg, who crops up in all the Wallander novels, tells Wallander he is going to retire to a cottage in the remote northern forests, where he can shrug off all the awful experiences he has had as a police pathologist and heal his soul close to the wonders of nature. Wallander can't understand this: he thinks the northern forests are bleak and depressing and remote. (But note that when Wallander comes close to retirement he buys a house outside town, and enjoys simple country pleasures and views.) Mankell seems to be split on this: in his autobiographical novels for so-called young adults, his child hero longs to get away from the remote forests and sail down the river to the sea and exotic adventures. (Mankell himself grew up in a northern forest environment and eventually went to sea as a young man; but he knows and respects the Swedish yearning for communion with nature in a remote northern forest environment.) In many of his books Mankell exploits this Romantic longing for "skogen" – *Italian Shoes* is an obvious example, but that isn't a crime novel. But the characteristic does occur frequently in the crime novels and it helps to be able to identify it. A similar Swedish trait is their love for lakes and islands – again, there are many examples of this in Mankell, who spends time every year on the island that was the home of his father-in-law, Ingmar Bergman. The British idea of summer holidays by the seaside with amusement arcades and kiss-me-quick hats is totally foreign to many Swedes, who prefer to mess about in boats on lakes or in one of the many archipelagos and to live in primitive cottages bereft of modern comforts. (I suppose this is a trait that is becoming less general as the years pass...) Being aware of such things helps to set the tone of the translation, although to reproduce it faithfully might sound "quaint" to an English reader.

'I used to keep abreast of Swedish politics when I was teaching Swedish. I haven't bothered in recent years – but then, the books I've translated tend to be set at least ten years ago. Mankell is politically a child of the 1960s, and his views reflect the (in my view) naive enthusiasm for far-left ideals – the little red book and all of that. Edwardson is both different and similar; for instance, he rants on about Swedes who leave Sweden and live abroad in sunnier countries – and repeatedly states that they ought to be paying Swedish taxes, not avoiding them. I would like to think that in *The Man from Beijing* when Mugabe is controversially praised for his policies – his confiscation of land from white farmers etc., and the problems of Zimbabwe blamed on former colonial powers and a white conspiracy – he is presenting a twisted view of reality in the context of the novel: but I can't help suspecting that Mankell believes it, at least to a considerable extent.

'I've learnt about the finer points of left-wing politics from Mankell and Edwardson. Most interesting has been things I've gleaned from Åsa Larsson. I knew about apparently strange plans to literally move the town of Kiruna in order to exploit the iron ore seams more efficiently and prevent the whole place disappearing thanks to subsidence, and I knew that there was quite a lot of sympathy with Nazi Germany in Sweden during World War II, especially in the north: but the details she supplies have been eye-opening. For obvious reasons the Swedes have tended to keep quiet about pro-German sympathies in the Second World War (until it became clear that the Allies were winning...); she is brave to focus on them.

'It would be nice to think that the British are beginning to realise that people who speak a Germanic language are much more like them than people who speak Romance languages (i.e. that we are closer to the cold North than to the sunny South) – but that is my subjective hope rather than a rational thesis.

'Obviously, all books to be translated provide challenges and satisfactions, in their different ways. But I have no doubt that the one who provides most of both is Håkan Nesser. Henning Mankell is a brilliant storyteller, and he uses language creatively to put over his message. But there is nothing innovative or experimental about his use of language. Nesser is much more of a challenge. Mankell's main "message" – if there is one – is social and political; Nesser deals with "eternal values" (one often has more sympathy with his murderers than with their victims, which makes one think about the human condition rather than social problems). Mankell can do this as well, especially in his non-Wallander novels – *Depths* and *Italian Shoes* spring to mind, although I think Mankell's final Wallander novel *The Troubled Man* also raises questions about "eternal values". But Nesser's use of language is much more subtle and clever and adventurous (and difficult for a translator!) – Åsa Larsson also uses language in an almost poetical way, but I think Nesser is one of Sweden's leading authors of the day, not "merely" a crime novelist (readers will be familiar with the dismissive attitude of academics...). Nesser uses quotations and references that need to be identified and checked – I usually manage to find them, but if I can't he is happy to explain (e.g. he has helped with films and books about films). A typical Nesser linguistic joke is the very name of his main detective, Van Veeteren: there is a Swedish curse "Fan vet!" or "Det vete Fan!", roughly "the devil only knows", although "fan" is a stronger curse in Swedish than in English. And although "vetare" is not really a Swedish word in itself, it is tagged on to the end of words like "kultur" to form "kulturvetare/n", i.e. one who knows about culture, usually somebody with a degree in a cultural subject: and so "Fanvetaren" (the "n" at the end is the equivalent of the English "the") could be interpreted as meaning "somebody who knows about the devil"! Unfortunately it's not something that can be translated into English – without changing the name, which would not be a good idea. But using the "compensation" trick one can invent similar plays on words occasionally.

'Of the novels I've been connected with, I found Nesser's *Borkmann's Point* was very satisfying – it is number two chronologically in the series, but was the first one published in English, and I think it's one of the very best. It is important when translating Nesser to get the length and rhythm of sentences right, and sometimes when he is evoking atmosphere (as in graveyard scenes in *Borkmann* and at the beginning of *Woman With Birthmark*) to try to use words of the right length with appropriate vowel sounds. It was encouraging to send Håkan the translation for approval and to receive the typical comment: "I've read a few pages here and there and recognise my novel – do submit it!" I tend to get a similar feeling of satisfaction after finishing any of the Van Veeteren books, but as *Borkmann's Point* was the first, it was a bit special. (Colin Dexter was a great admirer of the book.) Like Van Veeteren himself, most readers are sure to have more sympathy with the murderer than with his victim.

'Mankell's *The Troubled Man* was also very satisfying. I translated only three of the original Wallander novels – if the "lead publisher" was British, I was asked to do the translation: the Americans preferred to have a US translator in those days when they were the lead publisher. (I have translated fifteen books by Mankell in all.) This novel contains a lot of references back to earlier books and examines a lot of characteristics of Wallander that have been referred to in the past, and now draws the threads together, as it were. Obviously the "crime" aspect of the book is important and gripping, but at least as important is the character and life of Wallander himself, and his relationship with his family, especially Linda and, of course, her child. Henning never comments on translations of his books (despite his claim that the Gothenburg Book Fair recently that his translators are his heroes) but I hear on the grapevine that he approves of my translations. I found it satisfying to try to convey the character of Wallander which is presented in a more detailed and rounded way in this final book: it was a privilege to be involved in the "funeral oration" of such a fascinating man who I suspect is largely responsible for the interest in Scandinavian crime novels.'

3
Sweden: The Dream Darkens

The forthright Sofia Odsberg of the Swedish Nordin Agency (whose clients include such hot names as Mons Kallentoft) is not a woman to mince her words. She points out that it's considerably easier to market Scandinavian writers abroad today, especially to countries such as Italy, France and Spain. But Britain and America have broadened their perspective and become less suspicious of translated literature. 'I guess not many can afford to shun a trend as strong as this one,' she said. 'Scandinavian crime appears to have developed into its own sub-genre. But the crime wave has also paved the way for other types of Scandinavian literature, which is a very positive development.'

Odsberg lives in the Stockholm area, which, she says, is essentially similar to any capital city in the Western world – minus, that is, the diversity. It is very much a segregated place with a small privileged clique based in the town centre, as the numbers of rental properties are steadily declining. People with less economic capital are pushed out to faceless suburbs on the fringes of the tube map. 'Not surprisingly, Stockholm has the highest average income, and here you will also find the highest number of conservative voters. It is in many ways a radically different country to Northern Sweden.'

Crime novels, according to Odsberg, are probably the most accurate and unsparing contemporary portraits of society.

'In our crime fiction, the urban images of Stockholm aren't just perfect sunsets over the water or picturesque alleyways in the Old Town, but gritty snapshots of a world where some have it all and some have nothing. Not even the small provincial towns are as idyllic as one may think at first sight: globalisation has forced local industries to shut down and unemployment, intolerance and social problems ensue. In Sweden, many crime writers are also former journalists or teachers: professions that often go hand-in-hand with a strong social commitment.

'In a small country like Sweden these sorts of cracks in the social fabric are more visible because we are still a very homogeneous nation, unlike Great Britain. We don't have a long history of immigration and Sweden is a much more sparsely populated country. But I think this hatred and intolerance worries a lot of people here because we still like to consider ourselves open-minded and civilised, and the image of Sweden as a role model for the rest of the world persists – or is fondly maintained. Since crime fiction has such a wide readership, it is, of course, a good platform for the author to examine issues such as these – as long as they elect to describe cause and effect rather than deliver long and patronising speeches.

'American individualism is a popular notion with the current conservative government. But I think the Swedes are slowly realising that the social safety nets we have always taken for granted will no longer catch us when we fall. It's welfare vs. tax cuts, to put it simply. But globalisation and capitalism are turning most countries into identical copies of one another.'

Odsberg has an unvarnished view of the appetites of crime fiction consumers.

'I think most "average readers" simply consume what they are fed with, unquestioningly. Both publishers and book retailers know that crime fiction is a goldmine, and therefore these titles are more prominent in marketing, and less easy to ignore.'

The lengthy liquid lunches between publishers and agent that were so much of a fixture in the past may not be so plentiful in these more austere times, but the restaurants of London's Soho are still the venues for passionate cases being made over the Pinot Grigio for as-yet-unpublished authors. And in the second decade of the twenty-first century, these encomiums are often being presented for as-yet-untranslated Scandinavian authors. No British publisher wants to miss out on a new sales sensation in this new(ish) field, but many are distinctly wary – having learned just how much product there is out there to be sifted through. But visiting literary agents from Nordic countries are still given a decent hearing: after all, who knows what treasures they have in their portfolios?

One author safely signed, sealed and delivered is Camilla Läckberg. Those who read Scandinavian crime fiction have not been surprised at the revelations of violent neo-Nazi movements in the Nordic countries. This subculture has been laceratingly exposed by several writers, and the recent tragedy in Norway finds echoes in novels by two of the best female writers in Sweden, Camilla Läckberg and Åsa Larsson. Post-Sjöwall and Wahlöö, the growing army of Scandinavian crime writers such as Läckberg (a celebrity of J.K. Rowling proportions in Sweden) has demonstrated a considerable consistency of talent and achievement. She is known to be inspired by British crime writers such as Ruth Rendell – and comparisons may be drawn between modern Britain and Sweden, implying (for instance) that a lack of joined-up thinking is just as endemic to Swedish policing as it is to British.

Läckberg has a bushel of novels to her credit. The first to reach English shores, however, was *The Ice Princess* (2008 [2002]) – and if its remarkable acclaim in Sweden wasn't repeated in Britain, there was still a great deal of praise (perhaps insufficient compensation for her British publishers), with Läckberg hailed as Sweden's new Agatha Christie. And although that's a description with a soupçon of truth, it hardly tells the whole story. True, there is a Christie-style provincial village (here, Fjällbacka, in which the author herself was born) and a slew of suspects for a very unpleasant murder. Also Christie-like is the machine-tooled precision of the plot, but Läckberg is very much a contemporary writer, offering a picture of modern society that is as penetrating and allusive as her narrative is involving.

The writer Erica Falck has made a journey to her home town on the death of her parents, but discovers the community in turmoil. A close childhood friend, Alex, has been found dead. Her wrists have been slashed, and her body is frozen solid in a bath that has turned to ice. Erica decides to write a memoir about the charismatic but withdrawn Alex, more as a means of overcoming her own writer's block than solving the mystery of Alex's death. But Erica finds that her interest in Alex is becoming almost obsessive. She begins to work with local detective Patrik Hedström, and the duo soon find that some unpleasant secrets are buried beneath the comfortable surface of the town. More astringent novels have followed, such as the impressive *The Stonecutter* (2005), released in Great Britain in 2010 (as was *The Preacher*, in a translation by Steven Murray).

The latter was the novel in which Läckberg's credentials as both a storyteller of skill and a keen analyst of non-metropolitan Swedish society was consolidated. Her novels – all set in the coastal town of Fjällbacka – are immediate Scandinavian bestsellers, pleasing both critics and readers alike. Even her private life is of interest – her recent divorce was exhaustively covered by the Swedish tabloids (crime writers in this country might be grateful for the attention Läckberg is exasperated by). Her first novel to reach Britain, *The Ice Princess*, refracted elements of Golden Age writing through a hyperborean Nordic sensibility, but *The Stonecutter* demonstrated a less concentrated vision.

One of the reasons for the success of Scandinavian crime fiction in this country is its unsentimental readiness to confront the less admirable aspects of human behaviour (a readiness which is found more fitfully in British crime writing). That is very much the case with *The Stonecutter*, in which Läckberg's stamping ground of Fjällbacka – not a comfortable place to live, as we know from previous Läckberg novels – is the scene of a small tragedy: the body of a little girl is found in a fisherman's net. Has she drowned accidentally? A post-mortem suggests otherwise, and Patrik Hedström, the isolated resort's policeman, finds himself with the unenviable task of tracking down the murderer of a child whom both he and his partner, Erica, had met. Patrik's objectivity is coloured by the fact that he himself has recently become a father, but he continues with an investigation that is deeply troubling for both him and the cloistered society in which he lives. He finds he must make a community accept unpalatable truths about itself as well as bring to justice a cold-blooded killer.

As in *The Ice Princess* and *The Preacher*, Läckberg's job is to conjure anxiety – and that is one of her ironclad skills. But this novel adds another level cannily designed to unsettle us – a measured examination of the elements of determinism in human nature, and the readiness (which we all possess to some degree?) to cut adrift moral restraint when passionately held desires are frustrated. There is also a lacerating picture here of an unrestrained female psyche – one that is both attractive and monstrous.

The fact that a reality television show features in Camilla Läckberg's mesmerising *The Gallows Bird* (2011 [2006]) will mean little to English readers, but her fellow Swedes might discern a little score-settling here. Läckberg (as mentioned earlier) was the subject of much unwanted attention when the details of her divorce became headline news in Sweden. The most infinitesimal detail of her private life became a matter of public interest, so that when she began a relationship with a man who was also very well known in Sweden (a policeman who was the first winner of the Swedish version of the reality show *Survivor*), the scrutiny was ratcheted up to an even higher level. The important thing about Läckberg, though, is the quite remarkable success her moody and complex crime novels have enjoyed abroad. ⚜

In all her work, Läckberg examines her own sense of identity – both as a writer and as a Swede. She is a Scandinavian, but her literary inspiration (and spiritual home) is the sedate English town as evoked in Christie's St Mary Mead; large cosmopolitan cities have no appeal for Läckberg. And it's the vagaries of human nature that are her palette, in all their multiple aspects, with a Manichean sense of good and evil.

The Gallows Bird is the fourth entry in Läckberg's *Fjällbacka* series. Published in Great Britain in 2011, the novel has sold over 500,000 copies in Sweden. When a film version was shown on Swedish TV, it gleaned audiences of two million – neither fact, of course, necessarily creating a groundswell of interest in Britain.

A car crash in Tanumshede initially appears to be a simple accident, but a second, similar accident has Detective Patrik Hedström wondering if the victims in both crashes had, in fact, been murdered. At the same time, the town of Tanumshede is in something of a turmoil because of a reality TV show which is being produced locally. The frenzied attention given to the five-minutes-of-fame stars of the show has Hedström beginning to suspect that the killer is somehow connected with the phenomenon. The detective's own private life is distinctly unsettled, as he is tackling the problems of his forthcoming marriage to the writer Erica Falck (the couple are the continuing central characters in Läckberg's *Fjällbacka* sequence); problems sidelined when a chaotic alcohol-fuelled party ends with the death of an unpopular contestant on the TV show.

As with earlier books by the author (as ably translated by Steven Murray), there is an adroit manipulation of elements: the unpredictable plotting, the striking evocation of life in this idyllic (but flawed) community and – perhaps most satisfying of all – the intriguing interaction between Patrik and Erica, both loving and fractious. In *The Hidden Child*, Erica Falck is writing a new crime novel, but has made a significant discovery: her mother's diary from the war, along with a Nazi medal and a T-shirt stained with blood. She consults a local World War II historian, but then the elderly scholar is savagely murdered in a house he shares with his brother, who is tracking Nazi war criminals. Does the killing have anything to do with the burgeoning neo-Nazi movement in Sweden? And what did the dead man know about the clandestine activities of the country in the war years? There is an alternation between the present and the 1940s in the novel that Läckberg handles with steely skill, as she does the dangerous investigation into stygian secrets from Sweden's past.

It is Läckberg's particular skill to have created two of the most fully rounded characters in contemporary crime fiction, with a warmth that cuts through the Nordic chill.

Läckberg may be of little interest to the more salacious British tabloids (in contrast to their Swedish counterparts), but she should be firmly in the consciousness of readers of intelligent crime fiction.

Her publisher, Julia Wisdom of HarperCollins, numbers many estimable crime writers among her signings. Regarding Nordic fiction, she sees publishers as tapping into a rich vein of writing which has long been popular on the continent but not widely available here, and the growing acceptance of translated popular fiction is (she considers) here to stay. Läckberg, already massively popular in her native country, was personally recommended to her by a Swedish editor. The editor in question had pointed out that Läckberg provided something rather different to many of her peers, in that she was writing chilly psychological thrillers which nevertheless had something of a warm heart – the ongoing relationship of the detective Patrik Hedström and the author Erica Falck. And this element, in fact, holds true for all of her books. The only drawback for Wisdom is that she personally cannot read foreign novels in their original languages (except, in her case, in French) which means that she is dependent on reports and word of mouth, as with other key editors and publishers in England.

Regarding Läckberg, Wisdom employed carefully thought-through tactics for creating author awareness.

'With Camilla,' she said, 'we've very much built from the ground up: massive in-house PR, with intranet messages/desk drops/atrium giveaways/Scandinavian days in the cafe; lots of blogging; personal mail-outs; working hard with the high-street retailer Waterstone's; doing bespoke promotions; inviting supermarkets to try out "buy one, get one free" initiatives; bundling e-books. We've mimicked this activity in Australia and Canada, too. Working with reviewers has also been extremely important. We brought the author over for face-to-face meetings with key trade customers and critics before publishing her first book.

'Generally, such things require a great deal of hands-on work and revving up enthusiasm amongst reviewers, buyers and online opinion formers. We feel it's now paying off, given the response we're getting to Camilla. *The Hidden Child* is her fifth novel, and I'm convinced it represents her at her best. This book looks back to the scandal of those children born to Scandinavian mothers and German fathers, and is both powerful and provocative.'

Camilla Läckberg has examined her sense of identity – both as a writer and as a Swede – and what both these things mean to her.

'I am a Scandinavian, and I am a writer,' said Läckberg. 'I write about my country, my society, my world as I see it, and as honestly as I can. So the two elements of being a Scandinavian and being a writer are very hard to separate.

'When I started to forge the background for my crime novels I decided very early on to set them in my own small town of Fjällbacka, where I grew up, and where my mother still lives. I have been intrigued by small-town mysteries ever since my first encounter with Christie's Miss Marple and St Mary Mead, and, frankly, a small town interests me a great deal more than a big city. In my books Fjällbacka is actually one of the principal characters, and that was a very conscious strategy on my part.'

Any insights afforded the reader concerning Swedish society in Läckberg's novels is always an integrated element, along with the other necessary considerations.

'A crime novel is a wonderful way to be able to deal with the whole range of human emotions,' she says, 'and to address both the positive and negative sides of humanity. And, after all, that is what makes a society. It isn't the architecture or the institutions, the buildings, the companies, the factories – it's the human beings, in all their multiple aspects, with both their good and bad sides.

'I am, of course, dealing with Swedish society. For some reason, people in other countries seem to have fondly cherished a very idealised picture of Sweden. And now – perhaps because of tell-it-like-it-is crime fiction – they seem to have had a revelation: the country actually has crime, social problems, pollution, etc. Just like, in fact, every other country in the world. So I do think that there is perhaps a useful corrective in the picture of Sweden presented in crime.

'Political issues have a way of forcing themselves into one's work. In the novel I'm writing now, for example, I'm discussing a Far Right party that steams ahead in the Swedish parliament. Which, of course, is based on the truth. It has surprised and saddened me that people actually will vote for these small-minded individuals. Of course, having said that, I believe many of the old socialist ideas needed to be retired or thrown out, so a shake-up is not necessarily a bad thing.'

Läckberg is working on her eighth book.

'I don't know what the English title will be yet,' she says, 'but in Swedish it's a word used for women who in the nineteenth century would take in unwanted babies for money. Some of these women, in fact, actually killed the babies, and they were accordingly known as "Angel Makers". The last Angel Maker to be sentenced to death in Sweden was hanged in 1912. An element of the narrative centres on the daughter of one of these women.

'It's hard to single out favourite books from among those you have written, because it's a little bit like asking which one of your children you like best. Regarding children, *The Hidden Child* was a very special book for me, as I'm very interested in the Second World War, and with precisely how the Nazis were able to manipulate so many people. Mass manipulation is still, of course, endemic – sadly.'

A very different kind of writer is Camilla Ceder. Ceder (who lives in Gothenburg) originally studied social science and psychotherapy, disciplines that she has put to trenchant (and intelligent) use in her new vocation of psychological crime fiction – though Ceder has not given up the day job, and continues to work in counselling and social work. Her debut novel, *Frozen Moment* (2010), enjoyed considerable success in Sweden, though the dizzying succession in which new Nordic talents are appearing at present is making it more difficult for some authors to break through. Ceder excels in two particular areas: the adroit evocation of the chilly countryside around Gothenburg in western Sweden, with the mood and atmosphere of the landscape delineated in an almost poetic fashion. But like many of the best Scandinavian writers who have taken up the crime fiction form, she is particularly exercised by the darker psychological impulses of her characters (hardly surprising, given the other disciplines within which she works). Other issues that engage her in *Frozen Moment* include the decline of rural society, the fragmentation of family life in modern Scandinavia and the alienation and destruction resulting from the massive spread of recreational drug use. But (if the themes above were not challenging enough), she has other fish to fry, and makes cogent points about the state's role in tackling social dysfunction and breakdown. That's not to say that this debut novel is any kind of sociological tract: Ceder is well aware that the exigencies of powerful storytelling must always be paramount.

A rural town on the Swedish coast. On a frigid winter morning in 2006, Åke Melkersson is making his way to work when his car breaks down.

Finding a garage, he discovers that the garage owner is lying dead on the ground crushed by a car that has been driven over him repeatedly. Melkersson calls his neighbour Seja, a reporter, who quickly becomes interested in the murder. Seja finds herself involved with the enigmatic Inspector Christian Tell, the unconventional detective who is in charge of the investigation, and a sexual charge is sparked between the couple. A second murder occurs, and to his dismay, Tell finds that Seja has not revealed to him all that she knows – could she be involved in some fashion with the killings? There are a variety of elements to praise here, not least the way in which the youthful author has anatomised the psychological patterns of her protagonists, notably Seja, struggling to come to terms with the memories of a difficult and disturbed adolescence. Such is the assurance of this debut novel that readers had been keenly anticipating its follow-up, and the impressive trajectory has been maintained with her second novel, *Babylon* (2012 [2010]).

Ceder's British publisher, Kirsty Dunseath of Weidenfeld and Nicolson, a great proselytiser for her author, is confident that the enthusiasm for crime fiction from Scandinavia has 'legs'. 'I think that good books – from whatever country – will out in the end,' according to Dunseath. 'There is a particular – and keen – interest at the moment in the field, so numbers may surge – then, perhaps, decline. But, in general, if Scandinavia keeps producing great authors they will find a ready audience in Britain.'

Regarding Ceder, Dunseath was alerted to the book by luminous readers' reports, but she also talked to many European publishers who had bought *Frozen Moment* – and it also was on several bestseller lists, and had gleaned considerable accolades in its home country. 'When it comes to selling translated fiction such as this,' said Dunseath, 'we tailor our approach to each book individually – looking for the hooks and what will appeal to readers, who is the key audience and how do we reach them. The next book we will publish by Camilla is *Babylon*.'

Camilla Ceder has pointed out how she has been influenced by the environment in which she grew up.

'If you add to this the fact that there is a particular tone to Scandinavian crime fiction, perhaps in the spirit of Sjöwall/Wahlöö, weaving a sociological/psychological/social realist perspective into the narrative, then I think that as an author I am unquestionably influenced by my environment.

'For me, places often act as a source of inspiration in the form of an atmosphere that triggers my imagination, and I try to recreate this in the text. On the other hand, I feel no obligation to be faithful to reality in the first place; in many cases the atmosphere can be strengthened by the fact that I add or remove elements, with the best interests of the narrative in mind.

'My books are set in different locations. The first book took place almost entirely in rural areas – "well off the beaten track", while my second book was largely set in a city environment.

'As for the motivation of my characters, my particular area when I write is often discerning people's reasons for the things they do. Why we do what we do, how we choose to deal with our lives and why; communication, interpersonal relations – these things are crucial. My interest in the factors that push a person into committing violent acts is actually what made me choose to write crime fiction; in addition, the genre provides a climate in which it is possible to research the extremes of the human psyche. From that perspective, my focus with regard to corruption at different levels within society must, I feel, remain focused on how the individual is affected by these external factors. A common feature of my stories is that the psychological aspect of the crime is central; the narratives are about people driven to cross some kind of line for irresistible reasons such as envy, loneliness or social exclusion.

'I think that in many cases the Scandinavian crime novel has psychosocial undertones in which it is possible to highlight the loneliness and vulnerability of individuals within our society, a society which has otherwise been depicted (at least in the past) as a prosperous utopia, an ideal society. As globalisation spreads, the individual characteristics of our society diminish, and all varieties of social process leave their mark on crime writing, as on other literary genres. I am often inspired by crime novels, both Scandinavian and other nationalities, which have a slightly slower narrative pace and subtle, more indepth characterisation. I prefer less focus on the police procedural aspects and more on the inner life of the characters.

'I have no specific agenda when I write, but perhaps for that very reason there is a clear conviction (maybe because I am a social worker at heart) that it is possible to understand people if we use as a starting point their own life stories and the conditions in which they live their lives. I have always been interested in people, in how we justify the choices we make. I have heard it said that I make things very difficult for my characters, but that's absolutely the way I want it. It's important to me that my protagonists have the opportunity to be every bit as complex as in real life: those layers upon layers of experiences constantly influencing us in the present, our actions and reactions. And when we interact with others who have their own preconceptions, it is hardly surprising that things get complicated. But I've absolutely no doubt that this "complication" is what fires my writing.'

Ceder, her publishers hope, will be The Next Big Thing. But an enthusiastic supporter of the writer Mons Kallentoft – also heavily touted as TNBT – is his fellow Swede Camilla Läckberg, and she has cast a vote. Selecting several of her favourite Swedish crime novelists recently, she noted that Kallentoft came to crime fiction relatively late, after three other books – including *Food Noir* (2004), a collection of groundbreaking essays on food and travel. She praised his skill at plotting, as well as his ability to create strongly-realised female protagonists – the best, Läckberg said, she'd read by a male writer. Kallentoft's book *Sommardöden/Summertime Death* (2008) enjoyed a healthy stint on the Swedish bestseller list, while other things burnished his rising star: a three-book deal with a Swedish publisher, a French rights deal, and a film deal that included *Midwinter Sacrifice*, *Summertime Death* and two unwritten novels.

Kallentoft's British publisher, Nick Sayers of Hodder & Stoughton, is not to be drawn on the possible longevity (or otherwise) of the fashion for Scandinavian crime fiction.

'Making predictions has made a fool of many a better publisher than I am, but I think the auguries are that the interest will be long-lived. It's not as if Scandinavians come from Mars. There is a lot that we recognise in their society as being similar to our own, but enough that's different to make it intriguing to others. And the Nordic countries have some excellent writers who are getting established in other markets. Like it or not, the effect of brand-led marketing means that once established, people stay around and it becomes easier to direct readers towards other authors who might deliver a similar sort of reading experience.'

Choosing what foreign authors to publish is obviously problematic for English-speaking publishers such as Sayers.

'It's obviously a disadvantage not being able to read the books oneself, but a combination of buzz and good reports from trusted readers was enough to make me and my publishing house take the plunge.

'I think the British market still tends to regard anything translated as somewhat exotic, but things are definitely more open now, and

I hope translated fiction stands alongside the British and American product on our list purely on its merits. It's no longer enough – if it ever was – to simply say "this is an accomplished book". You have to have lots of intriguing angles to try to get attention for your authors, and being translated, opening up a different culture, is definitely one interesting angle to start with.

'The preliminary buzz on *Midwinter Sacrifice* by Mons Kallentoft was phenomenal. I think he has the kind of intense individuality that makes him stand out from the throng.'

Similarly enthusiastic noises have been heard at the mention of two newer writers, the Finnish Antti Tuomainen, and Kjell Eriksson (though the latter has been writing since 1993).

Kallentoft's first book *Pesetas* (2000) dealt with drug dealers in Madrid and gleaned the Swedish equivalent of the Whitbread award. Subsequently, the author's book of gastronomic travel writing, *Food Noir*, featured bizarre stories from the gastronomy scene worldwide, including tales of Basque chefs being threatened by ETA. The book read like a crossbreed between Hunter S. Thompson, A.A. Gill, Paul Theroux and Anthony Bourdain. Then came crime fiction.

Kallentoft is a peripatetic figure, travelling up to eight months of the year. 'I am not really at home in my own country, to be honest,' he has said. But his evocation of Swedish locales is particularly adroit. 'I use landscape as a backdrop,' Kallentoft noted, 'and I transform things to whatever fits my artistic purposes. That said, I base my picture of Östergötland, Sweden, on my emotional memories of the place. I grew up there, and I am forever attached to the landscape, whether I like it or not.'

The author's Malin Fors sequence is rapidly acquiring a devoted following.

'The whole process of creating the Malin Fors stories is a subconscious endeavour,' he said. 'I find that the images, scenes, stories that my subconscious creates when I sit down to write these narratives (although completely fictional) are much more "true" and "strong" than anything I can come up with by doing research. Frankly, I am not very interested in the minutely rendered "realistic" nature of things. Be it geography, the roof of a house, the right name for a model of a car... I choose all the details from whatever comes to me. If you just allow it to happen in a structured way, things usually work out more or less by themselves. The setting for me is mainly an emotional catalyst.

'Linköping is a very useful microcosm of Sweden. It's a successful town with a much-respected university, world-class hospital and advanced technology companies operating on a world stage. But at the same time it is a town rife with the problems of our time: factory closures, unemployment, class divides, tension with the immigrant population, prejudice of all kinds, drugs, etc. And all this is concentrated within a small area and a population of 190,000, including those people living on the margins of society.

'Of course, surrounding this turmoil is a typically Swedish landscape of open fields and dark endless woods. However, Linköping could be said to represent contemporary Sweden in a positive way. Many of my colleagues describe more tourist-friendly, scenic areas – but not many tourists come to Linköping... for me, Linköping functions as a stage for a Greek drama where virtually anything can happen.

'The crime novel can create an exaggerated sense of reality, and an urgency for enquiry – both into a specific issue, and, crucially, into life itself, for human beings living today. The crime fiction form can be a fulcrum for an examination of the very core of human existence, the questions, the doubts we all nurture along the lines of "what the fuck are we doing here?".

'I live in a very collective society, which sometimes leaves far too little space for the individual. And on a more concrete level there are many troubling issues that engage me; for instance I write about child abuse and molestation, and the Swedish judicial system. Our district attorneys have been shamefully slack in prosecuting the offenders in these areas. Writing about it might hopefully move it up the agenda for the authorities.

'In Sweden you cannot really talk in public about the problems with – and prejudices against – immigrants; it's the unsayable. This political correctness has created a void that the extreme right wing has exploited and used to gain parliamentary advantage. I try to discuss these issues in my books – we must be able to talk about such things, and listen to the people who feel excluded from modern society, and who blame immigrants for their misfortunes. Otherwise the far right will grow stronger, and this must be fought.

'At the core of Swedish society, many people still think that the state owes them a good life. And when they find out that the state doesn't provide this – not on any appreciable level – they become bitter and frustrated, and blame someone else for the things that are wrong with their lives.

'To be brutally frank, social democracy as an ideal is dead in Scandinavia at the moment. It needs to be redefined, with the values of equality re-examined as something that holds meaning for people in today's world, both from a local and a global perspective.'

Kallentoft adduces a long list of writers who have inspired him, including Walter Mosley, Cormac McCarthy, Sebastian Faulks, James Ellroy, Truman Capote, David Peace and Michel Houellebecq – along with the *sui generis* Hemingway and Fitzgerald. Of his own work, he is proud of *Midwinter Sacrifice*.

'I tried to create a new kind of hardcore police novel, infused with both a distinctly poetic feel and certain magical elements. The book, I'm glad to say, was my big break on an international level. I hope I succeeded in my ambition to write something that functioned as literature – but would also be entertaining in a "beach read" fashion. I'm also fond of *Summertime Death*, where I allow readers to get to know Malin Fors in more detail. I am proud of my heroine – she is a strong contemporary woman, but not a superheroine. Many women seem to care about Malin's life, and she seems to have generated her own autonomous life. What more can a writer want for his character?'

Peter Høeg is absent from Mons Kallentoft's list of inspirations above. But perhaps inspired by *Miss Smilla's Feeling for Snow*, Kerstin Ekman's 1993 Swedish Crime Academy prize-winner *Blackwater* made a few fitful appearances in English bestseller lists and then sank from view – but the book is well worth seeking out. Whilst the mystical, mysterious, introspective style makes it less accessible than *Smilla*, it both introduces throat-grabbing concepts and provides *inter alia* some cogent insights into the nature of landscape. The sound of a car engine wakes Annie Raft early one morning in her home in the remote Swedish province of Jämtland. Looking out, she sees her daughter Mia in the arms of a man she believes is responsible for an unsolved double murder in the area eighteen years before. Two-thirds of the book are concerned with those events from the past. We subsequently meet Annie, first on the scene of the tragedy, fleeing with Mia from the aridity of her Stockholm life to join an isolated hippy commune. Then we encounter Johan, a scion of the taciturn (and primeval) Brandberg family, also escaping, this time from the persecution of his peasant half-brothers. Also crucial to the narrative is Birger, the hard-working local doctor, losing his live-in lover to environmentalism, and the charismatic Dan Ulander, an important figure in the commune. Each holds a key to the solution of the mystery but eighteen years must pass before the trio meet again and the solution to this acrostic emerges. Along with the human figures, an important character, however, is the strangely lit northern Swedish landscape itself. Ekman describes her homeland with an intensity that makes the wilderness palpable, a living presence that shapes and defines the lives of her characters.

4
Sweden: Foreign Policy and Unreliable Narratives

The dislocation of expected patterns in fiction may sometimes have a salutary effect for the reader – and by employing what might appear to be an improvisatory approach to writing, the conditioned response of the reader may be propelled into terra incognita. Some will welcome this – even demand it – others will hanker for more linear fare. Crime writing functions by organising and controlling fictional forms in a more rigorous fashion than, say, literary fiction; the presentation of a concealed pattern or hidden logic presents a metaphor for the protagonist's psychological journey. The disruption of expected patterns automatically forces a closer attention to the text by the reader, along with an impulse to wrest order from what appears to be a series of haphazard events. Such strategies may function as training for a new rigour on the part of the reader.

Another index for new Scandinavian writing – and an index which demonstrates parallels between writers who otherwise share little other than a common utilisation of crime fiction tropes – is the attitude that the writer adopts towards his readership. To some degree, of course, genre function depends on withholding crucial information from the reader in order to give revelation and resolution the dramatic force required at the appropriate point in the narrative. More than British and American writers, Nordic novelists seem prepared to enter the hinterlands of opaque motivation and clouded psychology. Again, this has the effect of forcing the reader to make a more crucial engagement with the text than is customary and ask: 'what am I being told here?' And where crime writers from non-Nordic countries are more ready to supply the reader with the requisite payoff, the attitude in the Scandinavian countries is to say to the reader: 'You have the facts about the events of the narrative and the psychology of the characters I leave it to you to draw your own conclusions about the veracity of what you have encountered.'

It might be observed that out of the Scandinavian fashion for presenting a disordered and dysfunctional society as the backdrop to its stories of murder and malfeasance is a growing apprehension of how fiction from these countries are perceived abroad, as much as giving the indigenous readership what it expects. We are taken into a world where judgements are necessarily nebulous and the reader is obliged to seek for the social purpose (if any) beneath the surface of the narrative. Under that carapace, many of the best current novelists appear to be making non-negotiable points: that social history and political reality are too complex and multifaceted to lend themselves to easy analysis; certainly, these subjects are too nuanced to be addressed more than glancingly in a work of popular fiction, if they are to be granted the requisite gravitas. Nevertheless, the criminals and antiheroes of the crime fiction genre, with their damaged and malfunctioning personalities, are in many ways conduits to certain truths about the world we all now live in. In this brave new world, illusions are ruthlessly stripped away, and morality does not lend itself to any facile judgement system (religious certainties, too, are generally not to be found in this coolly existential universe). These Nordic novelists rightly accept no responsibility for the conclusions we draw from their work, and shrug off notions of social responsibility. It may seem fanciful to invoke James Joyce's *Ulysses* (1922) as an exemplar here, but the best Scandinavian writers share Joyce's willingness to allow the reader to take from his text exactly what he or she wishes to take; whatever allusions are made may not be the ones that the author intended, but they are perfectly valid in their own right.

Any conclusions we wish to draw remain, basically, our own affair, and the writers of the best Nordic fiction do not so much abnegate their responsibility but simply offer us a greater (and more flexible) range of choices. Much modern fiction, crime or otherwise, is bereft of any sociological context, and the detailed, intelligent commentary to be found in the best crime fiction demonstrates the immense possibilities in the genre beyond its entertainment value. The crime writer (particularly in a Nordic context) who is reacting to and commenting on modern society has to be aware of every important strand in the ever-more-fragmented social structure. Any commentary imported into the narrative may be seen as a kind of added value in which the novel engages with the intelligence of the reader and provides myriad possibilities apart from diversion: social and political analysis, subtlety of psychological understanding, a rigorous examination of the way in which society works – or doesn't work.

The workings of society (for good or ill) are at the heart of the work of one particular writer. For some considerable time, cognoscenti of the best in Scandinavian crime fiction have been aware that Mari Jungstedt's Inspector Knutas novels are among the most rarefied and satisfying pleasures afforded by the field, and that the Stockholm-based writer has a total command of character and menace. Her books (set on the island of Gotland) are unique in their steady accumulation of unsettling atmosphere; what's more, Jungstedt has a fresh take on the traditionally based utilisation of classic police procedural techniques. In *The Killer's Art* (2010), a battered and naked corpse is found in the pretty port town of Visby, hanging upside down from the town's so-called 'gate of love'. The body is that of an art dealer, Egon Wallin (hence, perhaps, the bizarre 'framing' in the gate), and it falls to the tenacious Inspector Knutas to discover why this very public murder has taken place. The dead man has recently been divorced and has begun a new relationship. Then a painting by a hot new artist is stolen from the murdered dealer's gallery in Stockholm; is there a connection between the murder and the theft? The investigation leads Knutas into a fascinating trawl through the glittering world of art society, where (the detective is to find) wealth does not remove the need for violent action in the pursuit of an implacable goal.

The Killer's Art is a classic demonstration of just why Mari Jungstedt is held in such high esteem; in Tiina Nunnally's adroit translation, the prose has a stripped-down, utterly functional quality that is perfectly at the service of the carefully orchestrated plot. Writers such as Henning Mankell may outsell Jungstedt in Britain, but – if there is any justice – she will not remain caviar to the general. As several respected critics throughout the world have noted, her books are the equal of most of her contemporaries (and, in some cases, they are considerably more accomplished).

'I have chosen the island of Gotland as setting for my books,' said Mari Jungstedt, 'and the island itself plays a crucial part in my work. It's perfect for crime stories – it is a version of the "locked room" scenario, because of the coastal parameters. The environment is immensely evocative: the flat, wild and dramatic landscape, the special light, the limestone rocks, the long, sandy beaches that lay empty most of the year, the historical town of Visby with the wall around it (6–10 metres) from the thirteenth century, the medieval houses, the big, ancient church and ruins in the middle of the town and the narrow cobblestoned streets.

'Element of Swedish society are, I think, reflected in my work quite naturally, through the characters and narrative developments.

For instance, the complicated love story between my protagonists Johan and Emma grant the novels an extra dimension and, *en passant*, say something about the time and the society we are living in. Similarly, there are points made in the detail of how the press deals with the victims of crime, and how Johan addresses this in his job as a reporter. Points are made about the dumbing-down of the media (for instance, in the fashion in which crime is reported). Ethical questions are always key for me, and when I worked for ten years as a news anchor for Swedish television I thought that the treatment of families of crime victims was one of the most difficult things to handle.

'My focus as a writer is on the relationships between people, and I work very consciously to develop my writing. After having written nine novels in a series, I can discern a pattern – the same themes recur, more or less, in each novel: how our childhood affects us, our relationships with our parents, our vulnerability during childhood and how exposed we are as children. It's important for me to address how adults must give children support, how we must listen to them, take them seriously and offer help. This is actually the reason why I write in the first place; my own childhood was quite complicated. My father was an alcoholic and my mother was struggling to cope alone with three children. She was not strong, either financially, socially or psychologically. My parents were divorced when I was nine, but they continued to see each other and continued to fight. When I was fourteen, my mother became seriously ill with cancer, and we children were terribly afraid. But nobody gave us any support – neither adults, nor the hospital. I think it is important to talk about these things – the things that formed my consciousness. Of course I want my books to be suspenseful and engrossing – but I also want something to be left working away in the reader's mind after the last page. *The Dangerous Game* takes place in the fashion industry; it concerns two young women from Gotland who are making a mark as models. One becomes a successful model, but the other ends up in a clinic for anorexics. This was my eighth novel, and I'm glad to say it became a great success with 120,000 copies sold so far. But I remain very pleased with *The Killer's Art*, in which I achieved everything I set out to.'

An even more astringent view of crime and society is served up by one particularly uncompromising writer. Jens Lapidus's striking debut *Easy Money/Snabba Cash* (2011 [2006]) consciously evokes echoes of the author's inspirations Raymond Chandler and Elmore Leonard – possibly a foolhardy move for any writer, but one that Lapidus has the chutzpah to bring off. The book has sold phenomenal quantities in Sweden (as well as being successfully adapted into a film). Lapidus has a lawyer's background, and has similarly enjoyed much attention for the gritty *Never Fuck Up* (*Aldrig fucka upp*, 2008). The edgy *Stockholm Noir* sequence has also occasioned comparisons with the current American masters James Ellroy and Dennis Lehane. The vividly evoked world of the books is stygian and uncompromising, with an unvarnished picture of the criminal fraternities of Stockholm (including Hell's Angels and a variety of brutal Mafia thugs from different racial groups) unleashing massive violence in a series of drug wars.

Somewhat less confrontational is Kristina Ohlsson, who obtained a British publisher without too much trouble, something of an achievement, given that neither book nor author have enjoyed much press coverage in Sweden. Ohlsson is a political scientist and has worked as a Counter-Terrorism Officer at OSCE (the Organization for Security and Co-operation in Europe). The author also sports an impressive pedigree at the Swedish Security Service, the Ministry for Foreign Affairs and the Swedish National Defence College, where she was a junior expert on the Middle East conflict and the foreign policy of the European Union. Born in Kristianstad in southern Sweden, Ohlsson now lives in Vienna. She was recipient of the 2010 Stabilo Prize for 'Best Crime Writer of Southern Sweden'.

Unwanted/Askungar (2011 [2009]), her impressive debut novel, is the first instalment in a crime series featuring her protagonist Fredrika Bergman. As rain interrupts a Swedish summer, a little girl is abducted from a crowded train en route to Stockholm Central Station. None of the many potential witnesses seem to have seen anything, and the child's mother has been accidentally left behind at the previous station. Inspector Alex Recht and his crack outfit of federal investigators are to be aided by the investigative analyst Fredrika Bergman – and find themselves involved in what initially seems to be a bitter custody dispute. But then the child is found dead in the far north of Sweden, with the word 'unwanted' inscribed on her forehead, and the team realises that they are dealing with an implacable killer. Kristina Ohlsson's debut novel adroitly juggles the intriguing details of a complex investigation that appears (initially) to be going nowhere with some strikingly defined characters, notably the dogged analyst Fredrika Bergman, and a degree of analysis of the social and legal services in Sweden. The British branch of the publisher Simon & Schuster bagged Ohlsson for British translation, and is also adding two more acclaimed Nordic names, Camilla Grebe and Åsa Träff.

Ohlsson has said that she is principally inspired by American and British male crime writers (notably Dennis Lehane, Peter Robinson, John Connolly and Stephen King). And although she reads such Scandinavian writers as Anne Holt, Åsa Larsson, Stieg Larsson and Jo Nesbø, she does not see herself as part of a Scandinavian 'authors' community'. Ohlsson prefers to think of her crime novels as fairytales for adults, and feels no duty to teach readers about Sweden or Scandinavia.

Of her own books, she has said:

'*Unwanted*, my first novel, is a very intense story about a little girl taken from her mother on a train and later found dead. With *The Daisy*, the subject is a priest who used to hide refugees who were not granted asylum by Swedish authorities, and who is found dead with his wife. I am particularly proud of this book because I attempted to write a much more intricate story than I had tackled before, throwing some light on the status of refugees in Sweden.

'Of my own books, *Guarded by Angels* is a favourite. I'm pleased that I was able to maintain the same accelerated tempo throughout the entire book. My latest book deals with the myths surrounding snuff movies. A young student who has been missing for two years is found buried in a small forest in Stockholm, with two other bodies interred in the same grave. The police investigation leads back to an elderly author who hasn't spoken for the last twenty-five years.'

In his native country, Leif Persson the man is markedly more famous than his books; a situation looking set to change. He is a well-respected criminologist who regularly features (with measured, judicious comments) on Sweden's equivalent to the British TV show *Crimewatch*. His calling-card novel is *Between Summer's Longing and Winter's End* (2011 [2010]).

In February 1986, Prime Minister Olof Palme was assassinated, a nationally traumatic crime that remains unsolved to this day. For many Swedes, this was the date when the country was dragged blinking into the same harsh world as the rest of us, and to some degree it marked the beginning of the end of a particular dream – a dream of a somehow sacrosanct Sweden, above the agonies of other countries. The ramifications of the murder have indirectly fuelled much Swedish crime fiction ever since.

The notion of utilising such a society-changing real-life crime (as Persson does in this first novel of a trilogy) might be regarded as an audacious strategy on the part of a novelist whose ambitions are weighty. Does Persson pull it off? Within a few chapters, it is clear that as well as being an intricately detailed crime narrative, this is a powerful state-of-the-nation novel – on a par with the best writing of the American crime novelist James Ellroy.

Though it should be said that for many readers, the immense rewards of *Between Summer's Longing and Winter's End* will be purchased at a price – this is not a book for the casual reader.

The mention of James Ellroy in connection with this sprawling novel is perhaps less apropos than that of another American crime master, Joseph Wambaugh. Was it cynical of the publishers to request an encomium from the latter for the jacket? He's happy to provide one – unsurprisingly, given that Leif Persson draws on and refines many elements from his acclaimed predecessor: a massive, caustically characterised cast, the squabbling, less-than-perfect coppers of a busy, chaotic police department. And misogyny – lashings and lashings of misogyny. But is the latter to be laid at the door of the writer? Or is it just the on-the-nail rendering of a particularly sexist milieu that makes the Sky Sports newsroom look like a 1970s feminist rally?

Before Olof Palme falls victim to his nameless killer, there will be other deaths in Leif Persson's novel. The first corpse is produced by a fall from a high-rise building popular with students, just avoiding a 60-year-old man walking his pet Pomeranian. The dead man's shoe follows some seconds after, hitting the dog's neck and killing it (humour of the blackest hue runs throughout Persson's narrative). Is the death of the man, Krassner, suicide or murder? Two bloody-minded policemen are exercised by this: one is the uncommunicative Lars Johansson, an old-school detective who is aware that an overdue promotion is just around the corner. His colleague, DCI Bo Jarnebring, is a member of the force's surveillance team. Both men are crusty and difficult, but they are at least characters the reader can find some tenuous human connection with; all of their colleagues appear to be the worst kind of sexist scumbags. Not since Wambaugh's *The Choirboys* have a police department and its employees been presented in such a scabrously unsympathetic light.

However, this is Stockholm, not Los Angeles, and it won't surprise regular readers of Scandinavian crime fiction to hear that this investigation of a single death opens up a truly malodorous can of worms, involving Olympian levels of corruption (from the police to deeply compromised politicos) and the dirty deeds of the terminally shifty security services (have the latter ever got a good press in any Swedish crime novel?). And there's the hatred of women on the part of many of the characters that fairly leaps off the page. The status quo of much Swedish crime fiction, in fact.

There is no denying that this is a political thriller that set its sights very high and (to a great extent) achieves its ambitious ends. Leif Persson is a real novelist, with a truly authoritative command of the edgy material he is shaping. But if there is a caveat, it's the fact that Persson (who has experience as an adviser to the Swedish Ministry of Justice and is also a psychological profiler) is clearly not overly concerned with making the readers turn the pages any faster. We are invited to fall under the spell of a steady, unhurried narrative that eschews crowd-pleasing suspense and violence. All is measured and precise here; Persson respects the intelligence of his readers and has no qualms about forcing us to play close attention to the often diffuse (even prolix) narrative. If you're not prepared to do that, Persson seems to be saying, then I'm not writing for you.

But how responsibly does the author deal with the central crime to which the book is building slowly (and invisibly – there is no artificial manipulation of tension)? In some ways, this is the real achievement of *Between Summer's Longing and Winter's End.* Underneath the dense layers of corruption and maladroit administration (by both the police and their political masters), we are given a sobering picture of the Swedish psyche, which has still not come to terms with the death of a politician – and, to some degree, the death of a dream. Certainly, impatient readers in search of meretricious thrills should look elsewhere, but those who feel that the crime fiction genre can tackle truly serious issues should pay attention to Persson's magnum opus. They may tussle with the 500-odd sometimes-intractable pages, but they will end up hungry for volumes 2 and 3 of this ambitious trilogy.

Serious issues are also on the table in the work of Lars Kepler. There were those who felt that Kepler was notably overhyped in Sweden ahead of the publication of a debut novel, principally due to the concealing pseudonym (which was subsequently revealed to be that of a husband and wife team – both hitherto little-known literary authors – writing in tandem). 'Lars Kepler' is, in fact, the authors Alexandra and Alexander Ahndoril. After publishing *The Hypnotist* – a novel that enjoyed much acclaim (and bestseller status) in Sweden – local media inaugurated a thorough search for the identities of the dual authors of the book. After the revelation, sales to a British publisher swiftly followed, with the mystery of the author's identity not such an issue for British readers.

The book has had some ambivalent reviews, but there has been considerable praise from its many admirers. The ebullient Patrick Janson-Smith of Blue Door is Kepler's British publisher, and (characteristically) needs little prompting to extol the virtues of his author. He is confidently trusting that the book will enjoy the success of similar fare.

'Sales of such books are buoyant,' he said, 'mainly because writers of Scandinavian crime fiction keep producing the goods. Mankell, Nesbø, Läckberg *et al.* aren't suddenly going to drop off the map – their legions of fans won't desert them unless there's a very serious dropping off of standards.

'At present, as a publisher I have only the one Scandinavian writer, Lars Kepler with *The Hypnotist.* I chose that book for a variety of reasons, not least being tipped off by the Swedish publisher, Jonas Axelsson. Also, when starting a new list (as I was with the Blue Door imprint), one needs to acquire a few 'statement' books – happily *The Hypnotist* was crowned 'Book of the Fair' at the London International Book Fair in 2009.

'I am becoming hungrier for translated fiction, as the market is becoming hungrier. My latest acquisition is a bestselling German thriller called *Sorry* (2011) by Zoran Drvenkar – such books suggest the rich potential lying far beyond the shores of the United Kingdom. Moreover, such books increase the appetite for foreign fiction.'

The translation aspect of publishing can be an arduous process (*The Hypnotist* was published under the pseudonym 'Ann Long', after various editorial differences between publisher and translator), often dependent on how good the original work turns out to be.

'In many instances,' said Janson-Smith, 'the "editing" needs to be shared between the translator, the publisher and the author. In the case of *The Hypnotist*, the author was immensely receptive to all our editorial suggestions (e.g. some restructuring, additions, more explanation for a foreign audience etc.) which we believe has resulted – dare one say it? – in an altogether better, more roundly satisfying book than the Swedish original.'

The Kepler duo see themselves as a writing couple who are very much aware of the strong crime novel tradition in their country.

'We enjoy taking our part in the tradition,' they have said, 'but we are also rebelling against it when we're attempting to incorporate something innovative.

'The forensic examination we have undertaken of Sweden can, frankly, be transferred with ease to many societies throughout the world. Our country – to other nations – seems simultaneously both exotic and comfortingly recognisable, and that is an attractive combination. We're always trying to utilise our setting as a crucial part of the story. *The Hypnotist* is set in Sweden, but the characters, the dilemmas and the unsettling murder cases we write about are universal, so that they have an application outside Sweden too. *The Hypnotist* is essentially about the strength of family bonds, which can be both positive and, at times, lethal. These are things we all can empathise with.

'Stories about greed, for example, have been told for thousands of years – we're always trying to excavate the essence of key human dilemmas, investigating unconventional angles and infusing the existing tradition with newly minted information.

'In the final analysis, our inspiration is actually film rather than the written word – we both love to immerse ourselves in a thriller at the cinema. It is exciting to examine if it is possible to transfer the filmic kind of tempo and suggestion to the novel form. We even utilise the filmic present tense for our narratives and try to create a kinetic, visually oriented presence in every scene. We're using these non-literary techniques to deepen the relationship we have with our wayward and headstrong Detective Inspector Joona Linna from book to book.

'Our latest book, *The Paganini Contract* (to be called *The Executioner* in Britain) was published recently in Sweden and has, we're pleased to say, been a huge success. It deals with the huge gap for humanity between the creative and the destructive (in this case music and the weapons industry). On a summer night, the body of a woman is found on an abandoned pleasure boat drifting in the Stockholm archipelago. Her lungs are filled with brackish water, but there are no traces of this liquid on her clothes or the other parts of her body...'

But there are still crime series as yet unknown to non-Scandinavian readers – such as Carin Gerhardsen's striking *Hammarby* series, an omission in British publishing of translated fiction that urgently demands to be remedied, as the sequence is a splendid achievement. Carin Gerhardsen is a mathematician who made her literary debut over fifteen years ago, but decided to put her writing career on hold in order to pursue a career in IT. The writing bug, however, reasserted itself, and she opted to try again – on this occasion with a crime novel trilogy (a trilogy that predated Larsson's *Millennium* trilogy). The enterprise was successful, and six years later she sold all three books – the *Hammarby* books – to

Ordfront (Henning Mankell's original publisher). The books are fast-paced and addictive: finely tuned pieces that virtually demand to be read in one sitting. In fact, once under the spell of her work, there is little opportunity to let the mind wander off in other directions. Her organisation of scenes and characters demonstrates a decidedly filmic quality, in terms of kinetic, cinema-style cutting and mise-en-scène, and there is a fierce intelligence at work behind the crowd-pleasing set-pieces. After the current fashion, the murders in Gerhardsen's books are uncompromisingly gruesome, the atmosphere throughout thick and dark, with the influence of contemporary horror fiction a prominent vein running through the narratives.

No such gruesomeness may be discerned in the work of Lars Gustafsson. Born in 1936, the Swedish writer is not a crime fiction practitioner, but has produced an unclassifiable novel, *The Tale of a Dog* (1998 [1993]), which, as well as being a quirky, sardonic meditation on existence and identity, features a protagonist who begins the novel by claiming responsibility for a savage killing. But is his word to be trusted? Gustafsson (who is also a poet and an academic) has lived in Austin, Texas – the setting for his remarkable Nabokovian novel (which has been adroitly translated into English by Tom Geddes). Caldwell is a judge in the Federal Bankruptcy Court. The body of his mentor, the Dutchman van de Rouwers, has been retrieved from a lake. Speaking to his friend, the district attorney of Travis County, Caldwell admits responsibility for a brutal killing – but not, he says, that of his associate. *The Tale of a Dog* defeats all expectations with its wry, playful narrative; existential examinations of the condition of life are juggled in a narrative that cannot be taken at face value.

The notion of taking things at face value is similarly not to be under-taken in the work of Karin Alvtegen, widely celebrated as one of the most provocative and challenging of Nordic writers, with a combative but nuanced approach to gender politics (married to a pronounced skill for ingenious plotting). Her novel *Missing* (2003) won for her (as for Peter Høeg and Henning Mankell before her) the Nordic Prize for best crime novel. When the reader first encounters 32-year-old Sibylla Forsenström, she's in the dining room of Stockholm's Grand Hotel, clad in designer clothes, drinking wine and skilfully reeling in an interested businessman at a neighbouring table. Is she a prostitute? No, that businessman will find her bedroom door politely but firmly closed in his face, his credit card nevertheless picking up the tab for her night of unaccustomed luxury. And the designer dress came from Oxfam – its waistband is secured with a safety-pin. For Sibylla is one of Stockholm's long-term homeless, the luxury she occasionally craves once a feature of a bourgeois but loveless childhood. Unsurprisingly, she hightails it the next morning when the police come knocking on her hotel door, only to find from a late afternoon newsstand that her over-friendly businessman has been murdered during the night – and that she is the key suspect. What follows is both a strong thriller with some expertly delivered twists but also a beautifully developed and written character study. Sibylla first makes some clumsy attempts at clearing herself. But the murders continue and she is herself forced to track down the killer, in the process calling upon first her intimate knowledge of Stockholm's homeless underground (vividly portrayed) and then all of her other resources, particularly those of a keen mind. It is ironic that many of these resources (such as the virtual telepathy she needs to protect herself against an increasingly hostile world) are the product of her harsh childhood and teenage years, detail of which threads its way throughout the book – and it is in these elements that some social critique is subtly shoehorned into the narrative. The result is a character allowed to grow both in appeal and in stature as the book proceeds. If there is a caveat, it is a piece of outrageous sleight of hand sets in motion the final confrontation, itself replete with many ironies. But *Missing* is a clever and involving novel with a trenchant take on the relationship between the sexes.

Karin Alvtegen has said that she draws her ideas and inspiration from the environment she is living in – the social climate, changing societal tendencies and – crucially – what she herself experiences in her daily life. Alvtegen's real interest is the extraordinary human brain and the dark, recessed hiding-places in the avenues of the mind – our fears, our driving forces and what forges them.

'For me,' said Alvtegen, 'the overriding imperative is to invest my characters with genuine psychological depth. I always try to build my stories around such universal emotions as shame, guilt, grief, betrayal. The consequences when such emotions take command of one's behaviour and way of thinking fascinate me. It is fundamental for me to really understand my characters, and to be able to sympathise with them – although of course, that does not mean that I always approve of their behaviour. With every book, I try to finesse my use of language and the complexity of the narrative. I'm always eager to surpass everything I've written before, although that ambition means, of course, harder and harder work. For instance, I wrote *Missing* in six months, whereas my latest book I laboured at for over three years. My books are translated into more than thirty languages but the only non-Scandinavian version I can read is the English translation. When *Shadow* was translated I worked quite closely with my translator Steven Murray, and for me that experience was genuinely inspiring and instructive.

'Speaking from a political standpoint, the socioeconomic divisions and differences in Sweden have increased considerably since the 1990s. Our generous subsidy arrangements for the poor and disadvantaged have been dissipated. Since 2006, when the centre-right Alliance won the election over the Social Democrats (who had dominated Swedish politics for the past eighty years), the disparities have notably increased. Among other things, the government has significantly cut income tax, reformed the unemployment benefit system and slashed access to long-term sick leave. Globalisation, a neoliberal world order and a global shift of power (whereby capital moves freely across national borders) are, considered together, a challange to every national welfare system. Today the global corporations enjoy total world dominion.

'Recently, I realised that all my books have a common theme. I always, it seems, write about exposed and vulnerable children, but in my books we meet the child when that child has grown up, and is struggling as an adult to manage and handle the difficult problems of life and relationships. I am very interested in all the unsaid things we inculcate over generations in our families. Our parents (to paraphrase Philip Larkin) make us what we are. The interactions we have with our caregivers are recorded as brain cell connections. Positive or negative: repeated interaction becomes memories and the foundation for future feelings and behaviors. As adults we tend to look for situations and relations that remind us of our childhood and confirm what we have learned in those early years. So those brought up in a violent home often end up in violent relationships, perpetuating their own misery. Similarly, children from a home rife with alcohol or drug abuse often become addicts themselves or marry (or live with) addicts. I believe our most important task in life is to teach our children empathy and respect for their fellow human beings. The key to a more reasonable world, I strongly believe, may be found via safe, respected and loved children.

'My latest book, *A Probable Story*, is not a crime novel. I wanted to challenge myself and write a suspenseful novel without incorporating any violence or criminality whatsoever. I have tried to infuse the suspense directly into the characters' inner life and their relations. It is a book about love, relations, grief, prejudices, quantum physics and our fear of change and the unknown. How we become lodged in our a locked-in way of thinking – and just how hard it is for human beings to change in any profound fashion. But it's not downbeat – I felt I needed to write something brighter, a novel with a sense of hope.'

A sense of hope is fitfully present in the work of Helene Tursten. The chorus of praise for her atmospheric writing has been growing in volume for some time. Tursten was born in 1954 in Gothenburg. Before her debut with the intriguing *Detective Inspector Huss/Den krossade tanghästen* (2003 [1998]), the author worked in the somewhat less romantic profession of dentistry. The highly-thought-of Irene Huss series now includes seven novels, all bestsellers in Sweden, and the German editions have similarly sold more than 1.5 million copies. The first six volumes of the series have been filmed (to some critical acclaim) by Illusion Film in Sweden in cooperation with German ZDF, with six new episodes filmed during 2010 and 2011. In early 2010, Tursten was shortlisted for the prestigious French literature prize *11e édition du Prix SNCF du polar*, for the French translation of her novel *Tatuerad torso* (*Tattooed Torso*). Her translators include Laura Wideburg, Steven Murray and Katarina Tucker.

'In my work, I'm always driven by narrative – always and ever the narrative,' said Tursten. 'The evocation of my region (Gothenburg, on the west coast) will always be an integral part of the novel, but only as it arises from the demands of the plotting. I've discovered on many occasions that people abroad are greatly interested in the natural locales of Sweden – and there is great foreign curiosity concerning everyday life in the country. I'm happy to supply these two requirements.

'Frankly, I'm not interested in what is considered by delicate souls to be "politically correct" – if I give offence, so be it. I'm energised by learning as much as I can about a given subject, then delivering my opinion, however contentious it may be. But – having said that – sometimes I decide to hide my views in the background, so that they are not easily discernible. I think that my readers will understand what I'm saying in a given book without me inscribing it "on their noses", as we say in Sweden.

'Political issues are no more relevant for Scandinavian writers than for anyone else, whatever the country. I read English and American writers who tackle such issues provocatively: for example Ian Rankin and Val McDermid in Britain, Joseph Wambaugh and Dennis Lehane in the USA.

'Although I respect Henning Mankell, who is a first-rate writer, it might be said that he perceives our society from a male point of view. In the past, we didn't have any women writers to redress the balance, except Maj Sjöwall, who, of course, wrote in tandem. So I decided to write the kind of books that I wanted to read myself – books that reflected different viewpoints. My debut was in 1998, with *Den krossade tanghästen*. (Published in an English translation as *Detective Inspector Huss* in 2003.)

'A recurrent theme for me is crime against children, such as grooming on the internet, trafficking and incest. These are dark, disturbing issues to write about, but it's important to drag them into the light. My last novel was published at the end of August 2010; the title is *Den som vakar i mörkret*; I think the English title would be something like *The One Who Watches in the Dark*. It's about stalking, both of the physical variety and on the internet.'

5
Last Orders: The Larsson Phenomenon

Leaving aside the phenomenal sales – and the posthumous nature of his success – of the late Stieg Larsson, it is possible to discern an examination of the far right and extremist organisations as refracted through the work of the world's bestselling crime writer, even though the books are closer to the mass-market blockbuster thriller than the literary crime fiction they were initially perceived as. Before his untimely death at the age of 50 in 2004, Larsson had produced three of the most remarkably successful crime novels ever written, and the first of his trilogy, *The Girl with the Dragon Tattoo* (2008 [2005]), has broken sales records throughout the world on a weekly basis. It is instructive to examine the mixed response by Swedes to the final nail driven into the coffin of the Swedish dream by Larsson's dark world of massive governmental corruption.

Very few crime fiction practitioners justify the sobriquet 'hero' – but it is a mantle that fits Stieg Larsson. Before his death, he had created a trio of the most ambitious (if imperfect) crime/thriller novels ever written, and the book that inaugurated the trilogy, *The Girl with the Dragon Tattoo*, is perhaps the most widely read thriller of the modern age, after the far inferior *The Da Vinci Code*. As a crusading journalist, Larsson was celebrated for publishing trenchant analyses of neo-Nazi organisations, and became one of the world's foremost authorities on right-wing and extremist groups. His frequent scrimmages – which often placed him in immediate physical peril – were not just political but personal. The author also identified and supported many groups whom he considered to be vulnerable (he was particularly concerned with the harsh treatment of women in fundamentalist theocratic regimes in the Middle East). But Larsson – a lifelong admirer of genre writing (from crime to science fiction) had another career dream. He was keen to undertake another discipline, very different from that of his crusading journalism – his project was to mould himself into a bestselling popular novelist, with ambitious state-of-the-nation novels, painted on the largest of canvases.

However, Larsson's signal achievement was to pull off something most crime writers would give their eye teeth for: fashion an entirely original kind of protagonist for the crime novel (though admittedly synthesising several pre-existing elements). The author's maverick security analyst and computer magician, Lisbeth Salander, is some distance from the drink-sodden detectives with chaotic private lives who haunt most contemporary crime fiction, though her own life is hardly admirable. She is a damaged, brutalised young woman, with an alienating carapace: her Goth death makeup, tattoos and piercings suggest – and forcefully at that – her pronounced sociopathic tendencies. But the appearance is deceptive – Lisbeth is no slacker, divorced from the intricacies of society (except on the level of socially interacting with people); she has a fierce intelligence and an ability to measure and analyse the depths of human behaviour, while standing outside ordinary lives. Larsson contrasts her rebarbative personality by aligning her (greatly against her wishes) with another rebel, but one perhaps more like the reader: a middle-aged journalist who has fallen from grace and is undertaking a kind of redemption by looking into a string of gruesome murders from four decades ago. But his surly computer hacker assistant turns out to be more than his equal when the duo take on the darker tributaries of the influential Vanger family (while Salander exacts revenge on a corrupt authority figure who has abused her). Their role reversal – in terms of generic (and gender) expectations – is one of the signal coups of the book.

Is it a political novel? A cutting examination of modern Swedish society? An analysis of duplicity and governmental corruption in the West? *The Girl with the Dragon Tattoo* (translated by Reg Keeland, aka Steven Murray) is an exuberant (if baggy) piece of popular fiction that confounds category – it is regrettable that its creator was never able to witness its unprecedented success. At the start of this weighty novel, Larsson appears to be testing his readers. He has up his sleeve the two extremely striking protagonists – and once these characters have appeared, our surrender to the novel is guaranteed. Before that, however, we are subjected to lengthy (and impenetrable) details of financial scams in which the reader (like the characters) seems to be being told – sharply – to pay attention. But just as our patience is being tested, Larsson finally allows us to luxuriate in some intriguingly labyrinthine plotting involving Mikael Blomkvist and Lisbeth Salander. The former is cut from a familiar cloth – the tenacious reporter who has taken on a dangerous enemy (as Larsson himself did – and frequently) – but Salander is that *rara avis*, something new in crime fiction (and crime fiction is what this novel remains, despite its initial perception as a 'literary' novel). Salander, much esteemed by her financial investigator boss (who is fighting his own inappropriately lustful impulses towards her), belies her professional expertise as investigator by an off-putting punk appearance: facial jewellery, outlandish clothes and the eponymous dragon tattoo. One of her subjects is Mikael Blomkvist, cut adrift after a disastrous legal defeat. Unconscious of Salander's report on him, Blomkvist is hired by an ailing magnate to look into the disappearance (and possible murder) of his niece on an island several years ago. The island was cut off from the mainland by an unlikely accident involving a blocked bridge, isolating a group of suspects – and before the reader can mutter something about locked room scenarios, Larsson second-guesses us, with his characters noting that this is classic English mystery territory. But not for the first time in the novel, we're being wrongfooted: what follows is much darker and bloodier than we seem to be being prepared for – more Thomas Harris than Dorothy Sayers.

Inventiveness reigns; for instance, just as we are worrying that such an extreme-looking anti-heroine as Salander might alienate the very people she is plugging for information, Larsson has her remove her face metal and don conventional clothes – she has, in fact, a secret identity. She is also, despite her insolent manner, vulnerable, tying in to a feminist undercurrent here, one that would have pleased the most militant in the movement (the novel's superscription is '18 per cent of the women in Sweden have at one time been threatened by a man'). But if this suggests a vitiating PC quality, the unsparing horror and torture the novel deals out banishes any such notions by opening up a debate that is still raging: Is Larsson really able to espouse feminist values while utilising the furthest extremes of sexual violence in his novels?

In the second book, *The Girl Who Played with Fire* (2009 [2006]), as in its predecessor, Larsson pairs Salander with an older man, journalist Mikael Blomkvist. This time, Lisbeth has cut herself off from everyone who knows her; she has surprisingly (despite her contempt for the opinions of others) had breast enlargement surgery, taken up with a naive younger lover, and she is soon the key suspect in three savage murders. But while the ex-security analyst is on the run from a nationwide search, her ally, Blomkvist (who has just published an exposé of the sex trafficking industry in Sweden), is on her side – even though she dumped him as a lover. As with Larsson's first novel, this is complex and ambitious fare limning a scarifying picture of the Swedish state and its compromised security services. The 600-or-so page narrative may be (like its predecessor) in need of pruning, but its rebellious, taboo-breaking heroine remains a winner.

For the last book in the sequence, it was necessary for Larsson to forge a notably powerful finale (leaving aside the possibility of a proposed ten-book project, which was Larsson's original intention). *The Girl Who Kicked the Hornet's Nest* (2009 [2007]), however, takes a route the reader could not have anticipated. Lisbeth Salander lies in intensive care, a bullet in her brain. A few rooms away is the man who has tried to kill her – her father. His body bears multiple axe blows (inflicted by the young woman). If she recovers, she will face trial for three murders – but not if the man down the hall is able to kill her first. There's no arguing that *The Girl Who Kicked the Hornet's Nest* hits the ground running, and the pace rarely lets up for an arm-straining 600 pages. It's an exhilarating (if exhausting) read. Salander's numerous enemies here include some very nasty types, from her hideous Russian father to equally murderous secret organisations and self-serving politicians. And these various nemeses all want her discredited – or dead. Larsson is unsparing in the area of grisly violence (another characteristic – along with a vulnerable heroine – he shares with fellow bestseller Thomas Harris), though this book is notably ratcheted down from its predecessor in this area. But this is a strong and challenging conclusion to a massively ambitious, assiduously detailed trilogy – readers were sorry to see *finis* written to the Lisbeth Salander saga.

Stieg Larsson's journalistic background is key to any discussion of his work. Kurdo Baksi, author of the memoir *Stieg Larsson, My Friend* (2010), is convinced that (both for himself and his late colleague) journalism is insufficient to present a complete and rounded picture of society. 'We need other forms of literature,' according to Baksi, 'and crime novels can be a perfect way to paint a picture of social tensions in different countries. For instance, Stieg Larsson was not allowed to write long, in-depth articles about racism, feminism and social injustice in the Swedish newspapers. And that, I think, is the reason why he wrote the *Millennium* trilogy – which deal with those issues.'

Non-Scandinavian readers, Baksi feels, are being given insights into Nordic society by contemporary crime fiction. Nordic crime writing shows that violence, the ill-treatment of women and endemic racism are components of daily life. He points out wryly: 'Crime fiction illustrates that even in countries considered to be paradise, you will find pockets of hell.'

The contentious immigration issue has a different resonance in Sweden from Britain, as the country does not have the same history as Britain. Sweden never had colonies so that immigrants and refugees have only begun to be a part of Swedish society relatively recently. 'In the construction of a new and multiethnic society,' he said, 'the inhabitants cannot avoid multicultural tensions. And these tensions are of course interesting and fruitful for Nordic writers to explore.'

6
The Fight Back: Anti-Larsson Writers

Inevitably, Stieg Larsson's all-conquering success has ignited a challenging critical response, notably in terms of perceptions of the late writer as an accurate commentator on Scandinavian politics and society (though Larsson would no doubt have pointed to his non-fiction as his real analysis of Nordic mores). The reaction of such writers as the sometime-London-based Swedish crime novelist Håkan Nesser (and others) against Larsson form a different political perspective (with a notably less dyspeptic – though clear-eyed – view of Swedish society, though, in fact, Nesser writes about a carefully unnamed country); the duo of criminologist and ex-criminal Roslund and Hellström also offer different analyses of Swedish society to such writers as Larsson.

Håkan Nesser, in two separate series, has utilised separate locales. There is the not-quite-Sweden in his novels featuring his detective Van Veeteren, but the author's own country is the setting for those books in which the protagonist is Gunnar Barbarotti. Both series demonstrate why Nesser is held in such high esteem by both critics and readers; just a few pages of *Borkmann's Point* (2006 [1994]) or *The Return* (2007 [1995]) demonstrate his effortless crime-writing acumen, from a notably more centrist political position than many of his more left-wing confrères. Nesser's work is splendid stuff: Scandinavian crime writing that is so rivetingly written it makes most contemporary crime fare – Scandinavian or otherwise – seem rather undernourished. Nesser's single-minded investigator, Chief Inspector Van Veeteren, is one of the most distinctive protagonists in the field (lauded by no less an authority than Colin Dexter, who said he was 'destined for a place among the great European detectives'), and the handling of the dark, labyrinthine cases he takes on has a rigour and logic all too rarely encountered in most modern crime fiction. But Håkan Nesser's is no overnight success story. Being brought up in Kumla, the most prestigious prison town in Sweden, may have helped put the author on the right criminal path (at least, the kind of criminal path where you're paid rather than arrested), but it was via his clandestine scribbling away at novels in the classroom for twenty years (when his teaching duties were put on the back burner) that allowed the writer to burnish his skills.

Borkmann's Point, dealing with two savage axe murders in a sedate coastal town, marked the British debut of Nesser's chess-loving investigator and instantly established a following. This second book in the Van Veeteren series was first published in Sweden in 1994. The detective is on vacation, conscious of his solitude after apparently failing to build the necessary bridges with his teenage son Erich, out on parole from a prison sentence. Van Veeteren's boss rings him with news of a double axe murderer in the nearby town of Kaalbringen, and instructs him to lend his expertise to the local force. What follows is a classic police procedural as the Morse-like Van Veeteren, first insisting on – and getting – his own man (the notably un-Lewis-like Münster). He then meets the local chief of police, and begins to assess the strengths (and weaknesses) of the local team. But as Van Veeteren gets to grip with the evidence in the case, and further painstaking investigations take place, it becomes apparent that the team is in stasis, in spite of their best efforts – including that of bright young policewoman Beate Moerk. Nesser incorporates a series of challenging developments before arriving at an unexpected, moving and highly ingenious conclusion. Nesser plays down the angst-ridden aspect of many of his Scandinavian contemporaries, and Laurie Thompson's sensitive translation serves him well.

The Return consolidated the success of the earlier book, with Van Veeteren investigating a corpse rolled up in a carpet in an otherwise sylvan beauty spot, while a double murderer prowls the area. The detective is lined up for a hospital appointment that cannot be avoided, when a body is found, minus its head and limbs. What little information there is points to a local suspect – a double murderer who had disappeared some months before after being set free on parole. Obliged to carry out his investigation from a hospital bed, Van Veeteren finds his talents sorely tested. The results of his investigation confound all expectations. The notion of a detective conducting a 'long distance' investigation by proxy is not a new one, but in the hands of a reliable practitioner is still fecund (think Nero Wolfe and – currently – Lincoln Rhyme). Unsurprisingly, Håkan Nesser shows that he's more than up to the task, and meets its challenges with aplomb. It is hardly surprising that layers of psychological verisimilitude are so beautifully built into writing of Håkan Nesser; one of his models is the writing of John le Carré, and there is no question that Nasser frequently demonstrates a similar adroitness when it comes to forging something more nuanced and ambitious in the genre of popular writing.

Inspector Van Veeteren is one of the most memorable of non-English detectives (and there's plenty of competition in that field). Van Veeteren, good-humoured, cultured and book-loving, is something of a contrast to the melancholy Scandinavian policemen we're so used to, and his sardonic take on the cases he deals with is echoed by Nesser's own off-kilter take on the crime genre: everything here is refracted though a mordant view of humanity and its foibles – but one shot through with sympathy. Perhaps the best entry-point for those new to Inspector Van Veeteren is *Woman with Birthmark* (2009 [1996]). The dramatist Terence Rattigan was generous to the generation of angry young playwrights (notably John Osborne) who were to supplant him; similarly, the composer Ralph Vaughan Williams championed the music of young pretender Benjamin Britten. In neither case was such generosity appreciated – a surly dismissal of the older men's work was the response. So it might have been hoped that history didn't repeat itself when Inspector Morse's creator Colin Dexter began showering encomiums on the younger crime writer Nesser. Dexter had said (as mentioned earlier) that Nesser's Van Veeteren seems 'destined for a place among the great European detectives', and on the contemporaneous evidence of Van Veeteren's third outing, *Woman with Birthmark*, it was hard to disagree. The detective's positive qualities may have been a touch muted this time, something very noticeable here, given the markedly dark narrative of the book.

A young woman is given a grim deathbed revelation by her mother. Slowly, calmly, she begins to draw plans for a bloody campaign of revenge. Her first victim is shot at point-blank range, first in the chest, then in the groin. Within a fortnight, there is another victim, and Van Veeteren is up against a baffling crusade of slaughter – made more pressing when it becomes apparent that there are a possible thirty targets in the murderous woman's gunsights.

If there's a reservation admirers might have with *Woman with Birthmark*, it's that the dialogue doesn't read as idiomatically as in earlier Nesser books (despite the best efforts of the admirable translator Laurie Thompson?). Sterling fare, nevertheless, and it appeared that Nesser appreciates Colin Dexter's fulsome praise, rather than making it clear (à la John Osborne and Benjamin Britten) that he's here to sweep the Old Guard away.

As with most of Nesser's novels, it is the use of language in 2002's *Dear Agnes* (*Kära Agnes!*) that most distinguishes the writing – along with the steadfast refusal (so characteristic of the author) to utilise the standard tropes of detective fiction – even though there is a playful spin on a recognisable plot. Henny and Agnes are prosperous, well-educated middle-class German women who share a close friendship, although many years have passed since the two were really close. Agnes' husband has died, and the women begin to correspond. But the subject of the correspondence takes a sinister turn: the women become mutually involved in a plan to kill Henny's adulterous husband, David. There is a clever diversionary tactic at work here: Håkan Nesser is well aware that the reader will be most concerned with the details of the planning of a murder, but fills in much incidental material about the women's lives; their financial independence, their interest in the arts. The author knows that we will be obliged to continue reading even though the central thread of the narrative is sometimes kept tantalisingly offstage. With the line 'My husband must die and I want your help,' the indomitable Agnes sets in train a series of events that will have grim consequences for everyone involved. Readers will quickly spot one element here that Nesser has cheekily borrowed from Alfred Hitchcock and Patricia Highsmith; a *Strangers on a Train*-style swapped murder. But Håkan Nesser has (*comme d'habitude*) some highly satisfying variations to add to this familiar basic scenario.

Nesser is well aware that (as crime in translation grows in popularity) it is no longer sufficient for writers from outside Britain and America to offer the novelty of unfamiliar settings, customs, etc. The prerequisite now is razor-sharp realisation of every conceivable element: narrative momentum, plot cohesion and (at the top of the list) powerful, distinctive protagonists. All of those factors are precisely what Håkan Nesser delivers in *The Mind's Eye* (2008). Inspector Van Veeteren remains one of the most distinctive of non-English coppers (and there's a slew of competition in that arena). Van Veeteren, amiable and well read, is something of a contrast to the dour Scandinavian investigators we're so used to, and his flinty perspective on the cases he tackles is mirrored in the author's own unconventional, highly individual take on the crime genre. Everything here is refracted though a clear – but not bitter – view of humanity and its foibles, and Nesser continues to eschew comfortable tropes of the left. Nesser is more balanced than some of his colleagues, and less judgemental. Unlike several others, Nesser's view is shot through with sympathy.

The Worms on Carmine Street (*Maskarna på Carmine Street*, 2009) was Nesser's twenty-third novel and is a highly individual standalone which concentrates on the psychology of the characters involved with the crime. The setting is an intriguingly realised New York, where a Scandinavian immigrant, Steinbeck, finds he has trouble with his wife after their young daughter, Sara, has disappeared. The wife, Winnie, has been under considerable mental strain at the beginning of the novel (having lost a child in a previous marriage), and had attempted suicide. But living in Manhattan throws up a series of problems for the couple quite as disturbing as those they have left behind. As so often with Nesser, it is the parlous state of mind of the characters that it handled adeptly; so rigorously, in fact, that the plotting in *The Worms on Carmine Street* seems almost an incidental aspect. That is not to say, of course, that the author is a slouch in this area. The resulting marriage of these two key elements produces one of the author's most intriguing novels.

The Inspector and Silence (2010) is one of the most striking entries for Nesser's astringently drawn copper, and the mystery he is given to crack is among the most ingeniously plotted in all the author's books – no mean achievement. Once again, there is a rich and penetrating picture of Scandinavian society (not, of course, directly Scandinavian – as Nesser writes about an unnamed country which may or may not be one readers might recognise), but with a subtle feeling that all is not heading to hell in a handcart; some kind of amelioration is possible (though, as ever, Nesser never openly grinds any sociological axes).

A very different writer is Johan Theorin, whose moody *Echoes from the Dead* (2008 [2007]) is easily one of the most distinctive novels featuring in the burgeoning invasion of Nordic crime writers – and its prize-winning status (Swedish and British) is massively justified. Theorin takes the reader on a memorable trip to the Swedish island of Öland, and the atmosphere of a windblown off-season Swedish island is handled in nonpareil fashion. The narrative shifts between past and present are impeccably handled, but Theorin is equally adroit at off-kilter characterisation: the relationship between a woman whose son has vanished in the fog and her father is strikingly handled. Theorin is better than even his accomplished compatriots at disturbing the reader – a key element of another equally accomplished novel of the writer's, *The Darkest Room*, which won the Glass Key Award in 2009.

Theorin's striking debut novel, *Echoes from the Dead*, was sold to eight countries even before it had been published in Sweden, and signalled the arrival of an unusual and unorthodox talent. The novel begins in the 1970s, when youthful Jens Davidsson vanishes on northern Öland. Police and volunteers search for him in vain. Twenty years pass, and the boy's mother receives a surprising phone call from her father, a retired sea captain, seeming to indicate what lay behind Jens' disappearance. Julia, Jens' mother and her father Gerlof have not lost their keen desire to know what happened to the boy. With some reluctance, Julia returns to the island on which she grew up, and begins to hear tales of an islander who had once terrorised an entire community. As with all of Johan Theorin's work, the crucial element here is exquisitely conjured atmosphere, and the accoutrements of the standard mystery tale are not be found – or, at least, are subtly diffused in Theorin's already-practised hands. Characterisation may be authoritatively handled (particularly with regard to the bereft Julia), but it is the sensitively evoked atmosphere of northern Öland which is the novel's principal and distinguishing feature. As a debut, *Echoes from the Dead* could not have been more auspicious, and created an instant readership for this highly unusual writer.

Theorin is lucky in enjoying the skills of one of the finest translators of Nordic fiction at work today, Marlaine Delargy. Delargy considers that the more challenging issues of translation vary from author to author.

'Johan, for example,' she has said, 'sometimes uses words absolutely specific to the island of Öland, and it can be tricky to find a suitable alternative in English. There are also the cultural issues, which sometimes have to be explained; for example, Christmas Eve is the main celebration in Scandinavian countries, and is very much a family day spent at home; this would be instantly understood by a Scandinavian reader, but can be confusing for a non-Scandinavian. There are also difficulties in finding equivalent ranks within the police force, and in clarifying procedures within the justice system. And sometimes knotty challenges tend to come via the publisher/editor rather than from the book itself; it is occasionally necessary to argue fiercely to keep a particular phrase or tone, and of course the publishers have the final decision.

'I am familiar with northern Sweden, and to a certain extent Stockholm, but my job is to translate and convey what the author has written. Having said that, I did translate Lars Kepler's *The Hypnotist* with a pocket map of Stockholm on my desk, because the author(s) included detailed descriptions of journeys by car around the city. Fortunately I think most of those have been removed or radically reduced in the editing process! It is occasionally necessary to check geographical details, but this is easily done via the internet or directly with the author.'

For Delargy, there is an element of pleasure in the things she herself incidentally accrues from the act of translation.

'I knew nothing about Öland, so it has been interesting to learn about the landscape and traditions of the island. I have recently translated two novels by the Norwegian Anne Holt (from the Swedish translations by Maj Sjöwall); I knew very little about Norwegian society, and have learned quite a bit about the economic success of the country, and the rights of its citizens.

'Too much emphasis is placed on the "gloom" of Scandinavian crime fiction; after all, P.D. James and Ruth Rendell have more than their fair share of such a quality, and Colin Dexter's Morse isn't exactly a bundle of laughs. I don't think Martin Beck or Kurt Wallander are necessarily any more dysfunctional than some of our British detectives, but what is missing is perhaps the humour we find in someone like Andy Dalziel or indeed Jack Frost. Having said that, I really enjoyed the acerbic wit of Hanne Wilhelmsen in Anne Holt's *1222*. Perhaps there is a perception that it's always winter in Sweden, but Johan Theorin's third book (*The Quarry*) is set in the spring, and as far as I remember Mari Jungstedt's books are set at different times of the year.'

Given the great appetite in Britain and America for crime fiction and crime series on TV, Delargy considers that it's not surprising that when one foreign author has broken through that it becomes easier for the English and Americans to overcome their natural reluctance to read translations.

'In Germany, Scandinavian crime fiction has been hugely popular for years and years; in fact I read the first Wallander novel in German while staying with friends – I'd never heard of Henning Mankell at the time. I also think translation itself has improved, or perhaps the editing process has improved in some cases. I have a set of the ten Martin Beck novels, translated by five different people, and the quality varies enormously. I think if you read one maladroit translation it puts you off the whole process; the aim is, of course, to make the reader forget that s/he is reading a translation at all.

'I thought Åsa Larsson's first novel was terrific. It was published as *Sun Storm* in the USA, but unfortunately Penguin then published the same un-anglicised version here with a lurid cover and an even worse title – *The Savage Altar*. No marketing, no effort at all. Laurie Thompson has translated her fourth novel for Christopher MacLehose, and I hope Åsa Larsson gets the success she deserves.

'My other favourite writer is Johan Theorin; I think *Echoes from the Dead* is one of the best crime novels I've read in any language. I love his characters, his description of the environment, and his plot twists. He is great to work with, endlessly helpful and accommodating, and I was so pleased to see *Echoes* and *The Darkest Room* receive the acclaim they deserve.'

Selina Walker of Doubleday, until recently Johan Theorin's publisher, has pointed out how the backlists of Scandinavian crime writers will ensure longevity for the current popularity of the genre – and in particular (she no doubt hopes), her star author. Her key requirements when searching for such fare to publish are quality of storytelling, and quality of translation. As for the translation process itself, Walker particularly enjoys nourishing a good relationship with the translator. With Theorin's translator, Marlaine Delargy, there are frequent conversations during the process about how the work is progressing. Delargy sees the copy-edited script, and also likes to check a set of proofs. Walker herself is unhappy with clunky or jarring translations. 'I prefer them to be as fluid and fluent as possible,' she has said. 'Johan Theorin's books, I'm pleased to say, are just getting better and better – no easy task, considering how accomplished his early work already was. We published *The Quarry* in 2011. It's moody and immensely atmospheric and, like Johan's first two novels, set on the Swedish island of Öland. He is a writer at the beginning of his career, with a big future ahead of him.'

Johan Theorin considers himself to be geographically specific as a writer. He said:

'I will probably always write stories taking place in Sweden, and if I do chose to write about other countries it would be stories about Swedes visiting them. It takes so much time to get to know a country and its people. I lived over two years in the US when I was young, but I could never write stories about Americans – they are still too exotic for me!

'The only goal I have in terms of place is to be true to my picture of the place I am writing about. I have written three books about the Swedish island of Öland and have tried to paint an accurate picture of what it looks like there, the feel of the place – and to make the island as much of a character in the stories as the people there. But I'm aware that you do become home-blind. I am reading something called *Fishing in Utopia* right now, a non-fiction book about Sweden written by an English journalist, Andrew Brown, who has lived in Sweden for several years and speaks the language. He has noticed strange and fascinating things about this country which I would never have bothered to write about, because I am too used to them. And surely it's the same for every writer, wherever they live?

'I have voted for at least five different parties from right to left throughout the years in the Swedish elections, so my political views are not very clearly defined. I grew up and became a reader of books in the 1970s, when Swedish children's books were much more political than they are now, usually with subtle or unsubtle left-wing political messages, and ever since then I have been wary of books with any clearly discernible political message.

'I'm well aware that the Swedish crime novel is considered abroad to be more specifically political than most other crime fiction, and – especially in Germany – I get a lot of questions about exactly what penetrating political messages about my society I am delivering in my novels. But to me, the finest fiction does not pursue a definite political agenda (with a few bright exceptions, such as the fiction of George Orwell). To say that people become criminals because something is politically wrong with our society is to over-simplify things. There have always been criminals in every society – totalitarian or democratic, rich or poor – and I think there will always be a small part of the population who for different reasons decide to break the law. I am much more interested in trying to see criminals, the police and the victims of crimes as individuals in a certain society rather than some sort of abstract symbols for it.

'I keep my batteries energised by a variety of approaches – for instance, by trying to tell stories about corrupted individuals and not targeting society *in toto*. Sweden is, in general, not a tarnished society and when it's exposed to the light, Swedish malfeasance tends, let's face it, to be very trivial – usually some political official with a little power in a commune who has been given a car to seal a building contract or something. Frankly, it doesn't make for stirring drama.

'Non-European immigrants and their children will see Sweden differently from those of us who have lived here all our lives, and I think they will write very interesting and provocative fiction about it. Some of them have already started doing so, but so far we have no immigrant crime fiction writers.

'Olof Palme was probably the last social democratic visionary with ideals he was willing to defend. Those who have followed him have been pragmatists. We have very few individuals with vision these days – mostly people just are *against* things.

'My subjects include the loss of innocence, people growing up and having to directly – or indirectly – face violence, crime, mendacity, prostitution, drugs and other things which really wouldn't exist in a perfect world.'

The British (more than most nations) have shown a readiness to assimilate fictions from foreign climes. This friendly omnivorousness may be due to the largesse that comes from British notions of superiority, but it is, thankfully, the enemy of parochialism in the ever-more-crowded field of the translated crime novel. The dour, fatalistic view of life in the novels of Henning Mankell and Karin Fossum is notably anglocentric, as is the casual acceptance of eccentricity. But while the ex-journalist and novelist Åke Edwardson hasn't yet enjoyed the success of his better-known colleagues, the auguries are good, with his protagonist Inspector Erik Winter (and his older, more philosophical colleague Ringmar) bidding fair to make a breakthrough in the fashion of Mankell's Wallander. But the urban settings in the novels of Edwardson demonstrate a focus on the minutiae of life within vital but dangerous cities, and incorporate a rigour rarely found in either current American or British equivalents (although, of course, it might be noted that the template for the novelist's narrative set-ups continues to be the 87th Precinct novels of Ed McBain). Interestingly, Edwardson is able to counterpoint such mechanisms as the workings of a police force with the angst-ridden, existentially tortured protagonist who has long been such a *sine qua non* of the field, with Erik Winter's anguished hero somehow remaining plausible despite being subjected to considerably more crises of conscience than most protagonists of genre fiction are subjected to.

Frozen Tracks (2007 [2001]), accomplished though it was, was not the calling card to carry the author into a higher sales strata. In this book, it is autumn in Gothenburg, and two unpleasant series of events have caused headaches for DCI Erik Winter. Two children have been lured into a car by a man proffering sweets. Reports are filed, but as different day nurseries and different police stations are involved, the reports are not correlated (Edwardson implies that a lack of joined-up thinking is just as endemic to Swedish policing as it is to British). But Winter has a more pressing problem: a series of university students have been violently attacked, seemingly at random. The assaults are bizarre: the unseen assailant has wielded an object that no one can identify – one that leaves a bloody cross on the victims' skulls. Then another child abduction takes place, with the boy victim discovered injured in a forest. As Christmas approaches, Winter is facing some truly nasty developments in both cases.

As in such books as *Never End* (2006 [2000]), Edwardson shows his skill in both his succinctly characterised investigators and a nicely labyrinthine plot. The unsettling glimpses into the psyche of a dangerous paedophile are intelligently and responsibly handled, and the narrative has all the fastidious skill of the best crime writing. However, readers of foreign crime are inevitably hungry for new milieux, new mores – something, in fact, both alien *and* familiar. *Frozen Tracks*, though, has far less of the local colour than that accorded readers in Edwardson's earlier books: change the place and character names, and the novel might seem very British indeed; the plotting here is clearly what engaged the author. This doesn't make *Frozen Tracks* less artful, but it sports less of a sense of place – and that's a key element in what admirers of Edwardson turn to his books for.

Edwardson's intriguing *Sun and Shadow* (2005), the first of his novels to be published in Britain, had a back-cover plot description that led the reader to expect something along the lines of a British or American police procedural, kinetic and edgy. What we were given was something rather different. That Edwardson's priorities may veer from the conventional is suggested by the book's opening pages. In the centre of Gothenburg, Sweden's second largest city, we encounter policemen Morelius and Bartram as they deal (amongst other incidents common to big cities everywhere) with the consequences of unrestrained teenage drinking. Meanwhile the jazz-loving, sharp-dressing Erik Winter, soon to be 40, and accordingly 'no longer the youngest chief inspector in Sweden', is contemplating a major change in his life. He is about to share his bachelor flat with his girlfriend Angela – and in a few months he will become a father for the first time. The third major element (subtly handled so that, initially, the reader is not really sure whether the scene described is real or imagined) is the introduction of a figure who may well be a murderer. The action of the novel takes place over seven months surrounding the city's millennium celebrations, and the murders that trigger the major investigation are discovered two months (a hundred or so pages) into this time frame. But meanwhile life (and low-level police work) goes on: we meet the force's female chaplain, her troubled daughter, the daughter's boyfriend. We are presented with further recollections by the potential murderer. Principally, however, we are taken on Winter's trip to Spain, summoned there by his mother after his retired father suffers a heart attack. There he dallies inconclusively with a Spanish policewoman. All is, thus far, measured. Nor does the pace increase when the murder scene is discovered. The investigation, absorbing in itself (with Laurie Thompson's skilful translation coping well with the various forms of death metal music that form part of the plot), proceeds in fits and starts. The pace remains leisurely (vital crime scene results take some time to appear, for instance). The writing, whilst often demonstrating a quiet humanity worthy of British writer John Harvey, is, like Winter himself, rarely demonstrative. And the climax, when it comes, is deliberately drained of drama. Edwardson presents throughout, instead, a strong sense of lives in transition, of endings and beginnings. It's as if Edwardson is consciously rebelling against the tyrannies of the Anglo-Saxon tradition. With three awards from the prestigious Swedish Academy of Detection, Edwardson is one of the most bankable names in Swedish crime writing, and for the patient reader, the rewards are there to be accessed.

The Final Winter (*Den sista vintern*, 2008) was the tenth book in which Åke Edwardson utilised his doughty protagonist Erik Winter (whose debut appearance was in 1997), and this book marks what is (it would seem) his last appearance. The reason for the valedictory note sounded here is the fact that Edwardson has expressed a desire to work in a field other than the crime fiction novel. The subject in *The Final Winter* is a man's overwhelming compulsion for revenge. Martin Barkner tells the police that the death of his lover Madeleine is something he has discovered by waking to find her suffocated, a pillow over her face. He has not seen the intruder who (according to him) carried out the murder. The police are not persuaded and, inevitably, suspicion falls on him for the murder. Shortly afterwards, there is another similar crime in which most of the circumstances of Madeleine's death are repeated. Once again, however, the police are only looking at the most obvious suspect (here, Erik Lentner) in the case of the murders. But police officer Gerda Hoffner, a tyro recruit involved at an early stage in both murders, spots a series of anomalies and persuades the reluctant Erik Winter that the two men are innocent. As ever, all the accoutrements of the police procedural are dispatched here by Edwardson with customary assurance, and the plotting (if occasionally, it has to be said, stretching the credulity of the reader) has a machine-tooled precision. If this is the last Erik Winter book, it is, thankfully, a truly splendid final curtain.

7

Criminals and Criminologists

To say that publishers are falling over themselves to find the next Stieg Larsson is something of an understatement; a headlong, frenzied, foaming-at-the-mouth dash might be a more apposite description. Hopes are pinned to an ill-assorted duo who have already enjoyed massive success in Sweden, but (as yet) not in Britain: one is a journalist and criminologist, the other a reformed ex-criminal. But just how good is *Three Seconds*, the heavily-touted novel from the authors who simply go by their surnames, Roslund and Hellström?

Börge Hellström – whose criminal activities are firmly in his past – is an immensely winning, wryly humorous bear of a man, and is perhaps Lennon to Anders Roslund's McCartney, the latter an articulate, award-winning journalist who shares his partner's sardonic qualities (a few days after the Swedish Far Right's electoral success, I asked Roslund when Sweden became the broken society that Stieg Larsson depicts. 'Last week at the elections,' he replied drily).

The first book by the duo to appear in translation in Britain was 2005's appropriately titled *The Beast*. It was a novel that took the genre into new, disturbingly visceral regions.

Two children are discovered dead in a basement. Their killer is caught, but four years later, escapes from prison. There is a grim realisation that if he is not tracked down quickly, he will kill again. But then the unthinkable happens: another child is savagely murdered in the nearby town of Strängnäs, and an atmosphere of low-level fear begins to escalate into hysteria in the media. The father of the dead child, Fredrik Steffansson, becomes deeply obsessed with notions of revenge. But his actions are to have far-reaching repercussions as the whole country is drawn into the incendiary situation. The two cops assigned to the case – Ewert Grens and Sven Sundkvist – are forced to deal with a cocktail of violence and mob hysteria. *The Beast*, for all its occasional unpolished writing, was a deeply disturbing novel, as well as being a judicious examination of even the capacity of rational Swedes for infectious mob violence. No easy conclusion – or possibilities of amelioration – were proffered. Despite critical acclaim, *The Beast* caused barely a ripple in Britain.

Box 21 (2008) followed (known in the US as *The Vault*). The novel is not quite as rebarbative an effort as its predecessor (the plot of *Box 21* hinges on sex trafficking and hostage-taking), but still pulls few punches, and is not designed for the squeamish. An injured woman is admitted to a hospital in Stockholm, where doctors discover that she has been savagely whipped. Her name is Lydia, and she is a pawn in a people-trafficking racket. Originally from Lithuania, Lydia's grim plight is the result of her callous boyfriend. Consigned to a Stockholm brothel, she is obliged to repay the money that she (against her will) owes. But present at the hospital are the hard-nosed police officers Sven Sundkvist and Ewert Grens, who are on the trail of a vicious mafia capo. Needless to say, the two plot strands are soon colliding, heading towards a hostage stand-off climax. As with Roslund and Hellström's earlier (and later) work, the vision presented here of several aspects of Scandinavian society is uncompromisingly bleak, and (on the Stieg Larsson scale of cynicism), as unforgiving as it is possible to imagine.

A new launch for the duo – via a different publisher (Quercus, in fact, who ignited the Stieg Larsson phenomenon in Britain) – created more interest.

Three Seconds (2010, translated by Kari Dickson) is a book that invites comparison with *The Girl with the Dragon Tattoo*. There is the same obsessive piling on of detail, the same endemic corruption of the authorities (police force, Ministry of Justice), and there's even Larsson's tactic of the slow, challenging introductory chapters that suddenly shift into higher gear. But these comparisons aside, Roslund and Hellström are very much their own men, dealing with a stygian drama of undercover police and the Polish Mafia's plan to corner the drug market in the Swedish, Finish and Norwegian Prison systems (more than most Scandinavian fiction, the duo are concerned with interconnectedness – on every level – of most of the Nordic countries).

A murder in Stockholm appears to be the bloody aftermath of a drug deal gone sour – what's more, undercover police are involved. Ace undercover man Piet Hoffmann has to infiltrate the Polish mafia's drug set-up in a maximum security prison, but finds himself linked to the killing of another undercover operative posing as a drug dealer. The first third of the book may be *andante*, but thereafter, the tempo is firmly *allegro* – and Roslund and Hellström have even managed to freight in some cogent aperçus about the nature of identity amid the clammy suspense; *Three Seconds*, without ever wearing its intelligence on its sleeve, is no dumbed-down blockbuster.

So are Roslund and Hellström the new Stieg Larsson? Or has Jo Nesbø already bagged the late writer's crown? Actually, it shouldn't matter who is at the top of the Scandinavian crime fiction tree to anyone except the bean counters at the various publishers.

Anders Roslund has remarked on his own relationship with Stieg Larsson.

'To me,' said Roslund, 'Larsson is not a global phenomenon; he is still local to me. This is because my dealings with Stieg Larsson were – and are – very important to me. I was – for some considerable time – involved in publishing investigative journalism concerning extreme right-wing organisations. At one point, I was high on top of their "death list" and was physically abused. In fact, I was referred to as a "Threatened TV Man" in all the newspaper coverage. I was obliged to have a bodyguard, and I was forced to live in a variety of hotels, then move as soon as my new number and address were known, I had to move – quickly – to yet another "safe house". Then the death threats would resume. At the time this was happening, I contacted Stieg, since I knew he had the same threats from the extreme right, and he had the knowledge and experience I needed to survive the Nazi threats. We shared the same problem, we worked it out together. I miss him immensely. After his death, as the economic crisis began to bite throughout the world, the extreme right made significant political breakthroughs in Sweden.'

Anders Roslund has admitted to being a literary heir of 'the great Swedish writers', with August Strindberg as his principal inspiration (it's possible to discern the bleak world view of the Scandinavian analysis of marital angst in the work of Roslund and Hellström – though their narrative focus is less personal than that provided by Strindberg's domestic conflicts). Like so many of his countrymen, Roslund discovered crime fiction via the work of Sjöwall and Wahlöö, as did Börge Hellström (who has also named the deeply unfashionable – and now largely unread – English writer Dennis Wheatley as an influence).

'Maj Sjöwall is a dear friend of ours,' said Roslund, 'and from our many talks and discussions I know that she and Per considered their ten novels as one complete work, one long book divided into ten parts. It really is necessary to read them all to get the full idea, to appreciate their full intention.' (Börge Hellström records a soft spot for Sjöwall and Wahlöö's 1971 novel *The Abominable Man*.)

Roslund worked for Sveriges Television, the Swedish equivalent of the BBC, for fifteen years.

'I started a daily programme called *Kulturnyheterna* (*Cultural News*), which was – and still is – a great success. As a news reporter and editor, I produced many ambitious reports about the consequences of crime on society that were shown on prime time television, gleaning millions of viewers. Most of the Swedish population watched – but I realised that no one remembered the subjects we addressed. And that's why I began writing; in fact, that was the starting point for this joint authorship with Börge. Producing TV reports was like writing in sand. I found my way into the sitting rooms of every home in the country, but somehow the content and the issues got lost along the way. Which is often the case with news programmes – what do you actually remember of them later? But writing crime fiction, creating tense thrillers that are primary intended to entertain and divert, but may also help to inform people about the way society works, and about a reality that, frankly, most of us know nothing about – this is a much better way of reaching people, and of making certain points. To entertain using a genre that is so well loved – and at the same time, possibly, educate a little.'

Roslund has talked about his first meeting with Börge Hellström, whose troubled past was very different from his own.

'I was making a documentary about the organisation KRIS (Criminals' Return into Society), a non-profit organisation that Börge had helped to establish for former criminals and drug addicts. I had for a long time worked as a probation officer in my spare time, supporting serious criminals, and so had Börge, and I had been looking for something like this – an organisation that operated beyond the establishment, made up of former criminals who knew how things worked, but had decided to change their lives, and for others who had also decided that they wanted to make the journey from prison to society. We were, so to speak, at the gate to meet them when they were released. Börge was one of five people who participated in the film, and when it was edited and had been shown on television in a number of countries, we continued to meet. We discovered that we were good at developing stories together, and that we could weave our knowledge of the criminal system into them.'

Unforgiving social commentary is, of course, a key component of the duo's work (but with a less overtly political tone than the Martin Beck novels of Sjöwall and Wahlöö), and they are clearly part of the now longstanding tradition of filtering social politics into Swedish crime fiction. According to Hellström: 'The filtering in of social commentary is perhaps one of the reasons why many Swedish crime novels have become so popular. The addressing of social issues has become a crucial element. What Roslund-Hellström are doing is to take such things one step further and force readers to question their choices and their longstanding ideas about particular problems. We want readers to think for themselves about what they read in our work rather than force-feed them our own notions and opinions. However, the social issues that pepper the narrative in our books are actually secondary; the most important thing for us is to entertain our readers.'

Roslund expanded on this element of the duo's work: 'Since Börge had a troubled background, and I had worked for quite some time producing reportage concerning the treatment of child molesters and paedophiles, we both had acquired knowledge of difficult issues from very different angles.' The theme of sexual abuse in their novel *The Beast* had a particular resonance for one of its co-authors.

'It's a matter of personal history for me,' said Hellström. 'As a child I was sexually abused by men on three occasions. And I did not tell anyone about it. But it was a trauma that I carried inside me for almost thirty years. I was 37 years old when I first started to talk about how those men had abused me sexually. As painful as it was for me to reopen that chapter in my life, it was important for *The Beast*, as it was our debut novel. It is a book (we're pleased to say) that has been honoured with awards, and it provided recognition for us as writers. But for each subsequent book that we wrote following *The Beast*, we have changed the way we write; we have also introduced new main characters in each successive book.'

Both authors believe that there is no such thing as a Scandinavian writer.

'If you compare Norwegian and Swedish and Danish writers,' according to the duo, 'there is quite a difference. You don't find any Larssons or

Roslund and Hellströms in Norway or Denmark. Stylistically, we may have an identity, but we are individually different. When comparing different Swedish writers, it's clear that we write books with distinct identities, using markedly different techniques – all the way on the spectrum from writers who are still very close to the Agatha Christie tradition to our books and those of Stieg and other more "modern" writers. This is not a value judgement on the genre and the various writers: this is a rich and varied field, and thrives on these differences.

'There is a unique tradition in this country. Swedish publishers have – commendably – for many years nurtured and treated crime fiction as a strong, independent genre, and shown respect for what authors such as ourselves are (hopefully) doing – telling a good story that is also imbued with insights into society and its problems. Of course, it helps that as Swedes we have so much darkness available to us, so many of those long dark nights that have the effect of creating a different attitude to time and human feelings. However, we try to consider ourselves as international writers.

'Our detective Ewert Grens is hardly an admirable figure. He sleeps on a worn-out sofa in his office, and sometimes struggles up, puts on an old Siw Malmkvist song from the Sixties, and dances in the middle of the room, remembering a time when everything in his life had a purpose. He also occasionally solves a murder. But we never tell a story solely from his perspective – it's simply not interesting enough for us to get stuck inside just one person's mind. It stimulates us as writers to understand both the detective *and* the criminal, a divided view of both aspects of society, to become part of their reasoning, their motives. We try to use multiple perspectives, because for us it forges so many more dramatic possibilities. We try not to politicise our stories, but the dilemmas we depict in our books are, bottom line, political. The welfare system that was once so lauded and celebrated in Sweden – which, indeed, the country was essentially built upon, was unquestionably an encapsulation of the social democratic ideal of solidarity and justice. Now we are slowly and inexorably disassembling this model under the pretext that we can't afford it.'

As mentioned earlier, while Roslund worked for many years as a journalist with prison connections and as a probation officer for prisoners with the longest sentences and the most serious convictions, his writing partner has seen prison from the prisoner's point of view (Hellström had been a drug user for a number of years). Together, the duo have a vast reservoir of knowledge of this world – from two very different angles.

To be able to sit side by side with individuals who have been inside for thirty years, and to be able to meet policemen who work with criminals in every area, to be able to glean key information from the heads of prison security about how things actually work: all of this requires a trust that the team have worked long and hard to attain – and it is, they maintain, absolutely essential to them.

But what image of their country does the duo feel they project with such in-your-face, deeply uncompromising fare? They have an unvarnished view of their role as spokesmen for Sweden – if, in fact, they possess such a role.

'We had a visit in Stockholm from a newspaperman from New Delhi, India. He came a considerable distance to interview us, two middle-aged Swedish authors who are not even very good-looking. The reporter made it clear that he really esteemed our books, but his first mock-humorous question was "Why have you ruined my image of Sweden as a role-model country?" He had grown up loving the films of Ingmar Bergman and the music of ABBA, and our books led him in a new, less acceptable direction. But, as we told him, for all its faults, Sweden is still a pretty safe place to live.'

Concerning the issue of translation, the team regards it as their duty to try to interfere as much as possible.

'Our books are currently translated into thirty languages – and of course, with the Japanese and Korean editions, we are completely in the hands of the translators. But we make sure we are always available to our translators, the very gifted people who are trying their best to give our books another life in another country. Our next book for English-speaking readers, for instance, is currently being rendered into English by the translator who did such a very good job on *Three Seconds*, Kari Dickson, a British-Norwegian living in Scotland – she is very talented. The Swedish title is probably unpronounceable (to English lips) – *Edward Finnigans Upprättelse*; the title for the English translation is *Cell 8*.

'We try in our books to alter perceptions of victims and perpetrators, which is now somewhat stereotyped – both in books and in the news media. Society has lazily accepted a vision of two distinctly different types of people, but the reality is considerably more shaded, neither black nor white. There is an enormous grey zone. One day you are a perpetrator, the next a victim.'

The team often use Börge Hellström's life as an example of this syndrome. He committed many crimes: assault, theft, fraud, burglary. As a criminal, he created many victims, but he seldom gave them much thought; it didn't concern him what they looked like, what they thought and felt about the crime they had fallen victim to. Hellström's victims were, to him, faceless, soulless. He had never seen them, so he never knew them – they didn't exist. An absolute lack of empathy was part of his modus operandi, but feeling empathy is, of course, of little use to a criminal. However, the tables had been turned. Hellström was also the victim of a variety of crimes. As a child (as mentioned earlier), he suffered sexual abuse. He has been assaulted and robbed. As a victim, he began to think about those who had hurt him. What they looked like, what they thought: they were no longer faceless or soulless. He had seen them – they did exist. And he now could feel empathy – for himself. He was both the perpetrator and the victim. But with this new perspective, did he conform to accepted notions of either good or evil?

'As the perpetrator,' Roslund suggests, 'he was evil. He was the devil, the bad guy. As the victim, however, he was the person who had been personally affected by a crime, the victim who everyone could empathise with, a good person who had been struck by evil. We have tried repeatedly to explore this theme in our books. Who is evil, who is good? Who is right and who is wrong? Who is the perpetrator and who is the victim, or do many of us play both roles?'

Role-playing, for Liza Marklund, has involved accepting the role of co-author. Marklund may now be better known in Britain and America for her collaboration with James Patterson on a recent portmanteau novel. Marklund had been initially published in paperback in Britain some years before and did not make a mark commensurate with her status as the first important modern female Scandinavian crime novelist, discounting Maj Sjöwall (though Marklund enjoyed great success in Germany). For *Postcard Killers* (2010), James Patterson's new co-author was not (as is customary for him) a lesser-known writer-for-hire with whom the reader may not be familiar, but a considerable novelist in her own right, chosen for canny geographical reasons – the gifted Swede Marklund, already celebrated for her own highly individual novels (which are, in fact, quite unlike those of James Patterson). The resulting book from this collaboration by an ill-assorted duo was controversial. The partnership in the novel here – between an American and a Swedish protagonist – was obviously echoed in the literary partnership that produced the book itself. Interestingly, while reading *Postcard Killers*, it is not always clear cut where Patterson ends and Marklund begins – perhaps a deliberate strategy on the part of the co-authors. Certainly, the book is markedly different from most portmanteau Patterson novels, though some Marklund fans may wish that she had more of a conspicuous input into the novel.

For Marklund admirers, her own solo novels remain the *locus classicus*: such as the powerful *Red Wolf* (2010, translated by Neil Smith). Marklund, who was born in Piteå in northern Sweden, has enjoyed something of a peripatetic lifestyle. She has lived in London, Jerusalem, America and Italy, among other places. Her training was in journalism, and she has worked on a variety of Swedish newspapers, notably *Aftonbladet* and *Expressen*. Her first novel, *On the Run* (*Gömda*), gleaned several enthusiastic notices when it was first published in 1995, with critics remarking on the book's freshness of approach. However, it was 2002's *The Bomber* (*Sprängaren*, 1998), part of a series featuring as heroine the resourceful Annika Bengtzon, which brought Marklund to a much wider audience, selling over half a million copies. It was, at that time, the most successful novel ever published in Sweden. Marklund has repeatedly written about her protagonist Annika in such books as *Studio Sex* (2002 [1999]) and *Prime Time* (2006 [2002]). In the United Kingdom, her success was consolidated with the innovative (and well-received) *Red Wolf* (2003, published in the UK in 2010).

Paradise (2004) is constructed on a smaller scale than other Marklund novels, though the multiple elements are ambitious enough: two brutal murders in Stockholm's international container port, an unnamed woman on the run from a cunning assassin, hints of Serbian criminal gangs, a new force in European crime. Peripherally involved is a younger Annika Bengtzon (pre-*The Bomber*), employed, against some opposition, by a manager within *Kvällpressen*, a Swedish tabloid, but now benched as part of the fallout from her self-protective killing of her abusive boyfriend. Subsequently, a promising story comes along: a woman wanting publicity for an organisation with 'a new way to protect people whose lives are threatened'. This appeals to the young Annika, her 'undeniable passion for justice' (as her employer recognises) still relatively unquenched. Especially when, soon after, the woman-on-the-run also contacts her. The parameters would appear to be drawn for a fast-moving thriller, taking the reader deep into new and (inevitably) fashionable waters. What is delivered is something subtly different. *Paradise* channels a theme present in all of the Marklund novels previously published in Britain: the abuse of women by men (key, of course, to the proposed organisation).

To this end also – seemingly with limited initial relevance – we are introduced to social worker Thomas Samuelsson and his more high-powered wife, undergoing marital difficulties as their respective careers conflict. Subsequently, Annika's grandmother, a key figure in dealing with Annika's own post-manslaughter trauma, herself suffers a stroke, provoking an intelligently drawn conflict in the family. Marklund demonstrates immense skill as she continues her subtle portraits of the stresses and strains within a major newspaper, though, of course, tabloid news in Sweden is a more decorous affair than in its English equivalents. Despite a capable translation by Ingrid Eng-Rundlow, it might be said that the various narrative strands never cohere as they should into a functioning whole. Nevertheless Marklund's command of the medium never deserts her. Her work has already enjoyed the attention of film studios, with a serviceable film of *The Bomber* (renamed *Deadline*) doing reasonable justice to the original novel. She has been the recipient of several prizes, including the Poloni Prize and her country's Author of the Year Award. *On the Run* deals provocatively and intelligently with racial issues.

'I've added what, for me, is a key perspective to my stories', said Marklund. 'Media criticism and journalistic consequences. It turned out to be a very commercial brew, not just for me, but also for my fellow countryman Stieg Larsson...

'I'm not very calculating when I write my novels. I write what I, myself, would like to read, about things that I find interesting and important. These things normally take place in neighbourhoods that I know fairly well. There's a Swedish saying: Why cross the bridge to get to the water? I use the places I know, because that's what I can write about with the keenest insight...

'I am absolutely a political writer. I use my novels to get a message across. I've tried to say the same thing in all kinds of ways over the last 25 years – in radio programs, TV documentaries and numerous articles and columns. The books are just another tool. For the first 15 years, I was always told that my topics where commercially "stone dead". All the "experts" told me that abused women and mistreated children didn't "sell". Nobody is more surprised – and gratified – than I am that they actually do... The trick, though, is to subtly "camouflage" the message so the book doesn't turn into a political pamphlet – which, frankly, isn't particularly difficult. Political corruption, power abuse and human injustice are generally extremely compelling topics.

'It's in the nature of the crime novel to be full of detail: descriptions of settings, social issues, and human conflicts in order to set in train the narrative – or, one might say (more directly) the killings – since basically all crime novels are about murder, which is the most egregious abuse of power known to man, and also the biggest blasphemy. But it is hard to say how accurate this picture is. Traditional crime novels are usually twisted, dark, and sport starker contrasts than reality, but they do strip-mine the current topics of their time.

'I've been a journalist and a columnist for a quarter of a century, which means I've read an enormous number of daily newspapers for the last twenty-five years. It's my profession to study and reflect upon social issues. For decades, the Scandinavian media (among other things) succeeded in spreading the picture of Scandinavia (and Sweden in particular) as Paradise on Earth. In our humble opinion (the perception is), the problem for the rest of the world is that it's not Sweden. This is clearly not true, of course. A lot of things are good here, but it's by no means heaven. We're way up there in the suicide league, for example. We drink too much, and too many men beat their women on a daily basis. Domestic violence is a severe problem here – one we tend not to recognise (us, of course being "The Best"). The risk of getting mugged is bigger in Sweden than in the US. Two of our major politicians have been murdered in the streets of Stockholm during the last twenty-five years, Olof Palme and Foreign Minister Anna Lindh (who was a very good friend of mine). In other words: our self-image of being "The Perfect and Peaceful Ones" is quite far away from the truth. So the pictures that British readers get through our crime novels are actually more correct than our propaganda brochures.

'We have a higher percentage of immigrants in Sweden than the United Kingdom (Spain and Sweden have the highest in Europe), but there are not very many Swedish crime novels about this topic, I don't think. (But I have to admit that I really don't read them all – quite a few of them are really badly written.) Speaking for myself, all my books are really about power – what people are willing to do to get it and to keep it. Violence against women, gender issues, child abuse and media flaws are my key topics.

'*The Bomber* is the latest book of mine to be released in Britain. It's about power struggles in the work place, what we're doing to each other in the office (there are some very strong emotions and power struggles there...). It's about three women who find themselves in quite similar positions at one point – but handle the situation very differently according to their circumstances. I have to warn readers – it's quite violent...

'The book is chronologically the fourth in the Annika Bengtzon series, but the first one that I wrote. It is the book that got me started as a writer.

'I'm proud of *Red Wolf*, which enjoyed some critical acclaim in Britain. It takes place in my home region of Norrbotten, and it was, I'm pleased to say, a huge commercial and critical success. In fact, everybody seemed to like it – except the people in my hometown, Piteå. They thought I described my birthplace as too cold and dark (we're talking the Arctic Circle, in mid-winter), but in a way I suppose I can understand them. Here they finally had a chance of having the town represented in a widely read book, and of course they wanted an upbeat description out of a tourist brochure (who wouldn't?). Actually, the people of Piteå were so angry that they wanted to dig up the plaque on Main Street that has been placed there in my honour. Finally, I was forgiven – and granted the Culture Award of Piteå (pretty much the equal of the Nobel Prize in literature, at least in Piteå)...

'Of my other books, *Exposed* was an interesting challenge for me. I was inspired to write the book after writing a series of articles exposing one of the biggest union leaders in Sweden for lying, riding in limousines and going to strip clubs at the union members' expense.'

Strip clubs and padded expenses were not to be found in the books that made Hans Koppel's reputation. *She's Never Coming Back* (2011) is the British title chosen by the publisher David Shelley for his company Little, Brown's launching of the talented Koppel in the United Kingdom. The author's real name is (Karl) Petter Lidbeck, and he has written some much-acclaimed and imaginative children's books. The Koppel alias is used when writing such books as the astringent *Homemaking* (2008) for a mature audience. In his adult novels, Koppel makes a point of rigorously avoiding proselytising, but he has said, with typical forthrightness: 'I believe that all political books are bad – but that all good books are political.'

Regarding the rise of the far right in the Scandinavian countries, Koppel has suggested provocatively that Britain may be 'half a generation' ahead in this area. 'I'm deeply embarrassed that the far right is on the move in my country. Embarrassed, more than worried, at least for the time being.'

In the area of societal and political issues, crime writers who Hans Koppel feels articulate serious concerns in their work are Leif Persson and the Roslund/Hellström duo – these writers, he feels, share his own passionate concern for human decency.

The latter is also a key theme for Åsa Larsson. Larsson is a very different kettle of fish from her late, male namesake – and she's still (thankfully) writing. Larsson was born in Kiruna in 1966. She was educated in Uppsala, and spent time in Stockholm before adapting a rural lifestyle near Nyköping with her family. *Sun Storm* (2006 [*Solstorm*, 2003]) received much attention for the rarefied quality of its writing, and the translation rights to the book were sold to a variety of countries before publication. *The Savage Altar* (as *Solstorm* was retitled in the United Kingdom) conspicuously did not initially make the impression it should have in Britain, despite being taken up by those seeking something out of the ordinary in the crime field. But Åsa Larsson has been republished by Quercus (the publisher of her namesake) – and that overdue breakthrough may be pending. Her compelling 2003 novel features a strongly drawn series protagonist: corporate lawyer Rebecka Martinsson, reluctantly enlisted by her friend Sanna, who is under suspicion regarding the grisly death of a famous writer of religious books, Viktor Strandgård; the latter has had both hands and eyes removed in a bloody killing in a church in northern Sweden. Also involved in the subsequent investigation is canny police inspector Anna-Maria Mella, dragooned into the case by a colleague, despite being incapacitated by her advanced state of pregnancy. Like Lynda La Plante's Jane Tennison, these are women who are struggling in a world of unsympathetic men (and Larsson peoples her cast with some extremely nasty males), but the Swedish author's writing is more ambitious than her British colleague, with a level of plotting that excels in both ambition and achievement. It will be interesting to see what the author cooks up for her beleaguered heroine in future books.

Larsson's long-term heroine Rebecka Martinsson made one of her most memorable appearances in *The Blood Spilt/The Blood that Was Shed* (*Det blod som spillts*), a beautifully turned novel from 2004. Struggling to come to terms with having been obliged to kill (though in self-defence), Martinsson has been on sick leave. Accompanying a friend from Stockholm, she finds herself involved in the murder of a woman priest, Mildred Nilsson. The dead woman was something of an unsung feminist heroine, inspiring a variety of oppressed women to change the course of their desperate lives. She had utilised her home as a refuge for battered women and even spread her largesse as far as attempting to save under-threat wolves in the region. Needless to say, all of this worthy activity created a healthy variety of enemies, including the husbands of the abused wives and women of a conservative bent in the town (not to mention a churchman bitterly opposed to the ordination of women). The fact that there are so many possible murder suspects stirred into the brew here is something of a nod to the golden age crime fiction of Agatha Christie, but Larsson is very much her own woman, and the real skill of this novel in its adroit orchestration of a large cast of characters, not to mention its cool anatomising of the repressive morality of a cloistered community. *The Blood that Was Shed* is a novel that clearly suggested that the distaff Larsson has something cogent to say about Swedish society. And the most recent book to be published in Britain, *Until Thy Wrath Be Past* (2011), continues the author's vigorous reinvention of the crime novel form in a piece crammed with minatory atmosphere. Rebecka Martinsson is working as a prosecutor in Kiruna when the spring thaw reveals the body of a woman in the river. Rebecka's sleep has been troubled by a threatening, accusatory spectre – what do these dreams have to do with the dead woman? Rebecka becomes part of an investigation into the disappearance of a plane carrying supplies for the Wehrmacht in the 1940s, but there are those who believe that aspects of the country's past must remain hidden – among them, a ruthless killer.

Top-selling Scandinavian writer Jo Nesbø's work has featured a murderous ideologue – all too prescient. *Until Thy Wrath Be Past* shows that Åsa Larsson is similarly ready to confront unpalatable truths about her society. Of the current batch of Nordic writers, the new Larsson is one to be followed with the most minute attention.

Åsa Larsson is, of course, one of the chroniclers of a country which was changed forever by a political murder. Of the books dealing directly or indirectly with the killing of Olof Palme, Jan Bondeson's penetrating *Blood on the Snow* (2005) is one of the most provocative and confrontational. The book is to some degree a thoroughgoing analysis and systematic organisation of a variety of conspiracy theories, set within the context of the actual police investigation itself. To some degree, the sheer amount of information collected here is dizzying, and a variety of theories examined are contentious, to say the least (such as the possibility that the killer was acting in conjunction with right-wing elements in the police). Bondeson painstakingly lays before the reader a panoply that to some extent defies interpretation by the non-Nordic reader. But the research here is prodigious, and offers an intelligent selection of possibilities.

Swedish writers full of promise are, it seems, appearing daily. Stefan Tegenfalk, born in 1965 in Stockholm (where he is currently living) made his debut with *Anger Mode/Vredens Tid* (2009), the first book of a trilogy about the cynical criminal detective Walter Gröhn of the Stockholm police and Jonna de Brugge of the Special Investigations Unit. The Swedish Crime Fiction Academy has already commended the novel as one of the best of the year, while *Dast* magazine invoked the celebrated Donald Westlake in praising Tegenfalk's adroit treatment of his villains.

Johannes Källström's *The Irrevocable Contract* (2010) is a dark tale of obsession, set in a small rural town deep in the wilds of a remote Swedish forest. With the local industry shutting down and the community threatened with obliteration, Svea Rudolfson, the local mayor, seeks a collaboration with the town's prodigal son Oscar Vigelius, now a fashion designer with a worldwide reputation; the aim is to reignite local industry. But Vigelius brings other things with him – such as sudden death and inexplicable disappearance. Källström's detective Owe Tycho is a strongly characterised protagonist in a piece that synthesises dark myth and horrific elements not a million miles from Edgar Allen Poe.

8
Norway: Crime and Context

Norway remains, in most people's consciousnesses, the most imposing of the Nordic countries, with the ancient legacy of the Vikings still casting a shadow over the country (and foreign perceptions of it) to this day. Foreign travellers, of course, are inevitably counselled to visit bustling Oslo and take obligatory trips across the breathtaking fjords, but there is always a sense that the visitor has – ultimately – seen very little of the country. Which is, generally speaking, usually the case. The population (such as it is outside of Oslo) is spread far and wide throughout the intimidating vastnesses. Norse tradition is, of course, celebrated throughout the world – and for a country of its size, Norway's cultural treasures are truly impressive. Apart from the writer Henrik Ibsen (perhaps the most influential playwright of the 'modern' era, the first to anatomise certain fraught psychological states in a fashion which is now the lingua franca of much crime fiction), the painter Edvard Munch and the composer Edvard Grieg, there are many artists who have encapsulated the national character – difficult and proud – in works of art that are quintessentially Norwegian (the complex political interrelationship between the various Nordic countries is as symbiotic as it has been – at times, acrimonious). The literary traditions of the country (heavily infused with a sense of the past) are prodigious and still relevant for modern practitioners. In terms of contemporary crime fiction, the country's forbidding landscape – and the possibility for both the good and the bad to lose themselves in the vast reaches – is reminiscent of (but different from) the sprawling America of such writers as James Lee Burke. Similarly, the appeal to British readers may be that such canvases are a million miles away from the more geographically restricted brand of crime fiction practised in the parochial environs of the British Isles.

Audun Engelstad has spent ten years in which his area of research has been film (his doctoral thesis, *Losing Streak Stories: Mapping Norwegian Film Noir*, 2006, is available at the British Library). His views on Norway and its literature are trenchant.

'Norway, I would say, possesses a literature that is less continental and more provincial than Sweden and Denmark. Our population is fairly scattered across the country, unlike Sweden where the rural areas are depopulated, and of course, unlike Denmark, which is rather small. In my bleakest moments I believe that Ibsen's critical depiction of the Norwegian people in *Peer Gynt* is fairly accurate. As for politics, our country is recognised for being (largely speaking) consensus-driven. It seems to me that we have more such consensus than in Denmark and Sweden, and my guess is that Norwegian crime novels do not depict crimes that stem from social needs, but are rather driven by greed or jealousy or are sexually motivated. Crime fiction practitioners often pride themselves on their social consciousness (and justifiably so), but I believe the real value of such fiction is to do with the shedding of light upon areas that otherwise are customarily stripped out of the agenda.

'I think the far right – which in a European context is not *really* far right – is given an exaggerated, over-heated depiction (at least in Scandinavian crime fiction, almost turning them in to some kind of monsters). In the most cases, this has little root in reality, at least concerning Norway, which is nothing like these depictions.

'As for the much-touted social democratic ideal – I believe, it still holds sway. In this regard, I recommend Andrew Nestingen's book *Crime and Fantasy in Scandinavia*, which addresses this issue provocatively.'

The Scandinavian countries (leaving aside Iceland – which, incidentally, has the highest book production per capita in the world) are at once both similar and markedly different. All boast a high standard of living, a high GDP, a pronounced level of social awareness and (until recently) extensive welfare arrangements. To outsiders, they may seem very similar – but among themselves, they display noticeable differences, both in culture, language, traditions, politics and economic life. All have common roots, however, and their ethnicity and language reflect this. Danish, Swedish and Norwegian are still similar and fairly well understood.

One notable difference is in topography: Norway is mountainous, with notably dramatic scenery; Sweden is mostly covered with forests and lakes; and Denmark is flat and agricultural. Another distinction may be drawn in political affiliation: although the three are united in the Nordic Customs Union, Denmark and Sweden are also members on the European Union (EU) whereas Norway is not. Indeed, the Norwegians voted resoundingly to stay out in the 1994 referendum on the issue.

Denmark is perhaps the most continental of the three countries, and Danes are perceived as easy-going and jovial. Swedes tend to be regarded as more formal and industrious, and traditionally more affluent and powerful than their neighbours. To outsiders, Norwegians (it might be said) tend to present as rugged, good at sports and savouring the outdoor life.

Over the past few centuries, Norway has traditionally been regarded as the 'poor relation', having been united over several centuries first with Denmark and then with Sweden. However, the discovery of North Sea oil in the 1970s altered this status, and Norway now has the highest per capita income of the three countries and in general performs well on most macroeconomic indicators. Several of these factors have, to some degree, filtered into the country's crime fiction.

Among Oslo-based authors, the talented Thomas Enger has already gained a reputation as one of the most unusual and intense talents in the field, with a notably trenchant eye for human misanthropy. His 2011 [2010] novel *Burned* (with its provocative religious fundamentalism theme and 'burned' protagonist) is already gleaning enthusiastic reviews – and healthy sales. His English editor, Angus Cargill of Faber, is keen to promote his new star, and is well aware of the risk of overkill in the current Nordic boom. But Cargill is confident that quality books and writers will survive and prosper in translation.

'At Faber, we don't really differentiate between translated fiction in our list alongside British and American authors. We have a strong tradition of publishing fiction in translation – Milan Kundera, Mario Vargas Llosa, Orhan Pamuk, Banana Yoshimoto, to name a few – and it's a very important part of the list. Such books can obviously give you interesting angles in terms of promoting the books – both for home and export sales, and, as with Scandinavian crime at the moment, it can be part of a general trend that the public embraces – good news for publishers. That can work both ways, though, of course – a trend can be both a help and a hindrance. As always, there are some good books that don't get recognised and some bad ones that do achieve success.

'The translation process can be tricky, but the most recent one I've been involved in – Thomas Enger's *Henning Juul* series – went extremely well thanks to an excellent and diligent translator, Charlotte Barslund (who has translated Per Petterson and Karin Fossum, along with Sissel-Jo Gazan's *Dinosaur Feather*), so I won't complain.

'This series is one which I'm very excited about. The first book in the sequence, *Burned*, is based around a fascinating murder case (what seems to be a Sharia-style religious murder of a young girl in modern-day Norway). Juul, the physically scarred and grieving journalist covering the story, is a superb character and I found the novel's closing pages to be absolutely electric in terms of the set-up for the ongoing series.'

'I am a product of my environment,' Thomas Enger told me. 'As is my protagonist Henning Juul. Although he lives in one of the richest countries in the world, he is not at ease. He is an introverted man, a thinker, with a pronounced sense of responsibility and injustice. Universal things, perhaps, but I think these are quintessentially Norwegian traits.

'The ultimate rationale of my books is to create a narrative that takes the reader for a ride. Essentially, that means creating an environment that rings true for the reader – an environment in which the characters can live and breathe and love and – yes, kill each other. Henning Juul lives where I live, so it's both important and quite natural for me to paint an accurate picture of the surroundings we are both familiar with. Frankly, I would have done the same if the story had been set in Kuala Lumpur. It's important for me to be able to nod my head and say "Okay, I can visualise that – I see that picture. The details are being presented accurately to me."

'It's almost impossible to paint a truthful picture of our society without being engaged with it on some level. But this doesn't mean that ready-made solutions easily present themselves. Human duplicity is never-ending and self-perpetuating, and people tend to evolve and find new ways to commit crimes. In order to write persuasive crime novels, the writer must keep up to date with such developments, from a societal or human point of view. I like to think that I stand in a very strong tradition of engaged crime writers, and it's impossible for me not to mention Henning Mankell and Jo Nesbø as inspirations. And nowadays I find I am hooked on Harlan Coben – an amazing writer. I have also read a couple of Mark Billingham's novels, which impressed me.

'I have enjoyed being able to interact with and discuss linguistic points with the English translator during her work on my book *Burned* – Charlotte Barslund has done a fantastic job.'

In egalitarian Scandinavia, according to Thomas Enger's translator Charlotte Barslund (mentioned above), people are often on first name terms or address each other by surname only, which can make it hard to establish a sense of hierarchy within the police in the translation. How does the reader know who is in charge or when someone is being insubordinate? It can also be tricky for the reader to determine the gender and marital status of some characters as salutations such as Mr, Mrs and Miss are rarely used, especially among younger people. The social status of a character's name may be lost. Imported English names such as Brian and Johnny usually indicate a lower-class character though imported names overall are gaining greater acceptance. Names such as Christian, Henriette and Caroline usually indicate a character with a higher social background. Occasionally, names of places or characters may be unintentionally funny to a British reader. Name symbolism can be difficult to reproduce in translation. Fortunately, most cities have a West End and an East End and thus the significance of smart versus deprived areas can easily be conveyed to the reader.

Barslund maintains that good solutions can be found to the vast majority of linguistic problems and a semantic translation will deal with text that relies on the reader's prior knowledge of an issue.

'When I first read Peter Høeg's novel, *Miss Smilla's Feeling for Snow*,' she told me, 'I was struck by his use of the geography of Copenhagen. I was mesmerised by the intrigue and conspiracy he conjured up in a city I thought I knew and regarded as a little dull and provincial. Scandinavia is such a well-run and uneventful place and I love the idea of an author taking a real location, a well-known building, and playing "what if" games with the reader.

'Not all novels are set in real locations. Karin Fossum, for example, sets her books in a fictitious town half an hour's drive from Oslo. If the location is fictitious you need to make sure the book's geography adds up. How long does it take the killer to get from A to B? Crime readers are sophisticated and will spot errors in internal consistency. When the author uses a real place – and most do – I try to visit them or, if that's not possible, I rely on maps of the areas to get a sense of place in my head. Google images are a great help as well.

'Though there are many similarities between Scandinavia and the United Kingdom, there are also considerable differences. Scandinavian children, for example, have far more independence than children in Britain. Consequently, a Scandinavian parent may seem irresponsible, even negligent in the eyes of the British reader for letting their 8-year-old child make their own way to school. There is less "stranger-danger" than in Great Britain and more of an expectation of safety. That's another reason why a crime is so shocking. Secondly, because the countries are ethnically homogenous, there is a real sense of shared traditions and ways of doing things. However, this is changing and sadly becoming much more artificial and regimented – by which I mean that officials, sales staff etc. now attend customer training courses and repeat scripted text when dealing with you rather than relate to you as a human being with shared values and expectations.

'Also, everyone has started telling me to "have a nice day" (in Danish, Swedish or Norwegian, obviously) – this never used to happen and I'm not sure I like it. It displays an excess of emotion and misplaced optimism that any self-sufficient, introspective Scandinavian should surely avoid. Can you imagine anyone telling Kurt Wallander to have a nice day? No, just... no.

'I find the internet useful for reading daily newspapers. Also, the Scandinavian belief in transparency means that public bodies publish information about their work through excellent websites, so it's easy to read up on anything you need to know. I also work occasionally as an interpreter for the English or Danish police force and courts, which informs my work.

'There is a frustration in the Scandinavian countries that even the best social democracy in the world doesn't equal a crime-free society – though this, of course, is a source of many excellent crime novels. Life should be good there, but it isn't. And if the Scandinavians can't get it right, what hope is there for the rest of the world? Similarly, their emphasis on the victims, the process of grieving is telling: the dignity of resilience in the face of great loss. In an age of emotional outpourings and counselling, the reserve and self-sufficiency of both detectives and the victim's relatives is very appealing. There is recognition that many people suffer loss and disappointment and still have to get up in the morning and try to make sense of it all.

'The characters are often people you would not look at twice if you met them in the street, but some turn out to have huge integrity, stamina and dignity. Alternatively, you see a life unravel in a way you understand can never be fixed. In both cases the reader engages with the characters and consequently feels greater compassion for their loss.

'Wallander's Ystad has a prodigious murder rate and readers accept this is part of the novel's conceit rather than a reflection of real life, but you probably have to be Scandinavian to understand how initially Ystad seemed an unlikely setting for a crime novel. It's too quiet and provincial. However, it has become much easier for people to travel since the building of major bridges, the opening of more ferry routes and the arrival of the Schengen Agreement in 1985, and this impacts on crime statistics. Scandinavians now have problems with international crime, something which rarely used to affect them, and writers explore this in their books. I don't believe that readers in England expect the murder rate in novels to reflect real life, but I think the picture of a modern, but if not broken, then fraying seriously at the edges society is fairly accurate. Like all good conspiracy theorists, the writers construct their plot on just enough fact to make it credible. The books also reflect the loss of innocence which Scandinavians struggle to deal with. Prior to the murder of Olof Palme twenty-five years ago (in 1986), public figures could go about their daily lives quietly and safely. The Queen of Denmark would visit a department store on her own. She would of course be recognised, but no one would pester her. After the murder of Palme everything changed. However, we still don't understand how it has come to this. In disbelief, we echo Brack in Ibsen's *Hedda Gabler* who says "People don't do such things!" Scandinavians strive to create a free and open society and are rightly proud of it. Violence is shocking because it suggests that our model cannot protect us. British readers get a picture of a country where the expectation is still that life should be fair and safe. The weather may be cold, the inhabitants morose, but they should be safe.'

Non-Nordic readers are attracted to Scandinavian crime fiction, according to Barslund, because they believe in the characters and the world it portrays. They may be entertained and seduced by the pace and glamour of fast-talking US crime fiction, but they connect in a real way with the dogged determination and repeated disappointments of Wallander. Like their Scandinavian counterparts, US private detectives also have messy private lives and rows with their bosses, but somehow that only serves to add to their glamour. Even the mean streets and ghettos of a big US city can appear oddly attractive. By contrast, Scandinavian detectives usually look dishevelled and careworn. They have bad haircuts, crumpled clothes – not in a cool way – and dysfunctional and strained personal relationships. For a surprising number, a dog seems to be their closest companion. They are repeatedly battered by life in general and their work in particular. Even apprehending the killer at the end doesn't convince anybody that life will get noticeably better, but it is a small victory for justice in a flawed world. Life was miserable to begin with and still is at the end. British readers appreciate that honesty.

'Working on Karin Fossum has been a great treat. She writes slow-burning plots which ultimately deliver a devastating emotional punch. And *Burned* by Thomas Enger, the first in a series of six, is highly entertaining. Set in Oslo, it features a badly burned reporter investigating a complex conspiracy. Each book is a self-contained mystery and an overall crime unites them all. It's one of those great highs for a translator when you get the tone of the book almost straight away and find pleasing solutions to every translation problem. I also value the good relationship I have with the author and I'm about to start translating the second book in the series. Similarly, *Death Sentence* by Mikkel Birkegaard was very satisfying to work on: a dark exploration of the genre and a neat conceit. I translated the last twenty pages with my eyes closed, it was so grisly. The author did apologise for putting me through that, but I had to agree that it is the right ending to the book.'

In this crowded field of Scandinavian crime novels, female writers have succeeded in developing just as many variations on the genre as their non-Nordic equivalents. Kjersti Scheen's feisty 40-something Margaret Moss is an original creation, subtly different from (and perhaps owing something to) her many predecessors. *Final Curtain* is Moss's first case (the title may be something of a hostage to fortune), published back in Oslo in 1994, but not appearing in England until 2002. And it's a truly irresistible entry in the genre. But in this tale of actress Rakel Winkelmann vanishing from a train somewhere between Oslo and Bergen, we have (*inter alia*) a cogent picture of a failed mid-life career change from bored actress to lawyer. Such a move has left ex-political radical, divorced Margaret Moss (offspring: one punk daughter, 17 years old) scrabbling for a living as a private eye. Crumbling home, old car, tailing aberrant wives for a living: these are her lot. Even so, she is reluctant to return the call from the son of an old theatrical colleague, the vanished Rakel. And when she does so, it is not long before she is knee-deep in old associations, not all of them theatrical – not to mention the odd neo-Nazi. Scheen writes in sprightly, humorous and often perceptive prose (deftly rendered by translator Louis Muinzer), with sharp dialogue a particular forte. Margaret Moss comes over as a highly attractive figure – instinctive, self-deprecating, plucky and astute. And realistic enough to recruit a fanciable passing truck driver (strong hints of a return in future books) to help out with the rough stuff. Nor does Scheen neglect her other characters, with her women (unsurprisingly) a particular strength. Her plot, if a tad conventional in theme, is intelligently developed, its disparate strands combining to engineer a climax of accumulating tension.

Similarly, an immediate impact was made by the highly accomplished writing of Pernille Rygg (translated by the late Joan Tate, the most prolific of translators from the Scandinavian languages, with over 200 titles to her credit). Both *The Butterfly Effect* (2004 [1995]) and *The Golden Section* (2003 [1997]) gave notice of a strikingly individual literary voice, with a particularly unusual rendering of a threatening Oslo, evoked with both atmosphere and geographical precision.

9
Norway and Nesbø

Those fortunate enough to have encountered the Scandinavian crime writer Jo Nesbø on his visits to Albion have observed his understated, rather British humour and laser-like awareness of everything happening around him – the defining traits, in fact of his tenacious policeman DI Harry Hole (pronounced 'Hurler'). Novels such as *The Devil's Star* (2005 [2003]), *The Redbreast* (2006 [2000]) and (notably) his imposing 2007 novel *The Snowman* (2010) have propelled Nesbø to stratospheric heights – and have made him the most likely inheritor of the Larsson crown in Nordic crime fiction – but apart from the sheer narrative nous, his work also provides a coolly objective guide to fluctuations in Norwegian society. There is also a universal feeling that his work is more strikingly individual than that of most of his Scandinavian colleagues. But that's perhaps inevitable, given the author's very varied background. At 17, he made his debut in the premier league football team Molde, and dreamt of a glorious future at Tottenham. But when he tore ligaments in both knees, Nesbø realised that his future lay elsewhere. He decided to try music, and succeeded – massively: his band's second album was Norway's best-selling album for several years. Finally, though, on a thirty-hour flight to Sydney, he began to write about detective Harry Hole. Aware that this might be seen as 'another crap book by a pop star', he sent it to a publisher pseudonymously. The novel, *The Bat Man* (1997) was, in fact, published under Nesbø's real name and won a variety of prestigious prizes – and is, finally, to appear in Great Britain (2012). *The Devil's Star* built on this success, and became the novel that introduced Harry to English-speaking readers. Those readers are now keen for more outings by a detective the pronunciation of whose name they are slowly catching up with.

The Devil's Star, Nesbø's first book to be published in Britain, was a marker that a unique talent had arrived. A heat wave is making Oslo swelter, and Vibeke Knutsen (one half of an uneasily co-existing couple) makes a grisly discovery among her boiled potatoes: small black lumps in the water, later identified as congealed blood from a body in the attic flat above. Harry Hole, 'the best detective on the sixth floor', would customarily be police chief Møller's first choice for the case. But Hole is also a lone wolf, a chronic alcoholic separated from his wife and child (admittedly, over-familiar territory for literary coppers) and haunted by the recent murder of a close colleague. So Hole finds himself working alongside Tom Waaler, Møller's other 'best detective', but one who, Hole increasingly believes, may have something to do with the murder of his friend and colleague. Nesbø confronts and explodes the clichés here, quickly establishing his protagonist as one of the most credible police officers of recent times. The body in the attic flat is that of a young woman, naked and with a finger severed from her left hand. A tiny pentagram-shaped red diamond is discovered, hidden behind an eyelid. Nesbø manages to keep a complex, baroque plot continually on the boil, the tension between the confident Waaler and the slowly healing Hole (as he scrabbles after salvation) strikingly well conveyed. The dialogue has flinty verisimilitude, and Nesbø also takes the time to fully establish all of his characters, even minor ones. What emerges in Don Bartlett's highly adroit translation is not only an atmospheric portrait of a major city caught in a heat wave, but a sharp picture of a tense Nordic society in flux, crammed with relevant detail as you might expect from an ex-freelance journalist, particularly where the role of the media is described.

The Redeemer (2009 [2005]) is a key Jo Nesbø novel. A cold Christmas in Oslo. A group of shoppers have gathered to listen to a Salvation Army band street concert. But then an explosion cuts through the music and one of the uniformed men drops to the ground dead, shot at point blank range. This murder is new territory for canny Norwegian policeman Harry Hole; he and his colleagues have nothing to work with: no weapon, no suspect and no motive. But it becomes apparent that the victim was, in fact, the wrong man – and dogged detective work soon has the team in a state of grim anticipation with the suspected killer in their sights. They have details of his credit cards, his passport – even an inkling as to who is paying him to commit his murderous work. But breathing down the neck of the assassin has a lethal corollary effect that Harry Hole hasn't foreseen – the contract hit man is driven to desperation, and becomes even more dangerous. He has nowhere to stay in a freezing Oslo, and only six bullets left. The clock is ticking...

This cocktail of urban decay, religion and gruesome violence is a blistering mix, with Harry chasing his prey from the former Yugoslavia though the desperate, squalid territory of the underclasses. The 'Redeemer' of the title may bring salvation – or death. The book, with its adroitly orchestrated, ever-mounting tension, is quite as grittily impressive as its predecessors.

Nemesis (2008) was the third of Jo Nesbø's novels to be translated into English (by Don Bartlett), and was another salutary reminder that a considerable talent had erupted into the Nordic crime scene. The novel kicks off with a bang: a violent bank robbery that ends in death, dispensed by a criminal who escapes leaving no clues. Harry Hole runs into an old girlfriend, Anna, and the couple have sex. But Harry, always at the mercy of alcohol, wakes up alone at home with no memory of the encounter. Then Anna is found dead in her flat – and Harry begins to receive a series of menacing e-mails. This is a novel of character – a Nesbø speciality – but above all else, it's the highly efficient plotting that marks this one out as one of the strongest of the author's outings.

It's a moot point among admirers of crime fiction as to what sort of issues we expect the genre to cover. Those who feel that personal responsibility, cracks in the welfare state and the problems of parenthood are fair game for the crime novel, then Jo Nesbø is the author of choice. All of these issues (and many more) are crammed into the weighty 454 pages of his *The Snowman* (2010 in Britain). If, however, the reader's taste is for tough and gritty narratives with a relentlessly page-turning quality, well... Jo Nesbø is still *de rigueur*. The fact that he is able to combine the urgency of the best storytellers with a keen and intelligent engagement with social issues may well be the reason why Nesbø is shaping up to be the market leader in Scandinavian crime fiction (now that Mankell has incapacitated Kurt Wallander and Stieg Larsson is *hors de combat*).

Publishers of crime in translation often cherrypick the novels they release into the British market when introducing an author established abroad – in other words, chronological sequences are not observed, as is the case with Nesbø. While *The Snowman* will (for English readers) be the first encounter between his laconic detective Harry Hole and a vicious serial killer, that's not the case for Norwegian readers. In fact, Nesbø's first novel had Harry encountering a similar monster. That book, *The Bat Man*, has now been mooted for a belated English publication (and possibly under a title that evokes the Dark Knight). *The Snowman* is certainly the most disturbing of Nesbø's books, with a spine-chilling quality that evokes the English master of the macabre, M.R. James.

It is a typical November night in Oslo, and the snow is beginning to fall. A young boy is awakened, and finds that his mother has disappeared. As he searches for her, he discovers wet footprints on the stairs. With a growing sense of horror, he looks out of the window and sees in the snowbound garden a snowman in the moonlight, the black eyes positioned to look at the bedroom window. And around its neck is a pink scarf – his mother's.

After this blood-chilling overture, DI Harry Hole has to deal with two problems: a forceful new female partner, Katrine Bratt – a woman who quickly demonstrates that she can give as good as she gets (readers will intuit that a mutual respect will grow between the ill-suited duo – standard territory in police procedurals). Harry's main problem, though, is an anonymous letter he has received, signed 'The Snowman'. Mothers and wives have disappeared, often on the day when snow begins to fall. Some days later, a gruesome discovery is made: the severed head of another woman, placed on top of a snowman.

This is the most ambitious of Nesbø's crime novels, though its successor in Britain, *The Leopard*, is considerably longer, with a globe-trotting scenario. The later book banishes any fears that the omniscient serial killer scenario has been exhausted with its considerable narrative grip. Winter in Oslo, and a killer is plying his bloody trade. He has murdered two women in a savage and gruesome fashion; both victims have been discovered with multiple puncture marks. The police are baffled, with nothing linking the victims. And as usual, the media are baying for results – so the head honchos of the Oslo police department opt to coax back to Norway the burnt-out detective Harry Hole. If he can be brought back from his substance-abusing haze in Hong Kong, he may once again demonstrate his skill at tracking down mass murderers. *The Leopard* may be one of the longer entries in Jo Nesbø's nonpareil series, but the author justifies every comma – and (largely speaking) keeps us comprehensively gripped.

Nesbø may be the kind of writer – like Stephen King and James Herbert – who wanted to be a rock star, but even though his band's second album was a Norwegian bestseller, he is self-deprecating these days about this particular blind alley – as he is about his stalled career as a footballer. It is fortunate that success as a writer has dwarfed his earlier endeavours; after all, who needs more rock stars or footballers?

At a recent crime fiction convention in Bristol, the authors who were the after-dinner speakers were dispensing the usual darkly humorous pleasantries to a chuckling audience; how they made a living from murder; how their spouses came up with ever-more ingenious ways of dispatching victims. But then the guest of honour, Karin Fossum, took the stage, and the bonhomie evaporated in a cool blast of Norwegian air. Fossum – possibly the most accomplished Nordic female writer of crime fiction at work today – was having none of the brandy-induced good humour that had preceded her, and her truly scarifying description of a real-life child murder was delivered point blank to a suddenly sober audience. People shifted uneasily in their seats, but it was a salutary reminder that crime – however pleasurable on the page – has grim consequences in the non-literary world.

Karin Fossum began her writing career in 1974. She has won numerous awards, including the Glass Key Award for the best Nordic crime novel, an honour shared with Henning Mankell and Jo Nesbø, and the *Los Angeles Times* Book Prize. Her highly acclaimed Inspector Sejer series has been published in more than thirty countries. She has worked in psychiatric wards, and even as a taxi driver.

Don't Look Back (2002 [1996]) was a psychological thriller that was both economical and forceful, and *He Who Fears the Wolf* (2003 [1997]) is an even more persuasive piece of writing. In an isolated village, a horribly mutilated body has been found, and the suspect (spotted in the woods nearby) has recently been committed to a psychiatric institution. Then a violent bank robbery occurs, with the thief grabbing a hostage and escaping. As the gunman becomes more and more desperate, paradoxically, a strange calm seems to descend on his hostage. And as the hunt continues for the murderer, only the young suspect's doctor maintains his innocence. Like the best of Ruth Rendell, this is a dark and unsettling novel about the reasons people commit crime and the devastating effect it has on the protagonists' lives. All the characters here are exuberantly drawn, notably the resourceful police inspector Sejer and the under-suspicion misfit Errki. But for the English reader, it is the evocation of Nordic society (not a million miles away from our own) that is so effective here. Fossum's novels featuring Konrad Sejer have been published in sixteen languages, and so it's only a matter of time before mainstream English readers take these books to their collective bosom.

In *When the Devil Holds the Candle* (2004 [1998]), Fossum tackles societal problems head-on. Stealing a handbag from a pushchair handle, two teenage tearaways, Zipp and Andreas, unintentionally commit murder when the baby inside is thrown to the ground. Not knowing they are now murderers, the duo pass on to their next target, Irma, an elderly lady who lives nearby. Andreas enters her house, tooled up with a flick-knife. Zipp waits nervously outside, but his friend never reappears. He will never see him alive again. Fossum cannily juggles the roles of victim and killer via the interior monologues of her protagonists.

What we see is what we get: all the crimes are clearly delineated for the reader, but the off-kilter psychology of the troubled characters place a queasy spin on everything we encounter. Are the teenagers straightforward sociopaths? As they discuss things with each other, Fossum subtly undercuts any pat stereotypical assumptions we may be harbouring: the shadings between good and evil. The former, theoretically, is represented by the cops, Sejer and his colleague Skarre, who fail to perceive a connection between the child's death and the reported disappearance of a town troublemaker. With Zipp too frightened to come forward, the police must wait for the evidence to present itself before a disturbing case can be resolved.

As yet, Fossum is still regarded as writer for the cognoscenti, known to a growing band of aficionados but not to the larger crime readership. In fact, Fossum's highly atmospheric and involving books are among the best being produced in the genre today, and her work certainly deserves the widest possible audience. *Calling Out for You* (2005) – originally *The Indian Bride* – is a Fossum novel that tackles another awkward social issue: intermarriage between Asians and native Norwegians, in a country less and less at ease with its immigrant population. Gunder Jomann is a careful, unassuming middle-aged man from a secluded Norwegian community who brings back a bride from a visit to India. The bride goes missing, and an Indian woman is found brutally beaten to death in a meadow. Fossum's long-term protagonist, Inspector Sejer, investigating, finds the community seething with mistrust. As with all of Fossum's work, this is Norwegian crime delivered with keen insight into the difficult issues involved; Fossum addresses her country's uncomfortable, uneasy attitude to what used to be called miscegenation, and while extending sympathy, refuses to dispense facile, politically correct conclusions. It is a provocative novel, not among the author's finest, but audaciously challenging the conventions of crime fiction.

Bad Intentions (2010), more fully realised, is a further reminder that Fossum is not in the business of offering readers a comfort zone. As her steely protagonist Inspector Sejer investigates a series of deaths that begin with an apparent suicide, we are some distance away from crime fiction cosiness. The book's first location, Dead Water Lake, is as bleak as its name suggests, introducing a narrative shot through with icicles of human malignity. Fossum's Norway is an apposite setting for a long dark night of the soul.

That's not to say, however, that reading *Bad Intentions* is anything but a bracingly pleasurable experience. By stripping away the usual excrescences of police procedurals, Fossum suffuses her fiction with something closer to the unsparing vision of her great predecessor and countryman Knut Hamsun. But this is still a thriller – Fossum never forgets that her primary duty is to entertain, and keeps her cut-to-the-bone mystery moving briskly. A young man dies in a nocturnal boating incident, and a fateful pact is subsequently made between the two friends who were with him. Inspector Sejer (armed with his customary profound scepticism about everyone he meets) sets out to crack the alibis of the survivors. Then another body – that of a teenage boy – is found in a nearby lake. With nary a wasted word (in the utilitarian translation by Charlotte Barslund), Fossum steers the ever-apprehensive reader to the novel's irresolute conclusion. It's not a relaxing journey – but then it would be foolish to pick up a Karin Fossum book for a soothing experience.

Karin Fossum has been writing since she was 18 years old, and fell into crime literature by coincidence. Her first story, *Eve's Eye* (1995), was never meant to be a crime story. 'I made the decision half way through the book,' she said. 'And because it turned out to be a success, I continued in the genre.'

Regarding such books as *Don't Look Back*, Fossum said:

'I never pre-construct a plot. I just start writing, and things happen as I move along. I never get inspired by real crime cases; I work very much in fictional terms. My books may include a great many facts and technical data but I do very little research. I might, perhaps, make a phone call, or I write a letter. My ideal is to write my books, sitting quite still in my chair, without having to get up and leave the house for information. I have no office – I work in my own living room, whenever the house is empty, and very quiet. However, a writer is always a writer. All day long I take notes in my head.

'I do not read much crime fiction. I know and admire the work of Minette Walters, but my favourite writer is another English novelist, Ruth Rendell. Generally, though, when I read for my own pleasure, I prefer other kind of books. However, as a young girl, I read a lot of crime stories – mostly the Swedish duo Sjöwall and Wahlöö.

'I think I have some things in common with my Inspector Sejer. We like the same kind of music – and the same kind of whisky. When I wrote about him for the first time, I fashioned him in the vein of the kind of hero that I grew up with in the 1950s and 1960s: the kind and serious type, like TV's Dr Kildare. Decent and good.'

In the year 2000, *Don't Look Back* was adapted as a TV series in Norway. Did Fossum find the experience of seeing her work on the small screen enlightening – or depressing?

'My impression was actually very positive. The TV version was very true to what I had written. As for the small rural community in *Don't Look Back*, well, it wasn't necessarily a typical Norwegian village. I live here myself, and I know every inch of it microscopically. The TV series was also made at this location. It is a small place with about 2,000 people, and it was easy for me to initially choose – and then describe – a place that I know so intimately. I could never write a novel set in a big city, because, frankly I don't know what it would be like.

'I believe I could commit a crime. We all can. It depends on which situations we find ourselves in. In despair, I would steal food if my children were hungry.'

Another challenging female Norwegian is the taboo-breaking Anne Holt, whose status as one of the key writers in current Nordic genre writing bespeaks a reputation that is being expanded as her work gains international footing via translation. While utilising the tropes of mainstream crime fiction in playful fashion, Holt largely stays within the culturally received parameters of the field. But there is something subversive in the lesbianism of her central character, presented unapologetically. In this regard, Holt is reminiscent of one of the most widely read of British/ Celtic crime writers, the talented Val McDermid. Earlier in her career, McDermid had written novels featuring lesbian characters which were well received but to some degree kept the writer in a midlist position with acceptable (if modest) sales. Only when the writer placed a heterosexual couple (Dr Tony Hill and DCI Carol Jordan) at the centre of her narratives (even though the duo are not lovers) did McDermid achieve the kind of phenomenal success that she enjoys today. This equation has its basis in the fact that the earlier books may have been regarded as being firmly in a niche market, whereas McDermid's current work is read by both straight and gay readers. Interestingly, McDermid's recent return to lesbian themes prompted some less enthusiastic reviews than her much-lauded, heterosexual-friendly work has enjoyed.

Within the context of a cool examination of the Norwegian Society, there is something subversive in the lesbianism of Holt's investigator Hanne Wilhelmsen, presented straightforwardly. Holt (who shares her character's sexuality) has kept this aspect of Hanne's character on the back burner – that is to say, it is not necessarily the central, defining facet of her persona.

This may also be the reason why the novels by Holt which were chosen for screen adaptation focus on heterosexual central characters. However, despite this, there is no denying that the current popularity of Holt's Hanne Wilhelmsen novels seems to suggest a ready acceptance of different sexual orientation within the once-hidebound crime fiction genre.

Aficionados of crime fiction's golden age sometimes rather prissily praise its avoidance of sexual misdemeanours; the few permissible were of the kind unlikely to upset the status quo – adultery and illegitimate children. Admittedly, Agatha Christie (whose cut-off locales are echoed in Anne Holt's 2010 novel *1222*) dropped the occasional sexually ambiguous character into her murderous scenarios – but what would she have made of Holt's steely sleuth, Hanne Wilhelmsen, married (with a child) to her lesbian partner? Christie's eyebrows might have been raised by this – and more so by the fact that Hanne's creator enjoys the same lifestyle. However, the fact that *1222* arrives with encomiums from another crime writer (as mentioned earlier), Val McDermid (who shares Holt's sexual preferences), demonstrates that the crime fiction community can finally stop regarding unorthodox choices as... unorthodox.

Of course, this new broadmindedness removes some useful plot devices (fewer secrets to expose), but the best writers can leap over that challenge with ease, and Holt (Norway's bestselling female crime writer) deftly marshals her perplexing narrative.

In a tunnel under the Norwegian mountains, a train crash results in only one fatality: the driver. The survivors – nearly 300 of them – are transported (during a massive snowstorm) to a hotel near the site of the accident called Finse 1222. As attempts are made to move the stranded passengers to safety, another lethal force begins to wreak mayhem among them. People are being murdered one by one, and a new terror is added to the suffering of those holed up in 1222. But among the survivors (as well as, possibly, members of the Norwegian royal family), is a difficult, antisocial woman who has had a ski pole driven into her thigh in the train wreck. But this isn't her only handicap: Hanne Wilhelmsen, retired from the Oslo police, is paralysed from the waist down after being shot on duty. She, however, is still a formidable opponent, as the unknown murderer is about to learn.

If the basic set-up here sounds a touch tired, the reader should not be fooled – there is a great deal of mileage still left in the well-worn tropes that Holt has channelled (recently, P.D. James similarly riffed on the 'murderer on the loose in a closed setting' theme). The clichés are resolutely seen off by the sheer energy and vitality of Holt's writing. What's more, the author (who cleverly parleys elements gleaned from her period as a former minister of justice in Norway) makes a telling stab at the contemporary conscience, with disquisitions on everything from the shifting sands of modern morality to the tendency of laudably intentioned people to be swept into mob violence (think of the turbulent London tuition fees protests). But such serious concerns are never worn on the sleeve; the large cast of potential victims are handled with prodigious skill – as is the uncompromising, short-fused policewoman heroine. As for the plot itself, it moves with the speed of the ill-fated train in *1222* – but, unlike the train, Anne Holt's storytelling never comes off the rails.

Anne Holt is aware of a particular literary legacy. She has said:

'I don't think any of the most popular crime writers in Scandinavia today can evade affinity with Sjöwall and Wahlöö, who wrote their Martin Beck series between 1965 and 1975. That duo in many ways founded what is now often – somewhat imprecisely – called "the Scandinavian socially realistic and socially critical crime novel". Today, almost half a century later, the diversity within this genre is, of course, greater than ever. Yet I would argue that most of us in the field have a Scandinavian foundation – something that is difficult to define but is nonetheless present. My novels are set in a rather rarefied stratum of society: a wealthy, highly educated, social democratic welfare state. (Fictional) crime that takes place in such a social structure will to some extent inevitably be influenced by this society. And I have to say that's true when it comes to myself as a writer, the act itself, and the total psychological structure of the novels.'

But Holt stresses the universality of the genre.

'I am convinced that crime fiction's tremendous popularity in many parts of the world, despite the great diversity and variation in the field, is because it deals in universal themes. Crime fiction is currently the genre that most acutely explores the great and eternal, one could even say biblical, issues: guilt, atonement, punishment, responsibility. Thus, it does not matter what country or region a writer such as myself comes from.'

This reluctance to foreground Scandinavia in Holt's books goes somewhat deeper for the author.

'First and foremost,' she said, 'I write about people, not about Scandinavia. In my novels, I am less concerned about "who did it?"

and far more concerned with "why the hell did this happen?" Especially in my last ten books (of a current total of seventeen), the psychological aspects of crime are most prevalent and central. Human psychology is a complex phenomenon, which can be roughly divided into two categories: the universally human that is basic for each individual, regardless of where you come from, and the attitudes and behaviour patterns that reflect the community you are a part of. In this regard, it is most important for me to tell a strong, consistent story with credible characters that the reader can identify with. This makes it crucial that I stick to characterising people who act in a community I am very familiar with. However, it is never the principal goal for me to describe my own region, it is purely the means to a narrative end.

'I am a political person but not a political writer. I would never attempt to present facile political solutions in my books. Since a crime cannot fully be explained without also truthfully depicting the society in which it occurs, I hope that I nonetheless raise important political issues. When it comes to the answers, I'm sure the readers will prefer to discover them for themselves. Fiction can never give a precise and all-embracing image of society. A society is enormous and complex, and impossible to describe precisely within a given literary framework. My challenge is – principally – to provide insight into the human condition. On the other hand, a good crime novel has the capacity to present an accurate glimpse of society, as the crime fiction genre relates to and anatomises society's darkest sides. I believe that literature in general and crime fiction in particular can help animate a picture more acutely than the other arts.

'By describing people who live, move and act within a given social framework, obviously one paints a picture of that very community – the framework for the novel. I've always said that if you are visiting a country which you have never visited, you should read a crime novel or an interior decoration magazine from that country before you leave on your trip. You will learn more than any travel guide can tell you.'

Holt is aware of the reach and intimacy of the global village.

'Increased globalisation and extreme developments in communication bring us all closer, and at an ever-faster pace. On the other hand, there is an increased polarisation because of this situation, both religiously and politically. The literature of a country will – and should – inevitably reflect this.'

Holt has a realistic, phlegmatic attitude to translations of her book.

'My starting point is that the translator always – inevitably – knows their language better than I do. In any case, it's only three languages – English, Swedish and Danish – that I could confidently finesse. My language skills don't stretch beyond that. I field a lot of questions from most of my translators during their work, and my involvement is limited to responding, as best I can, to those questions. I am a fairly prolific author – with seventeen books in seventeen years – and I find it more sensible to concentrate on new projects than on the translation of old ones.

'If I had to choose three of my own titles that have been significant for me. They would be *Death of the Demon* because in that novel I addressed for the first time the problem of neglected children on a serious basis; the most recent book to be translated into English, *1222*, because it is in many ways a literary experiment; and *Fear Not* as I feel it is probably the most important book I have written.'

The devil is in the detail in rendering from one language to another, according to Kari Dickson, one of Anne Holt's key translators. She told me:

'One of the features of Scandinavian crime is perhaps the acute attention given to detail. Inevitably, there are always the more general problems of translation, such as what to do about dialect, sociolects (though this is often easier), and the impact of a character speaking in English in the source text – obviously it's not so much of a problem if they speak in another language, as that can be kept, but when you're translating into English, how do you preserve that impact? It always feels a bit tame or even clunky to say, for example, "he said in English". In one text that I worked on, the characters spoke a specific enthnolect or pidgin Swedish, and finding the correct way to deal with this was very difficult, as Benglish, Afro-Caribbean or any other ethnolect from Britain doesn't quite match the breadth of that form of pidgin Swedish or "multiethnolect". Another issue was that I wasn't fluent enough in any of those ethnolects to make it credible.

'More specific issues for me have been the technicalities of police procedure and rank, though as I gain experience I'm becoming more familiar with the differences and similarities between Norway/Sweden and Great Britain. I now also have a not-quite-a-man-in-the-Met, but a contact in the Lothian and Borders police force. But there again, there are differences between the Scottish and English police forces.

Besides procedure, the details of daily life, surroundings, situations, weaponry, gunshot wounds, often give rise to considerable thought and research. Do you change the name of the local supermarket to make it more domestic or generic? Do you describe the social connotations inherent in the name? Many of these issues can be dealt with, such as the detailed forensic descriptions of wounds, cause of death, etc., but this often takes a considerable amount of time, and these days it seems that everyone is in a considerable rush to get these new hot books out as soon as possible, so you are often working under time pressure. Who knows what translators did before the internet!'

According to Dickson, the fact that Scandinavians are generally very adept at English can at times pose problems, but this also depends on the attitude of the author to their work in translation. Some authors are grateful that their work is being translated, but have a largely hands-off approach, and only make a few comments. Others are wholly involved in the process. A frustration well known to many a translator is when a Scandinavian author thinks that they know English better than the native English speaker. Also, they are not always aware of the differences between American English and British English. All things that can generally be ironed out, but that can lead to tension and frustration.

'I think that it is important,' Dickson said, 'to have at least some knowledge of the place and location in order to capture the ambience and feel. I know Oslo very well, whereas my knowledge of Stockholm is more limited, but I do know enough about the various parts of the city to understand the general social structure and aspects of the various districts and how they fit together. I think if I were to translate something that was from a place I had never been to, I would want to visit first, as it helps with the choice of words and descriptions. For example, I chose not to translate street names and place names, but if I have some idea of the topography, I can provide supplementary descriptions where appropriate to give the reader an indication of the contours of a landscape that they may not be familiar with.

'I'd say that it is perhaps more important to have a knowledge of a country and a people's mindset than a sound knowledge of location, as it helps you to understand what motivates people and responses, and why the author might have chosen to write about a particular topic and the significance it has in the country in question, in terms of values, etc. I like to know what the political trends and issues are, and any major changes in politics that will affect the country, as this often feeds through to the crimes that are committed in life and fiction. More recently, for example, immigration policy and the expansion of the EU, in particular, have affected the ethnic composition of the Scandinavian countries. I think it's interesting to note the predominance of Eastern European gangs and organised crime in Sweden, whereas I don't experience this as being as prevalent in Norwegian crime fiction.

'On the other hand, I recently encountered a very interesting and provocative crime novel by Tom Kristensen called *Dypet* (*The Deep*), which is about the divers' conditions in the early years of oil exploration and the Cold War. In Norway, compensation for these divers has been the subject of political debate for some time now, with various ebbs and flows.

'In Norway certainly, there is a long tradition of crime reading and writing. There is even the concept "Easter crime", which involves people buying a good crime book to take to the mountains with them at Easter. Quite why that is the case, I don't know, but I think that crime writing was accepted as a viable, "respectable" and serious literary genre in its own right in Scandinavia before it was in Britain and America. I also think there is an exoticism attached to Scandinavia – the bleak landscapes, the dark, the snow, all the elements that are prevalent. When the film *Fargo* appeared, this was similarly one of the unexpected appeals (pregnant women with guns in frozen wastelands), I would say. Another element is the very human aspect of the relationships that are described, and perhaps even the mundaneness of day-to-day lives, that quotidian quality that grounds everything.

'Having said all that, let's be frank: I also think that the hype is a major contributing factor. We buy into what we are told is good.

'I get great stimulus from the authors I work with. In Anne Holt's trilogy about Adam Stubo and Johanna Vik, Johanna has a daughter who is mentally deficient in some way, though it is never established quite why. She often talks in rhymes with word play and sings little ditties, which can be very challenging to translate. Anne Holt is very good at dialogue and I really enjoy working with that. Another issue that cropped up with this trilogy was that the publishers felt that the name of one of the main characters, Yngvar Stubø, was just too foreign and would have to be domesticised. It took us a while to come up with Adam, but I really do think that is the best name for him. Perhaps in all books, one of the greatest satisfactions is when you feel you have found the right voice for the various characters. And Holt's

The Final Murder is so well constructed, playing with various crime genres, and, crucially, the fact that the end is not final.

'A specific challenge in the Swedish duo Roslund and Hellström's books is that the detective Grens listens to Siw Malmkvist, a Swedish singer from the 1960s, who often sang Swedish cover versions of popular English songs. Fortunately, Anders Roslund has helped me unpick these, so that I can write the English lyrics, rather than starting to translate the Swedish ones. Every time I come across another song, my heart tends to sink. But as for the duo's *Three Seconds* – I love the political and social-ethical aspect of this book. And obviously, the fact that it is doing so well is highly satisfying! Also, the working relationship I have with the authors is so valuable and dynamic. The latest book I've done is *Cell 8* (the title was originally *Edward Finnigans upprättelse*) by Roslund and Hellström.'

The Roslund and Hellström duo are becoming better known in the UK – but perhaps the least familiar name in this survey (a situation that is likely to change) is the Norwegian K.O. Dahl. The author nevertheless deserves attention – as a strong novel such as *The Last Fix* (2009 [2000]) amply demonstrates. Katrine is a young woman struggling to put her shattered life into some kind of order. She is finishing a drug rehabilitation course at a commune for addicts in Vinterhagen, and feels confident enough to celebrate with her social workers at a party. Leaving her lover asleep in a car, she strays to the shore of a lake. And, as dawn breaks, she sees a man approaching her from the nearby trees. He is naked. It is the last thing Katrine will ever see. This arresting opening of *The Last Fix* instantly grabs the attention, and the book (the third to be translated into English – Dahl had written eleven) had British and American readers wondering why he is the least known of the ocean of Scandinavian writers washing over the current crime scene. We'd met Dahl's protagonists, Oslo detectives Frank Frølich and Inspector Gunnarstranda, in *The Fourth Man* and *The Man in the Window* (2005 and 2001, but published in English out of sequence in 2007 and 2008), and it's clear that the duo are among the most memorable foreign coppers in a now-crowded field. As the two investigate the vicious killing of Katrine, they initially suspect that associates from her days as an addict are involved – but then suspicion falls on the staff at the commune. And Katrine's experiences as a prostitute open up a whole new range of possible killers.

As in previous books by Dahl, we are presented here (in a subtly nuanced translation by Don Bartlett) with a dexterous synthesis of classic police procedural and novel of social critique. The details of metropolitan life in modern Norway are more than added value; such texture is, in fact, as pleasurable (and rigorous) as the working out of the whodunit elements. Particularly as the caustic observations of Frølich and Gunnarstranda on the absurdities and irritations of Norwegian society are so sardonically entertaining. If there is a discernible influence on Dahl, it's the matchless detective novels of the Swedish duo Sjöwall and Wahlöö; *The Last Fix* has all the skilfully orchestrated tension of that duo's Martin Beck series (the name of another Dahl should perhaps be registered here: the Swedish Arne Dahl, whose stygian *Misterioso* (2011 [1999]) is the first novel in his accomplished *Intercrime* sequence).

According to Dahl's translator Bartlett (who, of course, performs the same function for Jo Nesbø and Gunnar Staalesen), the challenges of translating Scandinavian crime fiction are not signally different from undertaking similar duties with other Nordic fiction. Issues involved consist of such things as home-grown concepts ('hygge' is one example) which have no exact correspondence in England, clarifying cultural allusions, dealing with the way the police force is organised (ranks, titles, divisions, etc.), reproducing humour and various forms of dialect. 'Hygge', incidentally, is closest to the German 'gemütlichkeit': congenial or cosy.

Bartlett makes an effort to familiarise himself with appropriate locales for the books that he works on. He described it to me as follows:

'For me personally, it's very important to do this. For instance, Oslo is actually a character in Jo Nesbø's novels, Bergen similarly in Gunnar Staalesen's, so I make sure that I spend time in both areas examining streets, houses, landmarks and so on. This may not actually make any difference to the translation but it gives me great confidence when I'm dealing with the places mentioned.

'Similarly, an immersion in the mores of a given country are very important. I am frequently in Norway and Denmark. Sweden too, even though I rarely translate from Swedish.

'Denmark has changed politically in recent years to such a degree that just keeping up with the news is fascinating reading. And it's intriguing to observe the degrees of influence from Britain and America.

'Readers might be slightly scared to set foot in Oslo now after reading the terrifying fiction, but it is actually very safe. Jo Nesbø and K.O. Dahl have made us think of Oslo in terms of a high body count. And the picture readers glean of other things is also a rather creative one. Regarding climate, the weather in winter can be severe but there are many days with striking blue skies and snow; stunningly beautiful settings, in fact. In the summer, the climate is better than in Britain. And people are kind, humorous, fair and flexible. Most commentators use the term "bleak" about Nordic novels, but that was never a term I used in the years I lived there. And, frankly, my opinion has not changed since then, either.'

Bartlett is not surprised by the burgeoning taste for Scandinavian crime fiction.

'Some of the novels are decidedly filmic, and there is the appeal of a change of scene and – to British eyes – new, exotic backgrounds. Scandinavian societies have been exemplary models for so long that when crime novels suggest fissures in the model, we are intrigued, particularly as these are our close neighbours who we feel are similar to us; these are like-minded cultures with a great deal of Anglo-American influence.

'As a translator, I particularly enjoy unravelling/recreating puns, jokes, idioms, humour, compressed language and witty dialogue. K.O. Dahl, Gunnar Staalesen and Jo Nesbø have all given me ample material for exercising this pleasure. *The Redbreast*, for instance, has some of these elements, and I still think it is Nesbø's best. It has a plethora of different, nuanced, views of fascism, some highly symbolic scenes, emotional depth, pace and humour. Similarly, *Lethal Investments* is the first of the Gunnarstranda/Frølich books and puts everything else K.O. Dahl has had published in context. I hope it will now allow readers to enjoy the four Oslo Detectives books in the correct order, and that will make a difference. Regarding Staalesen, *The Consorts of Death* was a pleasure to do as it reintroduced his signature character of Varg Veum after a long break.'

As this book has demonstrated, the trickle of Scandinavian crime in translation has turned into a flood, and even those who avidly consume such books are in danger of being shell-shocked. But attention has to be paid to Gunnar Staalesen, undoubtedly one of the finest Nordic novelists in the tradition of such masters as Henning Mankell. *The Writing on the Wall* (2004 [2002]) is a radical re-working of Mankell-style material, but his most striking novel was to appear seven years later. A phone call from the past sets the narrative of *The Consorts of Death* (2009), the thirteenth novel in the series about Bergen detective Varg Veum, in motion.

Gunnar Staalesen tries to avoid the parochial in his writing.

'As a Norwegian writer of detective novels,' he told me, 'I am definitely conscious of writing within an international genre, and the inspiration for my writing comes from both American writers (Raymond Chandler, Ross Macdonald), British ones (always Arthur Conan Doyle, and – in terms of plotting, at least – Agatha Christie), as well as the great Swedes Sjöwall and Wahlöö. But I have learnt a lot from classic Norwegian writers, too (even if they did not write crime novels), such as Henrik Ibsen and Amalie Skram. The small Nordic languages, in which we Norwegians can talk together and read each other's books in the original tongue, creates for Nordic writers one big family (and, to some degree, this also applies to writers from Iceland).'

The Consorts of Death is one of Staalesen's most impressive books. A phone call from an old flame brings the name 'Johnny boy' to Bergen private eye Varg Veum, resulting in memories flooding back. Veum started his career as a child protection officer in the Norwegian social services, and in 1970 2-year-old 'Johnny boy' (Jan Egil is his more formal name) became an 'acute referral' case, requiring immediate rescue from a terrorised mother at the mercy of her violent partner. Four years later Veum, still a social worker, is called to tend to a traumatised child at the scene of a murder. It is Johnny boy – and the corpse is his foster father. Still later, Veum, now a private eye, is asked to intervene in a hostage situation. This time both foster parents are dead, and Johnny boy is the key suspect. In the present, ten years on, Veum's old flame tells him that Johnny boy is on the run in Oslo, looking for vengeance on those who failed him – and Veum's name is on the list. It was no accident that Staalesen chose social work as the key background for his private eye, for the theme of the damaged lives resulting from family breakdown has recurred in his fiction. Coincidentally perhaps, of four Veum novels published in England since *At Night All Wolves Are Grey* in 1986 [1983], two others – *Yours until Death* (2009 [1979]) and *The Writing on the Wall* (2004 [1995]) – have both featured such themes. But here the writer (in Don Bartlett's translation) delivers his most trenchant treatment of the concept. But this is no British tabloid-style denunciation of the evils perpetrated by a hard-pressed social service system. In fact, right from the start, Staalesen is at pains to emphasise the problems of the dysfunctional family and, implicitly, the broader role of government in such cases. Stylistically, we are some distance from the studied similes and despairing romanticism of the two earliest books (perhaps over-emphasised in the translation of *Yours until Death*). Chandler's influence lives on mainly in the tarnished knight-errant character of Veum, but here it is the tangled web of human relationships that are at the heart of the book (as in the novels of Ross Macdonald, Staalesen's other key influence). The complex plot, incorporating four separate time frames (five if you include the real-life mystery, with its odd reverberations in the present, involving Mads Andersen and the Trodalen murder of 1839), not only affords consummate characterisation and striking evocations of the Norwegian countryside north of Bergen, but also some fascinating insights into the Norwegian state alcohol 'monopoly', and an affecting portrait of the damaged Jan Egil at key stages of his life, often tellingly juxtaposed with the flawed human beings (not least Veum) who surround him. Near the close of the book, Veum senses Jan's 'anger and pent-up violence' and asks 'was this the best we could achieve, the sum of our success?' Whilst the central mystery of the book is 'solved', the book's ambiguous conclusion leaves that question hanging tantalisingly in the air. Veum is also the subject of several successful film adaptations in Norway, discussed separately.

Staalesen has definite ideas about the individual character of Norwegian crime fiction. He described these ideas to me:

'I think the presence of nature is particularly strong – and pervasive – in most Norwegian (and Scandinavian) novels, be they detective or mainstream fiction. It's stronger and more pronounced than in the literature from many other regions of the world. Regarding this sense of place, it is important for me to draw a precise picture of my region, the West coast of Norway, the second largest city in Norway, Bergen, and the areas surrounding the city. I also need to register, of course, the ocean, the fjords, the mountains – but these aspects are not central to my books. They are a crucial background for the narrative, in which (if the truth be told) the main action could have happened in many other places in the world. Having said that, Bergen, which is known as a rainy city, makes the perfect background for my type of *noir,* private eye stories. Rainswept streets are a satisfying element of this kind of fiction.

'Regarding the area, the west coast of Norway from Stavanger to Kristiansund, I would say that it is very much influenced by the oil industry and all the activity linked to this. A great deal of the new money in Norway comes from this area, and even further north, and if you include the "old" money (deriving from the fishing industry and the energy resources from waterfalls), you could easily say that without the western part of Norway, this would not have been such a rich country as it is today. But all these fiscal resources are managed from the capital, Oslo, which results in some elements of conflicts between the powerful East and the moneymaking West. Politically speaking, though, in essence, there is no marked difference between my region and the rest of Norway.'

In terms of political undercurrents in his work, Staalesen attempts to avoid the tendentious if he can.

'I do not look upon myself as a political writer. I try to do as Henrik Ibsen did: I ask the questions. It is up to the reader to ascertain the correct answers. But, needless to say, the problems of modern society are a tangible force in my books, and it is not difficult to discern elements of political criticism in the long series of books I've written about Varg Veum. Through the plot of a crime novel you can move your main characters from the lowest levels of the society up to the highest, and (as a writer) you can take a scalpel to all those various levels, laying them open so that the differences or similarities between them are visible and evident. In a crime novel you can ask the crucial questions.

'It is important to keep in mind when talking about Nordic crime novels that they necessarily paint a picture of present-day Scandinavian countries that is darker and more filled with crime than might actually be the case in the real world. For most people living in these countries, everyday life is secure and safe, and the number of murders is more modest than in our fiction. Nevertheless, there is no question that Norway and the other Scandinavian countries are by no means as safe as they were forty or fifty years ago [recent tragic events have emphasised that], and the presence of organised crime is stronger, particularly in the bigger cities. This latter brand of crime is very often (as, let's face it, it is throughout the world) linked to drugs and prostitution.'

Staalesen hankers after a dream of the past: the perfectible Norwegian society.

'I think that the generation to which I belong (I was born in 1947) still has a dream about an ideal society, a functioning democracy based on welfare and solidarity. It seems to me that many of the politicians in Norway (even those from the right-wing spectrum) believe in the same ideals, because the differences between the most influential political parties in Norway actually do not go very deep. We still live in a version of social democracy. Admittedly, there is a strong right-wing in Norway (from time to time, they manage to achieve the biggest poll results), and it is possible that might represent a danger to Norwegian society. But I believe that even they are pragmatic enough (should they achieve power) to avoid destroying what generations before them have built. I'm aware that when I visit Britain, Germany, France and even Italy, most of the inhabitants of these countries still look upon Scandinavia as a sort of model region, whatever qualifying message crime fiction may convey. Are they right to sustain this belief? Frankly, at present, I'm not so sure...

'My protagonist Veum, before he became a detective, worked as a social worker in the area of the care of children. In many of my books the problems of young people, in our society, is an issue that repeatedly exercises me; very much so in the novel *The Consorts of Death,* recently published in Britain. My latest book about Veum, *Vi skal arve vinden* (*We Shall Inherit the Wind*), published in Norway in 2010, has as background the conflicts linked to wind power turbines on the western coast of Norway, but the main strand is a love story.

'Currently, four of my books are translated into English, and I consider that three of them best represent my work: *Yours until Death* (1993, republished in England by Arcadia Books in 2009), is the second in the Varg Veum series and still (I'd like to think) one of the best. It is a novel that attempts to challenge the traditional way of telling a detective story, and it is the first in which Veum is, I think, a fully rounded character. It's about a family tragedy devolving on the fate of a very young boy. *The Writing on the Wall* (2004) focuses on prostitution among young girls, and is one of the darker novels in the series (it's actually the tenth). Veum is confronted with his own past. *The Consorts of Death* (2009) is the thirteenth in the series and the one I'm proudest of. The time-span is almost twenty-five years; we encounter Veum as a young social worker, then as a private eye early in his career, and in the late 1990s, tracking the fate of a young boy whom he met years before – and who is subsequently accused of being a double murderer.'

Staalesen has pointed out that he cannot really distinguish between the various Scandinavian countries in terms of writing style or focus, but that Scandinavian crime fiction in general – particularly Swedish and Norwegian – had two characteristics: first, a focus on social affairs and current societal issues woven into the plot or murder mystery, often with a critical angle revealing the less salubrious side of Scandinavia's tenuously prosperous welfare societies; second, the frequent presence of nature as a key element in the narrative.

Urban rather than natural settings are the stamping grounds of Jørn Lier Horst, who was born in 1970, in Bamble, Telemark, Norway. Horst has worked as a policeman in Larvik since 1995, but the acclaim that greeted his debut novel in 2004, *Key Witness*, confirmed the possibility of a separate career for him. The novel was based on an actual murder case, and brought a striking verisimilitude to the often implausible developments of the police procedural form. Horst's *William Wisting* novel series – *Key Witness* (2004), *Goodbye, Felicia* (2005), *When the Sea Calms* (2006), *The Only One* (2007) and *The Night Man* (2009) – has been extremely successful in his native Norway, enjoying similar acclaim in Germany and the Netherlands. In addition to the *Wisting* novels, Horst has inaugurated a second series with *Codename Hunter* (2008). He has also written a book for children about police investigation procedures. *Dregs* (2011) is his first book to be published in English. The writer's career as a police chief has supplied a key ingredient for the crime fiction form: credibility. Intricacy of plotting is another Horst speciality.

10
Iceland: Crime and Context

For some years, the German book-buying public has been ahead of American and British publishers in demonstrating an appetite for Nordic crime fiction. There are several accomplished Icelandic crime writers (notably Ævar Örn Jósepsson and Viktor Arnar Ingólfsson) who are published in German (and who enjoy considerable acclaim in that country) but have yet to be translated into English (a situation echoed in the fact that there are several Danish writers who sell a substantial amount of books in Germany, and who similarly have not yet been made available to English-speaking readers). This neglect is as much a matter of dealing with the intimidating volume of foreign product available, jostling for attention as it is with a perception that Iceland is terra incognita for non-Icelandic or Danish readers. (English and American publishers not blessed with the necessary linguistic equipment are inevitably obliged to take several reputations on trust, or accept the blandishments of literary agents eager to make a foreign sale.) In the mid-1990s, the English writer Quentin Bates (author of the much-acclaimed Iceland-set *Frozen Out*) was approached by an agent at the Christopher Little Agency. The agent had clearly spent some considerable time finding someone who could speak and read Icelandic – not the easiest of tasks at the time. Bates was asked to read a book by an unknown Icelandic author and report back with a synopsis and an opinion. The novel in question was called *Synir Duftsins* (*Sons of the Dust*, or *Sons of the Powder*), and this was in fact the first book by the now-celebrated, then-unknown Arnaldur Indriðason.

Bates was not greatly impressed and reported accordingly, but when a year or two later the English publisher Harvill approached him with a similar request, he found that it was time for a second encounter with Indriðason, this time with the latter's protagonist Napoleon Skjölin. That second book (which has now been published in English) was

Operation Napoleon. The impression this time was considerably more favourable, and resulted in an emphatic thumbs-up from Bates.

Both Arnaldur Indriðason and his Icelandic contemporary Yrsa Sigurðardóttir have been fortunate in that their books have been translated by the late Bernard Scudder, and the acclaim for the translations is an index of the importance of the translator's art. Having read Indriðason's books in both English and Icelandic, Bates noted that he felt them actually to be better in English, courtesy of Bernard Scudder's exemplary work. And Scudder was not alone in burnishing the work of the writer he rendered into English – the phenomenon (after Scudder's death) continues to escalate.

Quentin Bates lived in the country for ten years, and told me that the excesses and malfeasance he studied while writing his novel have paled into insignificance in comparison to things that are still coming to light in the country today. Bates has characterised Iceland as:

'A bizarre place – a country that is in many ways out of step politically and culturally with the other Nordic countries. On the surface, Iceland looks notably idyllic, clean, safe and quiet, but under this patina there is a something of a rats' nest of intrigue in unpleasant motion. The Reykjavík area is also signally different to the rest of the country, practically a different country.

'It's the kind of place,' Bates continues, 'where you can leave your keys in the car ignition overnight and not bother to lock the back door when you go on holiday. But in Reykjavík you can be mugged in broad daylight, by a junkie or for that matter, in more civilised fashion, by a banker. These various conflicting facets are quite fascinating – "the Crash", as Iceland's massive financial disaster is called, has thrown a lot of the old hypocrisies into very sharp relief.'

Iceland was a colonial backwater of Denmark until World War II, when everything changed dramatically. Unlike neutral Sweden and Nazi-occupied Norway and Denmark, Iceland was occupied first by the British and subsequently by the Americans, who only abandoned their air base there recently. There has been a marked cultural influence from the United States that has shaped attitudes in Iceland much more than in the other Nordic countries (the latter have a tendency to look more to Europe). Marshall Aid after World War II was what forced Iceland to come to terms with the twentieth century.

Politically the country is somewhat diffuse and divided. Government is a matter of coalition between as many as four or five parties. In general, the country has been more right-wing than the more liberal Norwegian, Danish and Swedish countries with their Social Democrat leanings. The right-wing Independence Party has dominated politics for decades, and owes many of its present ideologies to the United Kingdom's Conservative party. The IP was in power for most of the last twenty-five to thirty years, principally as the dominant partner in various coalitions, and has been interpreted by fiscal pundits and others as having created the political and economic landscape that made the Crash possible.

There is a widespread perception that Icelandic politics are markedly corrupt – grist to the mill, of course, for its crime writers, who necessarily trade in this area as plot sources. A culture of cronyism is endemic, and Icelanders tend to see this as a simple fact of life (reflecting, of course, a variety of other countries, from Italy to Uganda). Icelanders would be unlikely to try to bribe a police officer, but would consider a senior figure in public life as infinitely more corruptible.

The poet W.H. Auden travelled to Iceland in the 1930s and wrote in *Letters from Iceland* (1937): 'I understand local politics are very corrupt.' Many observers, both inside and outside the country, would ruefully remark (in this connection): *plus ça change.*

The rise of the far right remains a deeply uncomfortable issue in countries that have been occupied in living memory, notably Denmark and Norway. This is still a grim spectre for older residents, not least (notes Bates) for the numerous skeletons rattling in closets.

Immigration is becoming an incendiary issue as this is a country that has not seen large-scale immigration until relatively recently. It is also significant that these are small, somewhat more cloistered societies. Hampshire has a larger population than Iceland, so it is evident that people who are ethnically different really tend to stand out. Iceland has a large immigrant population that became significantly smaller following the Crash, as a lot of the Eastern Europeans decamped to the Eurozone when the Icelandic currency lost – at a stroke – half its value. But the country has acquired the patina of a multicultural society, and the racism that has always been an undercurrent is certainly on the rise. The extreme example of this new focus is the Faroe Islands, generally recognised as a truly delightful place to live. (Interestingly, considering the issue of minorities, there is no gay community on the Faroe Islands; the reason for this being generally regarded as an antipathy to such a goldfish bowl society.)

But the Scandinavian countries are on Britain's doorstep. Oslo is a two-hour flight from Gatwick. The British are able to examine – at first hand – whether or not many of the old Scandinavian ideals have ebbed away. It is clear that there is a very strong, lingering egalitarian ideal and an innate suspicion of class differences. Instead, class differences based on wealth rather than social position or birth have been imported, almost unconsciously. Nordic countries are far less isolated than they were, particularly Norway with its huge oil wealth – but that doesn't necessarily appear to have granted the residents the largesse of happiness. Iceland is undoubtedly a special case, not possessing such a strong Social Democrat tradition. And the huge trauma of the financial crash has swept away many lingering, fragile ideals now that the government's piggy bank is empty – fertile territory for fiction that examines socio-political issues along with the customary sanguinary preoccupations of the genre. The prosecution of crime in Iceland is subtly different from that of the other Scandinavian countries, with a strangely understated 'embarrassment' quotient added to the disquiet created by crime's rupturing of the social fabric. The act of murder is, what's more, somehow even worse than the simple taking of a life; it is an intolerable imposition of will by one human being on another – both factors, of course, that hold true throughout both Scandinavian countries and the rest of the world, but which add another layer of the deeply unacceptable to the social context of Icelandic crime fiction.

Iceland is situated in the North Atlantic just below the Arctic Circle. The population at the beginning of 2011 was a mere 317,000. Icelanders are the descendants of Norwegian Vikings who settled there in 874 AD; the country's genealogy has elements of the Gaelic. The myth runs that the male Vikings raided Ireland to steal women to accompany them since the Norwegian women were not compliant. Whether or not this has any element of truth, it is commonly believed that the majority of the male settlers were Nordic but the majority of the women were Gaelic. The official language is Icelandic, which (because of the geographic isolation of the country) is notably close to the original Old Norse spoken by the settlers.

The geography of the country is unusual, as Iceland is situated on the mid-Atlantic ridge which separates the North American and Eurasian tectonic plates. Accordingly, the country is both volcanically and geologically active, and expands in both an easterly and westerly direction by about 1 cm a year. By this reckoning, Iceland should have quite a different geographical location in something like 140 million years.

Ninety-five per cent of all homes in Iceland are heated using geothermal energy, which is also harnessed to produce electricity, as is hydropower. House heating and electricity are, as a result, very inexpensive in Iceland. The country is a member of NATO, and is the only member state with no standing army. Wars have never been fought on Icelandic soil, although the disputes in the 1970s between Britain and Iceland over fishing limits were termed the Cod Wars (Iceland maintained that cod represented their principal industry, whereas it was a sideline for Britain). These were, however, mostly characterised by the clashing of fishing vessels out at sea and at no time resulted in any fighting on shore. Modern-day Iceland still remains peaceful, guns (other than those used for hunting) are not allowed and even the police are unarmed.

Volcanic eruptions occur approximately once every five years within Iceland. Thankfully, very few of these eruptions have a widespread effect akin to that of the Eyjafjallajökull eruption of 2010. It should, however, be noted that some historians believe that the impoverished crops in mainland Europe in the late 1700s (which resulted in, among other things, the French Revolution) were caused by an Icelandic eruption, the Skaftáreldar of 1783. A salutary fact (in terms of the country's crime fiction) is the fact that, statistically, only one murder is committed per annum in Iceland.

The publishers of the Icelander Arnaldur Indriðason (and the Norwegian Jo Nesbø), Briony Everroad and Alison Hennessey, are keeping a watchful eye on the Scandinavian crime fiction phenomenon; their stars may be riding high, but both believe that it's inevitable that the focus will shift at some point, either to crime from a different part of the world or to a different genre entirely, as people (inevitably) look for the next new thing. But both women are confident that the authors they publish will continue to be popular. 'Although Scandinavian crime fiction has reached something of a tipping point recently,' said Hennessey, 'the long-standing success of Henning Mankell and Sjöwall and Wahlöö's Martin Beck series shows that there has always been a dedicated core readership for the field.'

Regarding the positioning in the publishing market of translated fiction alongside British and American authors, Hennessey notes that the distinction is not between translated versus home-grown authors, but in essence between the different types of crime writing. 'Jo Nesbø's edgy thrillers are a world away from those featuring Arnaldur Indriðason's world-weary Icelandic detective,' says Hennessey. 'The "Scandi crime" label covers a huge variety of authors, who will each have their own dedicated audience. As for Indriðason's books, I'm a great proselytiser: the books form a haunting and atmospheric series that linger in the mind long after you've finished reading. *Jar City* was made into an award-winning Icelandic film in 2006 and is currently being re-made in an English language version.'

Briony Everroad notes that the Scandi-crime label has been something of a double-edged sword. In the past it could be seen as very much
a niche market.

'At present, even though the authors are markedly different (e.g.
Fossum writes in hugely different fashion from Jo Nesbø), it's gratify-
ing to put them all together in a brochure and encourage readers to
try new authors. Nesbø gave us a quote for Karin Fossum because he
is a huge fan of hers, but we're not trying to say Fossum is the next
Nesbø. That wouldn't be true. Equally, we try to solicit quotes from
British and American authors (for Fossum and others) so that the
broadest possible range of crime readers will take an interest.'

Everroad greatly enjoys working with the translators on Scandinavian
titles.

'The translators do a fantastic job of conveying the original, while
finding their own voice and rhythm in English. We discuss all kinds
of things, from tiny details in the original text to new titles for an
English readership. With Jo Nesbø's *Nemesis* we had a real challenge:
Sorgenfri, which is a reference to a famous song in Norwegian, translates literally as "Carefree", which totally loses the original sense and
is not a very menacing crime title, especially when paired with *The
Redbreast, The Devil's Star* and *The Redeemer*! We try to retain a sense of
the author's culture by keeping street names and certain police titles
in the original language. It's a delicate balance: you don't want to pat-
ronise readers – who can certainly figure out that "veien" is a street in
Norwegian – but you also need to make sure readers aren't confused by
terminology. And, of course, there are jokes that just don't translate.
You'd have to put in so much explanatory text that the comic timing
would be completely lost. Also, there are very Norwegian expressions
that sound silly in English. Norwegians are forever "flinging out their
hands", which doesn't quite work for us. Often the translator and
I work together to find ways round these issues. The translator has
spent months alone with the text, and as the editor you're usually the
first reader. You have to put yourself in the shoes of someone reading
the book in a comfy chair: you sit back and enjoy the story, but you
also need to be alert to areas that need a little more work. And you
have to think back to earlier books in the series: what term did we use
to describe a certain concept in the last book, is that character's height
the same as three books ago? It's a challenging process.'

Michael Ridpath, British author of a detective series set in Iceland featuring detective Magnus Jonson, believes that the distance of that country from the rest of Scandinavia is not just physical, but cultural as well. There are certainly similarities: long dark nights, windswept grey city streets, fjords, mountains and tall blonde twenty-first-century Vikings. But you do not have to scratch very far beneath the surface for differences to emerge. For every Linda Pétursdóttir, the blonde 1988 Miss World, there is a Björk. Indeed, a close examination of Icelanders' DNA shows that they count almost as many Britons and Irish in their ancestry as Norsemen. This all comes through the female line – a legacy of Vikings raping and pillaging.

Iceland does of course, have its long dark winters, but it also has endless summer days when the sun skims the horizon at midnight, and the population seems never to sleep. They are a manic lot: energetic, hardworking, creative, opinionated, quick-thinking and decisive. Planning is dismissed, appointments are for wimps, deadlines are there to be hit precisely. Because the country only has a population of 320,000 people, the Icelanders have to work hard just to provide the accoutrements that any self-respecting nation would expect: diplomats, choirs, football teams, politicians, writers. Most people do at least two jobs, all at top speed, and all passably well.

Everyone in Iceland seems to be on Facebook, yet everyone's granny has spoken to elves. At Christmas the gadgets flow, as do the tales of the thirteen Yule Lads, and their monstrous mother, the child-eating ogre Grýla. The architecture is modern – there are very few buildings over a hundred years old in the entire country – but the landscape is suffused with myth and legend. Trolls frozen to stone on mountain tops, hidden people slinking out of rocks and stones to meddle in the affairs of men. And of course the sagas permeate everything, those great medieval tales of the families that settled the island from Norway a thousand years ago. This literature is revered in Iceland in the same way Romans might revere St Peter's Cathedral or Athenians the Parthenon.

The landscape, too, is a mixture of the old and the new. Volcanoes bubble and blow, glaciers grind, and the North Atlantic nibbles away at cliffs. It is dramatic, it is alive, it is work in progress. And there isn't a tree in sight.

In his novel *Where the Shadows Lie*, Ridpath evokes the bleak beauty of this landscape as well as the contrast between the old and the new, as police in twenty-first-century Reykjavík unravel a mystery surrounding a lost saga, a ring and a volcano. His detective, Magnus Jonson, although born an Icelander, was brought up in America and became

a tough homicide detective in Boston. He is seconded to the Reykjavík
Metropolitan Police, and this allows him to view his countrymen through
the eyes of an outsider. He is able to portray Icelandic society in all its
glorious quirkiness.

There is a king and a queen of Icelandic crime fiction and they view
their country from different perspectives. King Arnaldur places Iceland
firmly in Scandinavia, whereas Queen Yrsa writes about a volcanic
island way out in the North Atlantic.

Arnaldur Indriðason portrays Icelandic society through his world-weary
detective, Erlendur. Although the name means 'foreign', Erlendur definitely views his country from the inside. He is old-fashioned, divorced,
uncomfortable with the way Iceland is changing. Arnaldur's books subtly explore the clash between the old and new Iceland: the breakdown
of the family, the sense of isolation, the migration from country to the
anonymous town. As such, although they are firmly set in Iceland, they
fit comfortably next to the gloomier work of his Norwegian or Swedish
contemporaries.

Yrsa Sigurðardóttir's books, on the other hand, display more uniquely
Icelandic traits. Her heroine, Thóra, is independent and headstrong with
a wicked sense of humour. A writer of children's books, Yrsa delights in
drawing the myths and legends of Icelandic society into her books. And
she deals with events in Iceland's history, such as witch-burning from
the reformation, and the evacuation of Heimaey, 'Pompeii of the North',
when its local volcano erupted spectacularly in 1973. She consciously
introduces a German character as a foil for Thóra and to provide an
outsider's view of Iceland.

Icelanders argue that, strictly speaking, their country is Nordic rather
than Scandinavian, and some will claim that they feel more affinity with
the Scots than their former colonial oppressors, the Danes. In Ridpath's
view, Iceland combines elements of Norwegian, Danish, British and
American societies with its own turbulent geology and its terrible weather
to create a uniquely fascinating setting for a crime story. There is plenty
to write about. There is also another notion to be entertained: that the
bland Scandinavian town is the twenty-first-century equivalent of the
charming, Christie-style English village, where people still hanker to live:
ordered, safe, a little bland, where everyone has their place. An environment where murder shocks because it is out of place (unlike Manchester,
Chicago, Berlin or Amsterdam).

11
Fringe Benefits: Icelandic Woes

Iceland has recently moved to a more prominent place on the stage of world events, with the striking dislocation between the country's industrial success and the catastrophic banking crash that virtually bankrupted the nation. An off-kilter vision of Iceland and its recent turbulent history may be seen through the work of such writers as Yrsa Sigurðardóttir (previously mentioned), who is also a highly successful civil engineer in Reykjavík, with prestigious hydro construction projects under her belt (one might contrast Iceland's recent industrial success with the banking crash). But different perspectives are provided by another Icelandic writer, Arnaldur Indriðason, who won a prestigious CWA Dagger Award for his novel *Silence of the Grave* (2005 [2001]). Indriðason is a novelist who foregrounds pronounced social concerns in his fiction, with his focus on the continuing influence of the Cold War. Remembering a time when idealistic left-wing students in Iceland would clamour to spend time studying in their admired communist East Germany, the novelist built into the mechanics of the police procedural an examination of Iceland's past and the ideological disappointments – the socialist ideals that inspired people to do something about corruption in society, only to realise that corruption is not the exclusive preserve of capitalist bosses.

If the children who so avidly consumed Yrsa Sigurðardóttir's juvenile novels accidentally leaf through *Last Rituals* (2008 [2005]), the author's first adult book, they might be shocked that it is a very different piece of work from her earlier books ('I had accumulated five books' worth of bad thoughts I needed to vent – *Last Rituals* was a kind of release for my darker side,' she remarked). In fact, new careers are a speciality for Sigurðardóttir; this was (at least) her third. But her non-writing work clearly wasn't slaking her creative instincts – good news for lovers of quality crime in translation, as *Last Rituals* showed that Sigurðardóttir had arrived (fully formed, it seems) as something of a unique talent in the field (as she might need to be – the once rarefied field of Icelandic crime thrillers is now becoming somewhat overcrowded). The body of a young history student is discovered in Reykjavík, his eyes gouged out. He has been researching witchcraft and torture, and his moneyed German parents won't accept the police theory that he was killed by his drug dealer. The dead boy's mother asks attorney Thóra Gudmundsdottir to discover the truth behind the killing with dubious help from rough diamond ex-policeman Matthew Reich. What makes Sigurðardóttir's crime debut such an exhilarating experience is the fashion in which she takes familiar (perhaps even overfamiliar) ingredients (e.g. ill-matched, combative detective duo, murder victims with their eyes removed) and throws off a series of dizzying and innovative riffs on these concepts. Sigurðardóttir clearly realises that women writers are obliged to be every inch as gruesome as their male counterparts in the field as it exists today, and matches such novelists as Tess Gerritsen and Kathy Reichs in the blood-chilling stakes. But like all the best Scandinavian writers, it's her acute sense of place that gives such individual character to her work, and readers may feel a keen desire to visit Reykjavík after reading *Last Rituals*.

Similarly, *My Soul to Take* (2009 [2006]) is an assertion of Sigurðardóttir's expertise in the field of Nordic skulduggery. Centre stage again is Reykjavík lawyer Thóra Gudmundsdottir, always prepared to take on difficult cases – and she has a prize assignment: a client is seeking to claim compensation after a farm he has purchased to transform into a hotel is (he believes) haunted. The sceptical Thóra investigates the locale and discovers a variety of unexplained happenings – along with disturbed, alienated people. Then the architect working on the hotel is raped and murdered – is Thóra's client responsible? This is more splendidly accomplished – and involving – fare from Sigurðardóttir.

Sigurðardóttir perceives herself as being Nordic by a roll of the dice. Her heritage, she considers, is a major influence on her world view and inner nature, and inevitably impacts on her writing – whether she likes it or not. She described this to me:

'I have tried to vary the locations of my books to add interest for the reader and I choose areas outside my closest surroundings. The first thing I do when beginning a new book is to visit the locale I intend to tackle and find that these reconnaissance missions provide me with many ideas that I am able to utilise. In *The Day is Dark*, which takes place in Greenland, I use this method, although the area was a bit further afield than I am used to. I cannot imagine having to write a book such as this without making the visits that I did; it would not have rung true had I relied on Google or the public library.

'I am from the greater Reykjavík area, Reykjavík being the capital, of course, and the only urban area with a large enough population to qualify as a city. All other such places are towns and the further from Reykjavík you go the more the feeling of immersion in the essence of the country is palpable. By this I mean the land itself – and the closeness and understanding of the inhabitants of the all-encompassing nature. Approximately half of the population lives in Reykjavík and the neighbouring suburbs, and half outside of this area. When you look closer, it's evident that those living in the more remote areas are less inclined to spend their days chasing after money or status, and are (as a result) less stressed. Also, the further afield you go, the more the population seems in touch with such things as how (in a broad sense) "the food is brought to the table", and bureaucracy seems somehow more inapposite than in the city. Loathing paperwork as I do, I really cherish this aspect of the more remote areas. Politically, Icelanders are pretty much across the country, choosing their party lines early on and then sticking to them fairly relentlessly. All parties are aligned along the middle of the political spectrum.

'I do not find that Icelandic politics merit being part of my novels; frankly, I find such things really boring – and ridiculous. It is enough to have them hanging over one's head like a dark cloud in one's everyday life.

'Corruption in Iceland often takes the form of nepotism, although recent events have brought to light double-dealing regarding money and the clandestine trading in bank and government assets. However, all these things are done in such a clumsy, greedy way that it does not spark my imagination as a writer, and to date I have not been inclined to shift from crime committed for psychological reasons as the focus of my books.

'Speaking for my native Iceland, the crimes involving murder are (for the most part) related to accidents rather than premeditated schemes. Most murders occur spontaneously, with violence breaking out too close to the knife drawer. Regarding crime, non-Scandinavian readers are in most cases getting snapshots of what the writer wants to show them, although this might be a very small part of a much larger – and more elegant – whole. What's more, Scandinavian criminals are shown in fiction as being harder and smarter than they really are – a characteristic, of course, of crime and mystery writing the world over.

'In Iceland, we have a tendency to mull over social issues and talk them into the ground – which is also a factor regarding the prominence of these topics. Perhaps it's easier to spot a problem and nip it in the bud when there are fewer inhabitants and people are accordingly expecting those in charge to act decisively when social problems arise. There is, also, more diversity in the population of Britain than in the Scandinavian countries and immigration problems here are not as urgent an issue. With Iceland, the very name of the country is not exactly beckoning to those in search of a place to live, and we are now – for the first time – having to undergo soul-searching when it comes to the matter of asylum seekers or migrant workers. Regarding the rise of the far right, this is such a small country it may be that we don't have enough fanatics within our population to sustain such a movement – a group of the four to five people one would expect to follow such dogma here will hardly constitute as an association and won't, accordingly, make much of a dent. Generally, social problems do affect the timbre of my work: the more of a mess the state of our nation, the gloomier I feel and write.

'A recent book of mine to be published in Iceland is not actually a crime novel but a stand-alone horror/ghost story, telling two parallel stories, one about three people from Reykjavík stranded in the middle of winter in Hesteyri, a deserted town in the remote Westfjords of Iceland – and finding themselves not as alone as they first assumed. The second tells the story of a doctor working in Ísafjörður, the closest inhabited town to Hesteyri, who has taken a job there to come to terms with the disappearance of his young son a year previously. Readers seem to say that I am to blame for many sleepless nights for my countrymen – which was absolutely my intention.

'Of my earlier work, *Ashes to Dust* is a book about which I feel I achieved what I set out to do, capturing the essence of the Westman Islands which are my favourite spot in Iceland and are therefore special to me. In *My Soul to Take*, I relished incorporating some of our rich folklore into the storyline and integrating it into a modern-day story. With *The Day is Dark*, I tackled one of the harsher environments of human habitation, the east coast of Greenland, with its lack of soil and abundance of ice. I located within this exotic area something very familiar to me, a construction camp of similar type to the one I stayed in for years in the Icelandic highlands. No one, however, was murdered in my camp, unlike the menacing one in the book. My protagonist Thóra is asked to participate in a trip to an Icelandic contractor's camp on the east coast of the country, as all attempts at establishing communication with the men there have failed and the bank which posted the insurance bond is worried it will have to cough up the money if the project cannot be salvaged. When Thóra's group arrives they find no trace of the men and the few natives in the nearby village believe the camp site is cursed. Before too long the curse seems less ridiculous than at first it appeared...'

When the writer Arnaldur Indriðason won a CWA Dagger Award for his novel *Silence of the Grave* (2005 [2001]), originally written in his native Icelandic, it alerted many people to a writer already celebrated by Nordic crime readers. After he won the CWA Gold Dagger, many felt that Indriðason would be the first foreign language crime writer to break the stranglehold that Henning Mankell maintained on this particular branch of the genre. So far, Stieg Larsson and Jo Nesbø have achieved that breakthrough (and prodigiously at that), but there is evidence that the remarkably talented Indriðason is perhaps the most plausible heir apparent. British and American readers may have problems pronouncing his name, but are fully aware of the highly distinctive merits of his Reykjavík-set thrillers. After the success of *Silence of the Grave*, *Voices* (2006 [2003]) was another taut and beguiling thriller. Indriðason's detective Erlendur comes across echoes of his difficult past when the doorman at his own hotel is savagely stabbed to death. The manager attempts to keep the murder quiet (it is the festive season) but Erlendur is, of course, obliged to find out what happened. As he works his way through the very bizarre fellow guests who share the hotel with him, he encounters a nest of corruption that gives even this jaundiced detective pause. The particular pleasure of these books is the combination of the familiar and unfamiliar – while the detective is cut from the familiar cloth, the locales and atmosphere are fresh and surprising for the non-Scandinavian reader, with a provocative interrogation by the author of the conventions of the detective narrative.

But his debut, *Jar City* (2004 [2000]), is, in many ways, Indriðason's signature novel (it has also enjoyed a successful film adaptation, discussed elsewhere). When the body of an old man is found in his apartment in Reykjavík, DI Erlendur has only an enigmatic note found on the body to go on. The murdered man's computer is found to contain pornography, and it transpires that he has been accused of rape in the past. A photograph of the grave of a young woman leads Erlendur towards a solution quite unlike anything he has encountered in his career. It was inevitable that this Scandinavian crime novel would be compared with previous successes by Henning Mankell, and that DI Erlendur would be racked up against the former's Kurt Wallander. Both readers and critics did not find Indriðason or Erlendur wanting in the comparisons. The protagonist here is much given to philosophical speculations, and has a very dark view of human nature, notions examined, *inter alia*, by both authors. Science (and not just forensics) are crucial integuments of the plot, and (as with Mankell) the scene-setting has a freshness and novelty that are very striking to the non-Scandinavian reader. As a debut novel for yet another saturnine detective, *Jar City* effected a variety of filigrees upon established forms.

In *The Draining Lake* (2007 [2004]), an earthquake rips apart the bed of an Icelandic lake, and the water level rapidly drops to reveal a skeleton. A hole in the skull suggests murder, and the body has been weighted down with a large radio transmitter inscribed with Russian Cyrillic script. The three detectives summoned (Erlendur, Elínborg and Sigurdur Óli) are the trio that Indriðason has made familiar in his series of confident and assured books. Very quickly, the trio realise that the secrets behind the death lie back in the fear-filled days of the Cold War, a time when left-wing students in Iceland would clamour to spend time studying in their admired communist East Germany. Erlendur and co. discover that there is more than a violent settling of arguments at the base of this mystery. Before the scales dropped away from the eyes of those who believed that the repressive regime in East Germany was the salvation of mankind, some heavy-duty espionage was the order of the day – and there are several Nordic citizens (now living respectable lives) who have very dirty hands.

Built into the intriguing mechanics of the police procedural here is a rigorous examination of the country's past and the Light That Failed, the limited success of socialist ideals.

It's these elements of social critique that lift *The Draining Lake* well above the level of most contemporary crime writing, but some will find it hard to keep track of the protagonists who are lightly sketched in this book; perhaps readers could have done with a little help here (although that's hardly the fault of Bernard Scudder's excellent translation). But if we have to work a little harder to keep up, our efforts are rewarded.

Indriðason's *Arctic Chill* (2008 [2005]) appeared at a time when British bookselling chains were aggressively promoting crime in translation (possibly on the assumption that bloodshed in unfamiliar foreign climes would tempt punters eager to escape from credit crunch Britain). So the appearance of *Arctic Chill*, a new novel by Indriðason, was timely – or was it? Although the book was as trenchantly written as anything by this talented author, it is probably not the best place for new readers to start, despite the persuasive promotion. While Indriðason's detectives Erlendur and Sigurdur Óli are as flinty as ever, aficionados of the author will be aware that narrative is always foregrounded; what little we learn about the personalities of the two male detectives is always supplied on the hoof – there is little room (in Indriðason's terse style) to dwell on the niceties of personality as he peels back layer upon layer of the mystery. Here, for instance, it is page 46 before we have anything involving the private life of Erlendur and his lover – and we're grateful for this release from a grim murder investigation when it comes. The details of the police procedural are, of course, as authoritatively handled as ever. On a freezing winter day in Reykjavík, Erlendur and his team are called to a block of flats where the murdered body of a young Thai boy has been found, frozen to the ground in a pool of his own blood. The boy's half-brother has disappeared; is he also a murder victim, or implicated in the killing? As Erlendur and co. talk to the boy's splintered family (along with unsympathetic neighbours and teachers), a dispiriting picture begins to emerge of the realities of multicultural Iceland. And it's here that Indriðason – unconsciously? – begins to sound uncomfortable echoes of British society, with its division and anger over the issues of immigration, and the concomitant working-class perceptions of disappearing jobs. But there is no knee-jerk liberal response from the author: intriguingly, his own sympathies are hard to locate. The immigrants, convinced that the boy's murder is racially motivated, are not painted as blameless victims of prejudice, and neither are the resentful native Icelanders tarred with the brush of unreasoning prejudice. As Erlendur realises, there are myriad points of view here: and it is his job to restore a balance before more people die. Rugged fare – but the stripped-down, sinewy prose (ably translated by Bernard Scudder and Victoria Cribb), with its economical characterisation of Erlendur and his fellow detectives, is not likely to win over those unfamiliar with Indriðason's Scandinavian mean streets.

Appearing somewhat late in Britain (in a translation by Victoria Cribb in 2010), *Operation Napoleon* (originally published in Iceland in 1999) was controversially received, and disappointed some readers. In 1945, a German bomber was caught in a blizzard off Iceland. The crew had no idea where they are, and eventually crashed on the Vatnajökull glacier, the largest in Europe. There is a mystery: why were there both German and American officers on board the crashed plane? One of the senior German officers suggests that the only route to survival is to attempt to walk to the nearest farm, and sets out on a trek with a briefcase handcuffed to his wrist, disappearing into the snowbound landscape. Half a century passes, and a US army investigation is trying (on a clandestine basis) to remove a plane from the same glacier. Two young Icelanders become involved in the enterprise, but they will find it a dangerous business. They are captured, but before this, one of the duo manages to get in touch with his sister, Kristin, who becomes obsessed with finding out the truth behind her brother's ill-fated involvement. Kristin finds herself on a lengthy and terrifying odyssey to find out the truth about the mysterious Operation Napoleon. While written in a markedly different style to most other novels by Arnaldur Indriðason, this is a book which bears all the casual mastery of the author's customary fare (predating as it does his much-admired *Reykjavík Murder Mystery* series), but even if it may not be to the taste of those who prefer the author's rigorous reinvention of the police procedural style, its rewards are copious. Those with a taste for Scandinavian thriller fiction will find that the requisite readjustment is worthwhile, and Indriðason fans will know that even less-than-top-drawer material by the writer is usually more compelling than that of a dozen other novelists.

On one of his visits to London, the author talked about writers who had inspired him.

'When it comes to influences, I must name the Swedish couple Maj Sjöwall and Per Wahlöö. I read all of their books when I was younger and, like them, I try to write books that incorporate aspects of social realism. I think I learned from them that crime stories are excellent arenas for writing about the society you live in and the things you want the reader to focus on and think about. So one of my books is about domestic violence. Another is about the dangers of storing great masses of personal information in a big databank. Also I read Ed McBain and, of course, the thriller writers like Alistair MacLean, Hammond Innes, Desmond Bagley and so on. I read a lot of crime fiction when I was a critic at *Morgunbladid*, the biggest newspaper in Iceland. I wrote about films and thrillers and learned from them both. I learned especially from the bad films because they can tell you so well how not to do things. I got tired of the books. They were all either British or American paperbacks that were sold in bookstores in Reykjavík: I tried to read all the newest ones and I found out that there really are very few very good crime writers working today. I have a degree in history and mostly I read historical stuff about old Iceland – much the same things my detective Erlendur reads when he is alone and sad in his dark apartment. What I don't like is to be preached to. I get very tired of writers with big agendas trying to tell us how to live our lives. It's very difficult not to be political today with all the things going on, but what I think is most important is that all sensible views and opinions are allowed to be heard. The only question is: what is sensible?'

Indriðason is always utterly focused on crucial narrative imperatives as the key element of his work, with the Iceland locales he is utilising lightly sketched in. He has even admitted that living in Reykjavík makes it difficult for him to render the country objectively, even though he is aware that some readers would like to have more evocative descriptive passages about the settings.

Politics, Indriðason has said firmly, bore him – though he is fiercely analytical about such social issues as domestic violence and rape. His books are almost all written in a cool but committed social realist style, which may be said to be the norm for many Nordic crime novels today. Unusually, the unfashionable institution of the family is a lodestone of both his consciousness and his writing.

Indriðason has made it clear, however, that he is not interested in limning an accurate, fully rounded picture of his society – that task, he clearly considers, is the prerogative of historians. Iceland, he notes, is something of a special case in terms of its crime. Sometimes a year can pass without a single murder being committed, while the tally may also be three per annum. Drug-related crime is, however, on the increase (a trend reflected in Indriðason novels), and to some degree, the author is conscious of the somewhat rose-tinted view foreigners have of Iceland (a view that doesn't extend too far beyond the clean air and beautiful landscapes).

Indriðason enjoys input into the English versions of his books, and has a very good relationships with his English translators, Victoria Cribb and Anna Yates (in the past, he was fortunate enough to enjoy the services of the late Bernard Scudder).

Indriðason is notably proud of *Jar City*, his breakthrough book (that novel's treatment of issues involving genetics remains à propos), but he nurtures a soft spot for *The King's Book* (not part of the Erlendur series, but a historical adventure concerning the most precious manuscript in Iceland). His latest novel, *Outrage* (2011), extends his forensic examination of his country's darker side.

12
Finland: Crime and Context

Finland – for many non-Scandinavians – remains something of a closed book, and few of the clichés that routinely spring to foreign minds about other Nordic countries present themselves in connection with this country. Finland's independence is a relatively recent phenomenon, dating from the beginning of the last century, and it bears many scars from incursions by near and not-so-near neighbours (notably, of course, the Swedish presence and the subsequent Russian invasion). In consequence, and as an impulse towards resistance, the *amour propre* of the Finn is notably well developed, and the visitor will often be proudly presented with a list of the country's achievements (which are, it has to be said, considerable, given the foreign influences under which the country laboured). The downtrodden image of a joyless, communist-era Finland (though the country became independent before that era) has been thoroughly banished, as have most of the other Russian influences such as language (the famous attempts to make Finns speak Russian were always doomed to failure and have perhaps led to the nationalistic desire to speak the Finnish language). Interestingly (regarding the contentious legacy of Russia), one of the country's finest composers, Uuno Klami (1900–61), struggled to escape the all-pervasive influence on Scandinavian music of Sibelius, who as well as being perhaps the twentieth-century's greatest composer of 'absolute' abstract music presented a nationalist case in such pieces as *Finlandia*. Klami's birthplace, Virolahti, was under the spell of St Petersburg, but his strategy was to plunge into a study – and thorough absorption of – Russian music (along with equally important French musical influences). Individual though Klami's work is, however, the Russian influences are outweighed by the shadow of his great Finnish predecessor.

There is, it is perhaps necessary to say, a certain uncompromising insularity to be found among many Finns, but younger residents (certainly from the baby boom era onwards) are as keenly receptive to modern notions and foreign influences as the residents of any other Scandinavian country. There may have been an attempt by the country to integrate itself more firmly with the West to help protect against any future aggression by Russia. Needless to say, as with all the Nordic countries, there are tears in the social fabric (notably among the many alienated, unemployed Finns living away from the populous areas), but the country itself boasts a particularly forceful pioneering spirit; useful when it comes to taking on and dealing with both the opportunities and vicissitudes of the modern world.

Crime fiction in Finland has long been a fecund genre. The country's crime fiction has a history that goes back to the late nineteenth century. Many Finns would claim Aleksis Kivi, the 'father' of both modern Finnish literature and of its theatre, as the distinguished precursor of the crime novel also. His classic 1870 novel, translated into English in 1929 as *Seven Brothers*, has a closing chapter in which a locked room mystery is solved. It would be some time, however, before another writer would build on this example. Finland was part of Sweden until the end of the eighteenth century, and Swedish still exists as an 'official' (if retreating) language of the country. It is, accordingly, hardly surprising then that the first recognised Finnish mystery, Harald Selmer-Geeth's *Min första bragd* (*My First Case*), which appeared in Finland in 1904, was, in fact, published in Swedish. The acknowledged 'father' of the Finnish mystery is Rudolf Richard Ruth, a versatile writer who, under a number of pseudonyms, published a series of mystery novels, starting in 1910. One of the most prolific writers was Mika Waltari (1908–79), a mainstream writer of historical novels with titles such as *The Egyptian* (1949), *The Wanderer* (1951), and *The Etruscan* (1956), who also created Inspector Palmu, who became an iconic figure in Finnish films. Today, Finnish crime fiction fans are well served by its contemporary crime writers. English readers may be familiar with Pentti Kirstilä whose short story 'Brown Eyes and Green Hair' was selected by Patricia Craig for her 2002 anthology, *The Oxford Book of Detective Stories*, and who also writes mystery novels. One of them, in fact, won the major Finnish award for crime fiction, The Clew of the Year. Another Clew winner was a novel by Harri Nykanen, one of a series featuring his tough detective, Raid. Other highly rated writers include Matti Rönkä (the 2006 Clew of the Year winner) and the novelist Leena Lehtolainen. Inevitably, J.K. Rowling,

Dan Brown and other translated writers account for a considerable section of the Finnish (and Scandinavian) fiction market. Which means that Finnish writers are alarmed at the widening impact of EU Public Lending Right (PLR) directives.

Whilst this means that those writers lucky enough to be translated into English or other languages can increasingly claim appropriate payment from the funds of the countries in which their translated work appears, there is most often a substantial downside. Where translated books dominate a particular market, as in most European countries, PLR payments claimed by 'foreign' writers are likely to be at the expense of locals – unless local funds are increased accordingly, an unlikely scenario. Generalisations are less and less appropriate as to the character of the various Nordic countries in the twenty-first century, as so much has changed. The Finns, once noted for their taciturn qualities (the rather worrying silences something of a challenge to other nations), have become much more loquacious in recent years. (Ironically, since the Nokia company came to prominence; after all, how can a nation be parsimonious with words when its inhabitants all carry telephones manufactured to satisfy the demand for small talk and chit chat? Nevertheless, Finns, even now, tend to be concise and to the point on their mobiles and avoid verbosity.)

Most readers of crime fiction might balk at the notion that their preferred field of entertainment was being used by writers as a platform for barely concealed point-making and the grinding of political axes. A conversation with most of the novelists discussed in this book would make it clear that they regard their principal job as conjuring a fully realised fictional world for readers, rather than social or political proselytising – though, equally, few would want their work to be free of such pithy undercurrents. Insofar as the experience of reading these books is not a collective one, it is significantly different from that of a cinema audience where the fine-tuning of effect is more straightforward (via music, mise-en-scène, editing and so forth); the act of reading – being solitary – demands both more and less from the participant, and the degree to which the reader chooses to read between the lines of a page-turning narrative for subtext is entirely up to them. The writer's relationship with the person engaging with their work is a very intimate thing, and requires an element of give-and-take which is not to be found in other art forms (such as, for instance, opera).

Finnish crime fiction, more than the varieties to be found in other countries, has something of a playful relationship with the conventions which have been set over the years for the genre. These conventions are, of course, useful when beginning any novel. They are a method by which the reader may take a compass reading regarding the tenor of the experience they are likely to have. Convention-shaking Finnish writers such as Kjell Westö enjoy setting up these expectations then ruthlessly tearing them to shreds, ultimately offering a very different experience to the reader than the one they may initially have been thought they would have been receiving. This playing fast and loose with conventions is an audacious strategy, given that the comforting traditions of the crime novel afford their own peculiar pleasures, and an author is obliged to come up with something equally persuasive and satisfying if these traditions are to be tampered with – or abandoned altogether. But to a considerable extent, Finnish noir routinely suggests that a real engagement on the part of the reader is *de rigueur*. These books are notably more personal than many entries in the genre, and demand a degree of commitment on the part of the consumer: we are obliged to keep our intelligence finely tuned and alert, constantly monitoring the density of the text and keeping ourselves open to allusions and subtleties which may lie just beneath the surface of what appears to be a generic murder mystery.

Fortunately, there is a new and informed public ready to undertake these journeys that more challenging writers are proffering for us, and while the greatest market will always be for undemanding, comfort-food books which simply press the expected buttons for the reader, the experience offered by the most ambitious Nordic crime fiction will always be richer and more satisfying: quite the most nourishing experience, in fact, in all genre writing.

Finland, whose soundtrack may be said to be the plangent symphonies of Jean Sibelius – once considered uncompromisingly modern and rebarbative, now firmly canonical – is (to some degree) shaped by a societal influence that is seen ambiguously in the twenty-first century: the Russian legacy in Finnish society (most keenly anatomised by its representation in the work of such writers as Matti Joensuu and Reijo Mäki). However, the country's crime fiction has, as yet, made no commercial breakthrough along the lines of the other Scandinavian countries – although a body of work is shaping up from a variety of Finnish writers that may fuel such a happening.

One such writer is Matti Joensuu, who was born in 1948. (The birth-name Yrjänä is sometimes added to his byline to distinguish himself from one or two of the other Matti Joensuus that populate Finland, at least one (at one time) associated with the World Council of Churches.) Briefly a journalist, Joensuu then became a full-time policeman in the Helsinki police, a career he pursued for thirty-five years, latterly in the Arson and Explosives Unit. (He has since retired.) His first novel and the first to feature his Helsinki policeman Detective Sergeant Timo Harjunpää emerged in 1976, some five years into Joensuu's police career. He produced a further nine Harjunpää novels in the seventeen years to 1993. Praised for their stringent social criticism and linguistic facility, many of his books have been translated into various European languages. His 1983 novel *Harjunpää and the Stone Murders* appeared in English in 1986. Two of his novels have been shortlisted for Finland's major literary award, the Finlandia Prize, giving him a certain cachet in the field of Finnish crime fiction. After a lengthy gap, Joensuu produced *Harjunpää and the Priest of Evil*, published in Finland in 2003. A major success in that country, it was nominated for the Glass Key, the major prize for crime fiction competed for across all the Scandinavian countries. Translated by David Hackston, it was published in Britain as *The Priest of Evil*. Dealing with Harjunpää's investigation into the apparent suicide of a young man who has thrown himself under a Helsinki underground train, it is a thoughtful and provocative work in which all of Joensuu's sterling qualities as a writer are in evidence, along with the trenchant realism accrued from a lifetime's experience as a working policeman. Also evident is Joensuu's ability to explore the dark interior landscapes of his characters, notably their persistent self-delusions. More recently, Joensuu has published the critically acclaimed *To Steal her Love* (2008).

Joensuu's publisher, Gary Pulsifer, whose enterprising company Arcadia Books has shown a keen and continuing commitment to crime fiction in translation, relies on a variety of elements to alert him to possible titles for the list.

'Overseas visits are very important,' according to Pulsifer, 'along with national literature organisations, embassies, foreign publishers and, of course, recommendations from our translators.

'At Arcadia, we publish writers from over thirty-five different countries, and even those of our authors writing in English might not come from the US or Britain but from India, Pakistan, Sri Lanka, etc., so it's all part and parcel of the same thing with us. At one point not too long ago, 50 per cent of our books were in translation, but we have had to reduce this figure due to arts council and national literature funding cuts.

'There is no specific process for promoting such books, apart from treating them as if they were home-grown titles. As I said, we enjoy a close working relationship with a number of embassies and national literature organisations which can use their influence and financial resources to help promote the authors from the individual countries – it is part of their remit.'

Pulsifer is particularly proud of three Nordic crime writers who are doing very well for the company at present: Gunnar Staalesen from Norway, Leif Davidsen from Denmark and Matti Joensuu from Finland, authors who continue to perform well in the English market and sell better with each new novel published here. They are gaining both in recognition with crime aficionados but also with the critics, and – a useful adjunct – they regularly tour Great Britain.

Matti Joensuu is conscious of his Finnish identity and considers that his task (because of his work as a policeman) is to talk explicitly and unapologetically about violent crime in Finland.

'It's very important for me,' said Joensuu, 'to create – in a very concrete fashion – the scenes and settings of my novels. I make a point of visiting them, studying them, photographing them. It's impossible to underestimate the importance of the locales in a novel – they are like the bones under the muscles in a human body.

'Helsinki is the only metropolis in Finland, which inevitably creates a special emphasis. The possibilities of disparate types of crime and other social upheavals are multifold there, compared to the small towns. My examination of these issues is not specifically political – I'm certainly not a political writer in the sense of party politics, but I am socio-political. In my work as a police officer, I was constantly exposed to the grim effects of crime and violent death – the unvarnished "behind the scenes" view I was party to was endlessly sobering. Transmuting this experience into my books can hopefully achieve a kind of truthfulness, perhaps not available to those who have had no direct experience of these things. I know all too well that part of the society that is kept away from the eyes of respectable citizens. Having said that, it's a little painful to read my older work, where I first addressed such things – I know that today I would approach these books in a very different fashion.

'My subject – again and again – is the mechanism of human evil. The wide and pervasive effects of evil, often hidden from the general public. The books in which I feel I have dealt most successfully with these issues are *Harjunpää ja rautahuone/Harjunpää and the Iron Chamber* and *Harjunpää ja pahan pappi/The Priest of Evil*.'

Crime fiction journalist Bob Cornwell spoke recently to Joensuu, along with the latter's English translator David Hackston, and obtained some intriguing aperçus. 'To write or be creative,' said Joensuu, 'you have to have some sort of order or balance within yourself, and if that crumbles, then you have a problem.' At the start of a creative hiatus, he had discovered some of the underground tunnels that burrow beneath parts of Helsinki. Such mysterious places are now rare in modern Helsinki, a problem also noted by those melancholy masters of Finnish cinema, the Kaurismäki brothers. So the Brocken, a key location in Joensuu's novel *The Priest of Evil*, is a real place? 'Yes,' says Joensuu. 'It does exist and it is situated at the meeting point of a number of railway tracks. There is a bridge that goes across this area. At one point I climbed over some railings and ended up in this terrifying place, or a place that you could imagine as being terrifying.' Further investigation revealed that 'beneath Helsinki there is over 300 km worth of tunnels and infra-structure, places that we don't know about, right beneath the city.' It is within these tunnels that we discover the Priest of Evil, conversing with himself in what appears to be Latin, as he goes about his curious ritu-als, one of those characters whose 'inner world' is explored with great thoroughness.

'I really enjoyed writing the chapters written from inside the Priest's mind, because I could let my imagination run loose,' said Joensuu. Did his approach to this book differ very much from those he has written in the past? 'In my earlier novels I have also explored the minds of the different characters, and the different narrators,' he says. 'But in the past I have always attempted to explain what has contributed to making someone a criminal. In this book, that is left unexplained, an absolute inexplicable evil.' The novel touches on many other ideas: the welfare of children, the treatment of mental illness, for instance, explored through an unusual range of characters, an unborn child for example. Are such themes a response to specific trends in Finnish society? 'The question of the welfare of our children is one that has come to fore particularly in recent years, in Finland and, I'm sure, everywhere,' says Joensuu. 'In that new born child, like Sinikka in the book, there is not the capac-ity to kill someone. It's the way that children are treated and brought up that makes them emotionally damaged, and which causes them to do things that might have been prevented. So criminals are made. The cause is fundamentally a lack of love.'

As for mental illness, there are echoes of Britain's controversial 'care in the community' policies:

'In my police work, in the arson and explosives section, you often meet serious pyromaniacs who are so mentally ill that it is impossible to interview them, and that often you have to call in a doctor to refer them to a mental hospital, rather than communicate with them.

On the other hand, in Finland, you can't commit people against their will. And if they don't want to go to a hospital there is no real way of forcing them to do so. And then they are just left drifting...'

Are such themes important to Joensuu?

'Yes, very important and very deliberate. Whilst it is a misconception that it is the only genre in which one can comment on social problems, crime sells well. I felt that I could actually have an effect. Subjects that come up in a novel, this novel, which then several years later are talked about in the media as if they are a new problem. The issue of women's violence against men comes up in this novel, published several years ago in Finland, but that issue has recently emerged again and is discussed as something new. As a police officer you have a ringside seat, and you can see the way things are going. You can almost predict trends before they happen. In an earlier novel (*Harjunpää and the Stone Murders*, 1983), I wrote about crimes committed by children. Then in 2001, this problem hit the headlines with a double murder committed by teenagers.'

There are also a number of autobiographical parallels in the book. Another key character, for instance is Mikko Matias, once a successful writer, now 'blocked' and with a problem teenage son. Amongst the many poignant details of a writer struggling to regain his lost creativity, is a mention of the fact that his fellow-workers in the post office where he has worked regard him first as a writer, rather than as a colleague, thus reinforcing his isolation. Has that been a problem for Joensuu in his career as a policeman?

'I did have such a problem,' he replies. 'In the 1980s for instance, there was an attempt to push for a sort of equality, and I as a writer stood out. Now the situation is the opposite, and my work is seen more as PR. They see me more now as "our Matti"! The younger generation of police officers is very different; the whole spirit of the force has changed. For instance, they are educated to a much higher standard than was available to the older generation.'

A less obvious autobiographical parallel concerns Matti, the withdrawn, troubled teenage son of Mikko Matias. Elsewhere Joensuu has spoken of using his experience of his own 'creative reawakening' in his depiction of Matti's mental landscape. Can such autobiographical parallels be read into other areas of the book? Joensuu: 'Ultimately the book must stand by itself; it's just a book. But undeniably there are elements of things that I myself have experienced. It would be quite impossible to write about things that you haven't.' It is also apparent to the reader of *The Priest of Evil* that Joensuu has a taste for unsettling and disturbing his readers. The narratives are not always straightforward, nor quite what they appear to be. This trait is apparent throughout the book, but is used most effectively in its disturbing closing pages. 'In the planning of the novel,' said Joensuu, 'I have a pretty good idea of its scope, but only halfway through the work, you realise that this is the way it has to be. Many of these things only become clear once you are in the middle of the work.' Does a downbeat ending reflect his own innate pessimism? 'Deep down I am something of a pessimist,' he says. 'After working in the police for thirty-five years, you realise that as one case comes to an end, another one is immediately on your desk. And you realise that the evil you see is not only restricted to that one case.'

Joensuu, with a successful series under his belt, and with many of his novels available in translation across Europe, was reluctant to leave his job and live solely by his writing. Did this have to do with the nature of the Finnish market for crime fiction? 'If you are the kind of writer who writes a book a year,' replied Joensuu, 'a book that sells at least 30,000 copies (which in Finland, is a lot), then you could live off the proceeds. But in the past I did not dare to leave my job because, when I finish a book, I always have this feeling that this book may be the last one.'

Did the young Joensuu read widely as a child?

'Yes, I went to libraries, to bookshops. In particular John Steinbeck was a writer that I admired, and I thought, if only one day I could write like that. And as far as subjects at school are concerned, Finnish was the subject that I excelled at. Then I wrote short stories, thrillers, and they were published. But the final push to write crime fiction was discovering the discrepancy between reading crime fiction and its image of police work, and what police work really is. Georges Simenon was an influence; I bought and read all his novels. Otherwise I would describe myself as an omnivorous reader. I don't just focus on crime fiction. Also, on a practical level, if you write crime fiction, and crime is your day-in, day-out job, the last thing you want to do with your spare time is sit down and read crime fiction.'

Specifically Finnish influences include Mika Waltari but also Väinö Linna (who wrote a seminal war epic in the 1950s translated as *The Unknown*

Soldier) along with Hannu Salama, whose 1964 novel *Midsummer Dances* led to the author's appearance in court, accused of blasphemy. Joensuu has observed that the influence of crime fiction has grown over the years. 'In the 1970s things were very different. Crime fiction was ridiculed. But I was the first writer to win the Finnish State Award for Literature (in 1982) with a crime novel. This may have helped to give crime fiction a higher profile and contributed to a boom.'

Similarly raising the profile of crime fiction is Kjell Westö, born in 1961. Westö has steadily consolidated his position as one of that country's most respected authors. He is a Finland-Swede, writing in Swedish (interestingly, though the use of Swedish is fading in Finland – the Swedish-speaking population has dropped from about 5 per cent to 4 per cent, with most intermarriages giving rise to Finnish-speaking children – the literary output in terms of numbers published has placed Swedish-language titles higher than 5 per cent of complete book production in Finland; meaning that the output of books in Finland is greater per capita for Swedish than Finnish – a fact the Finns are perhaps reluctant to acknowledge).

Westö's novel *Lang* (2005), a dark and erotic story of modern Helsinki, fuses a variety of elements to create an economically written tale of lust and violence. Christian Lang is a writer and television personality, keen to keep his romance with the seductive Sarita clandestine; she, too, has her own reasons for not revealing the affair. To his dismay, Lang discovers that Sarita's violent ex-husband has him in his sights, but finds himself unable to break free from the passionate affair. As events spiral out of control, the behaviour of all the characters becomes increasingly erratic – and dangerous. Westö's novel functions on many levels: as a scarifying picture of the psychology of modern relationships, as an analysis of the violence lurking beneath the surface of even the most middle-class characters (Finnish, but, by extension, universal) and as a sardonic analysis of modern-day media.

Jan Costin Wagner may not be a Finn (he was born in 1972 in Langen/ Hesse near Frankfurt), but his impressive work has to be taken on board in any serious consideration of Finnish crime fiction. After studying German language, literature and history at Frankfurt University, he went on to work as a journalist and freelance writer, and now divides his time between Germany and Finland (the home country of his wife). His adroitly written, acerbic crime novels featuring Detective Kimmo Joentaa are *Ice Moon* (2006) and *Silence* (2010), with the next in line being *The Winter of the Lions*. All have complex, beautifully judged narratives and a solid command of the crime fiction idiom. *Silence* won the 2008 German Crime Prize.

Wagner's subtle, mesmerising and atmospheric *Ice Moon* begins as Sanna, beloved wife of Kimmo Joentaa, finally (and quietly) dies, Kimmo by her bedside, after a long battle with cancer. Kimmo, numb and not knowing what is expected of him, leaves the hospital and returns to his work. Kimmo is a police officer with the Finnish CID, based in Turku, a coastal town west of Helsinki. Resisting attempts to extend his compassionate leave, Kimmo is assigned to the mysterious murder of a local woman, her husband absent on business. This woman too, appears to have died peacefully without pain or violence, perhaps by suffocation; like Sanna's, the corpse that Kimmo sees 'might almost have been asleep'. Struggling with memories of his wife, Kimmo begins his investigation, his intuitive senses seemingly heightened by his grief. But before the culprit can be apprehended, two more similar murders occur. Crime fiction has always been a liberal dispenser of death, currently delivered in its most commercial modern form, the serial killer novel. But while it may utilise the form, Wagner's book refracts elements of it in a markedly unorthodox and productive way. The killer's viewpoint, for instance, introduced from the second chapter, immerses the reader in the schizophrenic mind – while the writing, finally, delivers a perfectly credible, disturbed individual, far from the usual unrealistic monster of such fare. Principally (and this is a rarity in the genre), the subject allows Wagner to explore the tragedy of individual death and its corollary, grief, not only through Kimmo, but through a gallery of similarly deftly drawn characters. What's more, the author does not deal with just the negative effects of death, but the more random consequences. A serial killer will perhaps die, but a man movingly rediscovers his love for his wife, and Kimmo slowly becomes reconciled to Sanna's death. And as late summer segues into harsh winter, the carefully judged atmosphere of the book is enhanced by Wagner's hushed, simple but beautifully written prose (with translator John Brownjohn alert to every challenge). Jan Costin Wagner is in total command of his material. This is the second of three highly acclaimed novels, the first of which, *Nachtfahrt* (*Night Trip*, 2002) deservedly gleaned for him the Marlowe award from the German Raymond Chandler Society.

Jan Costin Wagner refuses to accept the notion of a prescriptive (and adoptive in his case) 'Finnish' identity.

'In the first place,' said Wagner, 'a novelist should not be reductively identified as an American, Scandinavian or a British writer. These notions are limiting. Each author is trying to find a voice for the same topic, essentially, the human being, and each author should forge his or her own way.

'Similarly, the region I want to paint is an internal one – I'm aiming for a picture of the interior lives of my characters. Finland is a major element in my books, of course. To me, the Finland of the novels is, of course, the real Finland – but it is also a landscape of the mind – the mind, specifically, of my protagonists.

'As a writer, I'm eternally engaged by stories which are, to some degree, timeless. But I do attempt to deal with specifics, and, in particular, cutting-edge issues; my latest novel *The Winter of the Lions* can be read as a media-critical study and as a (hopefully) clear-sighted reflection of the society we are living in, a society at the service of phoney morality, such as that of TV talk shows (with their deadening parades of platitudes).

'I try to convey a relatively realistic picture of my adoptive country, but, of course, it is simultaneously a vision refracted through my own perspective; an individual vision is something true of all art that aspires to substance, popular or otherwise. It is always the perspective of one novelist or one artist that fashions a worthwhile vision. A good example is the film-maker Aki Kaurismäki, who is a very strong and unique storyteller, and people often ask me if Finland really is as strange and unsettling as in Kaurismäki's films. I usually reply that it is partly the real Finland and partly, of course, an artistic, fictitious Kaurismäki-Finland. As, hopefully, with me and my books.

'My creative juices are activated by some very different writers – for example, the Swiss Friedrich Dürrenmatt (the ambiguous ending of his novel *The Pledge* (which was filmed with Jack Nicholson) is amazing). I'm also influenced by Patricia Highsmith, notably because her pitiless narratives seem to be (in a Nietzschean sense) beyond morality; and by the writer Max Frisch, because he bravely attempted to forge his own language; I'm also perversely inspired – in some way – even by Adalbert Stifter who initially seems to be such a pedestrian author, but beyond the idylls of his tales I always feel an abyss lurking.

'My work has transmogrified over the years. I couldn't write my first novel *Night Trip* today, but when I wrote it, it was exactly what I wanted to produce at the time. This initial novel utilised a very aggressive protagonist and the language of the novel was, I felt, also obliged to be his blunt language. In my second book, *Ice Moon* – which was the first of the *Kimmo Joentaa* series – I was reflecting more, marching on slowly and carefully, just like Kimmo himself, the central character of my Finnish novels. Basically I think that everybody is experiencing different things all the time and those experiences (and, perhaps, people's changing perspectives) should be reflected in the novels. It is important not to stand still.

'In the final analysis, all my novels deal with death. Not initially, perhaps, with murder, but with the question of how death – or the fear of death – transforms the lives and thinking of people in different, fraught situations. How is a young man like Kimmo Joentaa coping with the death of his wife Sanna? How is a mother living with the death of her child? How is a killer living with the guilt? I want to discern and encapsulate the language that is crucial to the moment of understanding.

'In my latest novel, *The Winter of the Lions*, I've tried to establish an important new character, Larissa, who is bringing a new dimension to the life of my protagonist Kimmo. Important books for me personally have been *Silence*, which was published in 2010 and, from 2005, *Ice Moon*, which I mentioned earlier.

'The latter was a key book for me, establishing my youthful protagonist Kimmo Joentaa, whose wife Sanna is dying from cancer; by the time of *The Winter of the Lions*, his life has taken a turn for the better. He is feeling alive again.'

13
Death in Denmark

The citizens of Denmark coolly regard themselves as blessed; repeated surveys have suggested that the country is considered one of the most pleasant places on the planet to live (a fact that does much to burnish national pride – and the Danes certainly have plenty of that). However, British and American observers, while accepting this conclusion, struggle to find the precise reason for the Danes' satisfaction. Denmark is a country that does not lend itself to easy dissection or analysis (analysis of the kind that – rightly or wrongly – foreigners feel they can apply to Sweden). It is a very European country (Denmark is an EU member state) and many people live in what might be considered to be very comfortable circumstances by British standards. A further comparison with Britain is not necessarily to the advantage of the inhabitants of John Bull's island: consensus politics, distinctly fraught territory in Britain, seems to function with relative success in Denmark. Another comparison with Britain might be noted in the fact that both countries have had to come to terms with the loss of empire; the British Empire is much celebrated (and criticised) but less well known is the fact that Denmark – despite the modest dimensions of the country – held sway over considerable parts of Europe (as, of course, did Sweden). And in some ways, the national farewell to the imperial instinct seems to have been a less painful exercise for Denmark than it was in Britain.

The Danes have put centre stage an appreciation of the cultural life of their country, celebrating it in a non-jingoistic fashion, with none of the problematical aspects that England has shown in this regard. The most cosmopolitan city in Denmark – and clearly the country's beating heart – is Copenhagen, which combines both exquisite historical aspects with a very modern cosmopolitan zeitgeist. The comfortable tourists' eye view of Copenhagen, of course, includes Hans Christian

Andersen and the Little Mermaid, but also boasts more heavyweight fare in the person of the influential philosopher Søren Kierkegaard. The sense of history of the city is encapsulated in the mediaeval architecture (notably on display in the city's many haunting echoes of the Middle Ages). Copenhagen's pace of life in the twenty-first century, however, is somewhat more frenetic and this is a very modern city. One of the less salubrious aspects of the city is, of course, its notorious trafficking in women from the Third World, with the porous borders making it easier for the traffickers and criminals to run prostitutes. It's an unlovely aspect of the city that has provided fecund material for Danish crime writers.

The American writer Donald Spoto (whose three-volume study of the life and work of Alfred Hitchcock is definitive) has made his home in Denmark for many years. Spoto told me he would not now consider living anywhere else – Denmark, according to the writer, is as close to a model society as one could hope to find.

Spoto's area of Denmark, the island of Sjælland, also the home of the Danish capital, Copenhagen, is much more cosmopolitan than regions farther from the capital (Jylland, for example, or the island of Fyn). It is also strikingly rural and so offers the best of both worlds – a quiet life in the countryside and close proximity to one of the great cities of the world and all it offers.

Regarding the vision of the society that non-Scandinavian writers are receiving from crime fiction in translation, Spoto is not persuaded that readers are necessarily influenced in this fashion.

'It's possible that certain people accept such fiction as an accurate representation,' said Spoto. 'Some readers are always a bit dense, after all, and take a part of a book, or an author's take on a situation, as representative of the whole truth – as if people years ago were to believe that Ross MacDonald, Dashiell Hammett or Mickey Spillane had once given accurate pictures of American life. It's easy for people to mistake a part for the whole.'

Spoto regards Scandinavian society as remarkably open and liberal compared with just about everywhere else (particularly the USA).

'Danes have other concerns than the private lives of individuals,' he says. 'Here, people want to work hard, have a good education for their children and guaranteed free healthcare in a successful social democracy (Denmark is not a socialist country, which is something very different). Unemployment is very low here – less than 3 per cent, compared with 10 per cent in the USA, for example. There is no time for – or interest in – any sort of prejudice, actually; certainly no time for sexual intolerance. Very many couples with children are (for a variety of reasons) unmarried. Society in Denmark doesn't blink an eye at that. Very many people live happily and openly as gay men and women, alone, with partners or married to them. Danish society doesn't blink an eye at that. This is just one reason why I call it a model society.'

Spoto acknowledges that there is a divisive conservative renaissance in Denmark – but it is very much the minority, and that fact must be stressed.

'Divisive? Yes, the right-wing here can be shrill and divisive. But there is not even the remotest possibility of a Tea Party here in Denmark. Good sense, thankfully, prevails. Remember, seventy years ago Denmark was an occupied country. Freedom and individuality are prized here very much indeed. Two recent studies conducted worldwide found that Danes are the happiest people in the world, and fewer Danes want to emigrate than citizens of any other country. Without "waving flags with one hand and picking pockets with the other" (as Ingrid Bergman memorably says in Hitchcock's *Notorious*), Danes love their country, support it and want to stay here – and with good reason.

'Denmark still stands for a "social democratic ideal", and is very different from other nations. The French cherish fond notions of working four days a week, having three months' holiday and retiring at 60. In Denmark, these sorts of cloud-cuckoo demands evoke loud laughter. One must remember that Denmark is very much a middle-class society. There is an unofficial motto here: "In Denmark, you will find very little excess [wealth] but even less want [poverty]." We have one of the highest tax rates in the world, but I have not, in almost a decade, heard anyone ever complain: after all, healthcare is free; all education is free – right up to advanced professional careers. Child care is free. These are more of the reasons why I call Denmark a model society. When I first moved here, I asked another American resident – a man who has lived and worked here for thirty-five years – what major difference he found between life outside and within Denmark. He replied: "That's easy to answer: here, people care about one another."

'Denmark is a bookish country. Serious works of history and non-fiction, for example, are as high on the bestseller lists as popular fiction. One sees people on trains and buses reading good books, not, for the most part, meretricious trash. For meretricious trash, people can (if they want) turn to TV programmes imported from the USA.'

The Danes have a noted affection for the British because of common cause in the last war, and an earlier generation was wont to display to English visitors the guns with which they'd resisted the Germans. However, many Danes speak German, as parts of the country have been German satellites at various times. It is no revelation that in Jutland, German TV was available before all channels became accessible. How many of these disparate elements are reflected in the country's crime fiction makes for intriguing study.

There is a perception among the reading public that the best Scandinavian fiction (of both the crime and literary varieties) possesses something oracular – not so much in the sense of holding the mirror up to nature, but in freighting in analysis of the fraught state of modern Western society and the shifting sands of human psychology. Such elements may sound a touch forbidding (if, for instance, the reader holds to the rigorous view that crime fiction must perform the simple and straightforward task of entertaining without educating). In practice, such elements of social criticism are (in general) fully assimilated, rather than protruding from the text in attention-grabbing fashion. Also, it might be argued, such elements are easily assimilable for the intelligent reader – in the sense that not too much winkling out of the author's socio-political intention is generally required even within the context of a page-turning thriller. Points about society may be inscribed in the interstices of the narrative, but the real business of the day remains the movement of the plot; characters being obliged to dance to the music of the author's ingenuity, with lives casually dispatched to provide a body or two, set things in motion and launch the detective on his or her dangerous odyssey.

The deepest imperatives of the crime thriller, Danish or otherwise, represent the manipulation of frustration and deferred resolution (springing from the labyrinthine mystery that the protagonist is confronted with – not to mention the non-cooperation of virtually everyone around them – notably his or her superiors), and the sense of vicarious relief when the mystery is solved and the status quo is (after a fashion) restored. Scandinavian crime fiction is more ready to provide this juxtaposition of elements than the (for instance) Italian variety, which is less given to tidiness, closure and the satisfying delivery of moral justice. The progress described here – in the work of several Danish crime fiction practitioners, has an angular, unfinished quality which makes for a challenging read (in the best sense of the term). All of this dislocation is reflected within the startling structure of the Danish language itself (perhaps reflected in the abrupt octave leaps of the country's greatest composer, Carl Nielsen).

Generally speaking, crime fiction from the Nordic countries touts its strategies in terms of straightforward realism, without utilising very often elements of surrealism or phantasmagoric incident (favoured by such American and British writers as Carl Hiaasen, Colin Cotterill and John Connolly) to grant the text an off-kilter, non-realist feel. If there is an element of the metaphysical, it is introduced by the novelist's parallel journey into the Nordic soul, sometimes forbidding territory that has the effect of lowering the emotional temperature of the narrative, and according the reader a cool, balanced appraisal of the situations and characters that are presented to us.

The Northern view of life, of course, is sometimes famously bleak, and the destruction of the lives of the characters frequently has an implacable quality that is reminiscent of nothing so much as the fatalistic Wessex novels of the English writer Thomas Hardy. But whatever challenge the reader is presented with in Danish crime fiction, the dividends provided are considerable and make the rite of passage (however lacerating it may be) well worth the undertaking. Like Coleridge's wedding guest, we rise sadder and wiser on the morrow morn.

For a foreigner, as Jesper Hansen of the Scandinavian Studies department at University College London has noted, Denmark, Sweden and Norway often coalesce into one: the amorphous mass of Scandinavia, which is principally dominated by people's perception and knowledge of Sweden above all else. Sweden is famously known for its attempts at seeking political compromises to both national and international conflicts, along with (on a more prosaic level) the ubiquitous Ikea brand, and people immediately think about efficiency and simple yet elegant design.

Denmark is a special case. While an abstract notion of tourist-trap Copenhagen sits comfortably with many people, and most are aware that it is the Danish capital, the country of Denmark itself is terra incognita, apart, perhaps from cosy images of Hans Christian Andersen and the Tivoli. These factors, perhaps, combined with half-assimilated knowledge of the Danish royal family, might explain the general perception of Denmark as a fairy-tale country. The association of the country with stress-free happiness and a relaxed, laidback lifestyle (which includes liberal laws relating to alcohol, sexuality and drug use) also incorporates visions of healthy, flaxen-haired Vikings who cycle everywhere, and beautiful girls in short skirts; all aspirational images that are (unsurprisingly) emphasised and touted by the Danish tourist board.

However, despite clear congruences between Denmark and its Nordic neighbours, there are striking divergences, often emphasised in conversation by the Danes themselves. Danes characterise themselves as more easy-going than the Swedes, who are often unkindly perceived as mindless 'gammas' doing precisely what the state tells them to do. Similarly, the Danes pride themselves on being considerably more social than the Norwegians, who favour (according to one of the fondly held stereotypes) skiing alone through a forest covered in snow. Danish self-image devolves on their nation (and especially the capital) as being the cultural nexus of Scandinavia, boasting a smogasbord of modern design, tolerance and innovation. Sweden is, by contrast, regarded as being markedly more retrograde in its thinking and more resistant to new ideas (Ikea excepted), whereas Norway is envied for its enormous oil resources. Danes have no hesitation in acknowledging the genius of August Strindberg and Henrik Ibsen – while simultaneously emphasising that the literary movement to which the writers belonged was sparked by a series of lectures given by their own Georg Brandes.

In the cold light of reality, of course (and *pace* Donald Spoto), Denmark is no fairy-tale country. The government is under the sway of right-wing politicians (to the dismay of its more liberal inhabitants, notably those in the arts); immigration laws are routinely criticised by the UN, and Denmark has been engaged in the conflict in Iraq (the observation is made by Danes that this is an 'offensive' war, rendering ironic the term 'forsvaret' – which means 'the defence', customarily used about the Danish army), and Copenhagen, like other big cities, has its own extremely violent gangs, prostitution, poverty and drug problems. Also, as with so much of the rest of the world, sordid political scandals are an integral part of political life, and examples of the abuse of power crop up repeatedly – within the police, the armed forces, among politicians.

It is, accordingly, no surprise that one of the most highly regarded and bestselling Danish crime writers, Jussi Adler-Olsen, tackles precisely these issues – and in uncompromising terms. His edgy novels deal with corrupt individuals, social outsiders, manipulative psychopaths, and all of this strips away the fairy-tale varnish that has been Denmark's prerequisite since the nineteenth century. Perhaps this clash between non-Danes' rose-coloured expectations concerning the country and the bracing 'reality' (as it is presented in the crime fiction genre) might explain some of its success: the spectacle of the abuse of power in the 'perfect' social democracies of Scandinavia; the grim vision of maiming and torture in this sylvan setting has a lacerating force.

As writers tear the fairy-tale wrappings to pieces, this might be seen as the ultimate personal and social reassurance: for the foreign reader encountering such unsparing crime fiction, reassurance is proffered: perhaps our own countries are not so benighted after all; and the corollary might be that for the Danes, it is possible to just look out of the window and be comforted that life as portrayed in crime novels is, in the final analysis, still a fiction. Thus crime fiction itself becomes a varnish, and we can all collectively relax – cleansed and consolidated in the untorn fabric of our lives, our moral compass and our society.

The Danish lecturer in Scandinavian literature Jakob Stougaard-Nielsen has wondered if it is possible for any work of art, any film or piece of fiction to 'accurately' represent an entire society.

'Certain genres in fiction have for hundreds of years done their best to describe and reveal the "hidden" and sometimes darker sides of societies in a way that made readers feel immersed in the unknown or suppressed lives of others. The reason why Scandinavian crime fiction is often considered to offer something new to the genre, is that the field, in its rather short history, has not been viewed as offering critical insights into various societies. Significant voices in Scandinavian crime since the 1960s came out of a period in Scandinavia where social criticism was central to art and literature informed by social movements and the rise of the left in the political spectrum. This turn towards social and cultural issues has become a mainstay in the genre, and has taken many shapes since then from the obvious programmatic critique of the perceived failure of the Social Democratic party in Sweden to remain faithful to its left-wing Marxist heritage in Sjöwall and Wahlöö. This also applies to some degree to Henning Mankell's post-Cold War engagement with transnational challenges such as human trafficking and immigration, and his main character Wallander's repeated doubts about the security and social equilibrium traditionally offered by the welfare state. Wallander became a voice expressing a perceived change in not only Swedish society since the early 1990s, but perhaps more generally in Scandinavia, of a growing insecurity with a perceived rise in violent crime, anti-democratic forces and the demise of homogeneous nation states following increased globalisation and a more integrated EU.

'Of course, Stieg Larsson should also be mentioned in this context for his fairly well-documented references to a hidden past (and present) of right-wing extremism in Sweden, and his (and Mankell's) social interest in the gender conflicts still apparent in the Scandinavian welfare states that (at least since the 1970s) have prided themselves on being the most egalitarian nations wherein social equality is inevitably tied to gender equality at home, in the work place and in public discourse. I think these Swedish writers have been the inspiration for much crime fiction written in Scandinavia. Most crime writers published these days are not as explicitly engaged in social issues as these examples, but they have had an impact in allowing crime fiction to engage explicitly with the everyday, with the relationship between genders (as in the Danish TV series *The Killing*, in Liza Marklund, etc.), where traditionally these traits have been either left out of the genre, or turned into clichés, subservient to the plot. But we also find novels engaging with socio-political issues, such as Arnaldur Indriðason's backdrop of genetics and social welfare in Iceland; and while Jo Nesbø in Norway seems less interested in the everyday or the political, his books being more American and British-seeming in their form, Karin Fossum's novels could equally be regarded as socially concerned fiction as crime novels.

'So, I would probably rephrase the question slightly: do Scandinavian novels attempt to paint a picture of the Scandinavian societies? And I think the success of the genre at home and abroad has something to do with the social engagement, with their interest in the struggles of their characters amidst changing social conditions, and the everyday struggles of ordinary people in Scandinavia trying to be dynamic and independent individuals, finding their place in society with all the uncertain challenges and responsibilities that this entails.

'To claim that crime novels paint an accurate picture of Scandinavian societies would be mistaken – the level of violence and crime obviously doesn't represent reality; but I suggest that the crime depicted should be taken as symbolic of a sense of growing insecurity not only pertaining to Scandinavia. And the interesting protagonists capture the readers' imagination exactly because they are also struggling to negotiate their individual ambitions, their roles as social beings in the workplace, at home and in society – in societies where social interaction and responsibilities have for generations been highly regulated as a consequence of the welfare states.

'We also have to remind ourselves that crime fiction is a truly international genre, and many of the Scandinavian crime writers are modelling their stories on British, American, German, Spanish and other crime fiction. That being said, I think the picture readers abroad are left with is that (for all the exotic qualities) the Nordic countries are not markedly different from cultural expressions elsewhere today. What I think we see in Scandinavian crime, and in contemporary crime fiction generally, is a fairly typological lonely and ordinary detective/ journalist/lawyer who finds him/herself in extraordinary situations that (however dramatic and unrealistic) represent struggles within the individual, expressions and situations that allow this individual to negotiate (or fail to negotiate) struggles within herself dealing with ambitions, social relationships, love, strained family relations, ethical behaviour in a complex world where most traditions have been dissolved. Everything has to be mapped anew, and all behaviour has to be negotiated based on individual needs and challenges. In this way, I think crime fiction has become the perfect postmodern genre in that the rules pertaining to the extremes of society do not apply to the ordinary lives of individuals. While detectives may succeed in establishing some form of order as regards to the criminal transgressions, they rarely succeed in managing their own lives, hopes and dreams in the same way. This, I think, is an interesting paradox in contemporary crime fiction, and a central preoccupation of Scandinavian crime.'

Concerning hot-button issues such as immigration and the rise of the far right in Scandinavian countries, Stougaard-Nielsen seeks for shadings of opinion.

'There are differences in the Scandinavian countries on these issues. Denmark has had a fairly determined right-wing movement opposing immigration since the 1970s, a movement which has had a significant say on the tightening of immigration laws in Denmark throughout the 1990s, and Dansk Folkeparti (the Danish People's Party) as the fourth largest party in Denmark presently enjoys much power as the party providing the final votes for the present liberal-conservative government. In Denmark there is a tradition for allowing people to express themselves freely without much in terms of social sanctions (such as political correctness or self-censorship), possibly due to the nation being fairly homogeneous culturally and ideologically up until the 1970s–1980s. This may possibly also be one of the explanations for why the Mohammed cartoons appeared in a Danish newspaper, where the publisher's agenda was exactly to counter a perceived sense of a growing tendency towards self-censorship when it came to speaking openly and critically about the religion of many recent immigrants to Denmark. This would probably not have happened in

Sweden five years ago, though there were signs in the most recent election that similar right-wing nationalist, anti-immigration parties gained in representation. The reaction to this development from the political parties and from the press was and still is very negative in Sweden, and there were moves to suppress the viewpoints of the far right in Swedish media. I imagine that the populations in the Scandinavian countries view the challenges of immigration to the welfare states in similar ways: some find immigration inevitable and something that the rich Scandinavian countries need to take part in as much as possible, whereas a significant minority of citizens find the open immigration policies problematic. (They used to be open in Denmark, and are now one of the most restrictive in EU; in Sweden they are still the most open in Scandinavia, but there is a concern that this will change. I am not so sure about the current policies in Norway, I am afraid.) There have always been far-right movements beyond the political parties in Scandinavia, and interestingly the most violent ones have come from Sweden and Norway. But these are different from other such fascist or neo-Nazi movements in other European countries. In the Scandinavian countries there is concern over both the political move to the right (many voters moving from Social Democratic parties to the nationalist, anti-immigration parties) and the pockets of anti-democratic groups. My impression is that they are perhaps not more troubling in Scandinavia than in other EU countries, but they shatter the self-image of the Scandinavian welfare states as open, socially responsible, rich, ethical, egalitarian and caring countries. That is probably why the problem seems larger from abroad.

'I think we are presently witnessing a trend in Scandinavian crime fiction that is becoming more global, and I think this is a general reaction to perceptions held in the Scandinavian countries. In the main Scandinavian countries, my impression is that generally the ideals of the Welfare state (the high level of redistribution of wealth; the strong role of the state in almost all aspects of life from cradle to grave; the belief that a strong state will make it possible for citizens to live a life where they are free to realise themselves and their potentials no matter their social heritage, their gender etc.) are still very much central to all political parties in Scandinavia from left to right. There is, however, a growing concern with whether the welfare states can maintain the level of service and social impact in a globalised world with the impact of immigration and free mobility within the EU, and, as in other countries, the social welfare system is already showing signs of weakness confronted with an unbalanced distribution of age groups: fewer people to provide the taxes that will pay for the deserved entitlements of an older population with growing needs in terms of well-being. The Scandinavian countries are surely today not that different, generally, from other countries, also in that many Scandinavians live in a globalised world through international media and easy access to travel and working abroad, but to my mind what is still significant for the Scandinavian countries is the level of political consensus about the value of maintaining as much as possible of the traditional Welfare states, though, as I said, it is currently facing challenges and needs reformulation, in which parties on the right and left are struggling over the details of what this will involve.

'Regarding translation of crime fiction, I am afraid that I have not studied the actual quality of translations closely, but gather from my correspondence and conversations with colleagues in the translation community that a good many of the current translations of Scandinavian crime fiction are done by highly skilled translators who also translate contemporary Scandinavian fiction and the classics. Laurie Thompson, for instance, has translated both Nesser and Mankell, and his translations are recognised by both Swedish organisations and his peers in Britain and in Sweden. The Swedish translators are particularly well organised in Britain. Don Bartlett is another great translator of the Norwegian crime writers Staalesen and Nesbø. He also translates contemporary Danish fiction, and is, as Thompson, delivering translations of a continuous high quality. Tiina Nunnally is an American award-winning translator who has translated Karin Fossum and the Danish blockbuster author Peter Høeg's *Miss Smilla's Feeling for Snow*. She received an Independent Foreign Fiction Prize for *The Royal Physician's Visit* by Per Olov Enquist in 2003.'

But do the British have a more accurate apprehension today of the distinctions between various Nordic countries?

'This is really difficult to have a general opinion about, since "the British" are not a very homogenous group. Some Britons have astonishing insights into either general cultural differences or very specific knowledge about certain particularities: for instance, some have great knowledge of the different Scandinavian film-makers, some are aware of the different social systems (though they are not easy to tell apart), some know a great deal about different rock, pop or metal bands from the Scandinavian countries. Most people recognise national icons such as Ikea and ABBA from Sweden, and, regarding Denmark, they know about the Mohammed cartoons (if not Hans Christian Andersen); then there is Henrik Ibsen from Norway and Björk and volcanoes from Iceland – but generally, I would say, that individual Scandinavian particularities are mostly lost in what appears in British and American media; Scandinavian countries have, obviously, very little place in the school curricula (apart from the history of the Vikings, I would suppose), and have – as with most other foreign language cultural products – a very difficult time entering the English language market. That Scandinavian languages and cultures are now taught at fewer British universities than a decade ago further adds to the fairly limited access British people have to learn about cultural particularities of the Scandinavian countries, as both similar and different cultures. Many people obviously travel to the Scandinavian countries and learn from first-hand experiences, but my assumption is that Scandinavia still is, despite the cultural success in foreign markets for film, literature, music, etc., considered an indistinguishable entity, interesting for the social systems, and also slightly eccentric in the apparently idealistic attitudes towards redistribution of wealth.

'I think generally that these days British people have a better knowledge of (and different examples of) what it means to be Scandinavian – but I also think that Scandinavian countries are mostly perceived in terms of a roseate image of their egalitarian past, their high living standards, impressive levels of education, etc. while naturally, Scandinavian countries are faced with many of the same challenges – culturally and socially – as other north European countries. Perhaps Scandinavian crime fiction will have the effect of demonstrating to British readers that Scandinavians have many of the same concerns as themselves – for different reasons, with different backgrounds and cultures, but should be studied for how they try to find different solutions to similar challenges. Books are a passport.'

Books are at the centre of *The Library of Shadows* (2009) by the talented Danish writer Mikkel Birkegaard; his protagonist Jon Campelli inherits a second-hand bookshop after the sudden violent death of his father. Jon's mother similarly died under strange circumstances, and he had not seen his father for many years. Shortly after Jon receives his legacy, there is an arson attack on the bookshop and he realises that the shop (a meeting place for book aficionados) is the repository of a strange and dark secret. He discovers a remarkable tradition passed down from the time of the fabled library of Alexandra – and his life is on the line. Mixing elements of intrigue, conspiracy and the power of the printed word (a resonant notion in Denmark), *The Library of Shadows* is stylish, engrossing fare.

As is *The Exception* (2006) by Christian Jungersen. The writer made a considerable mark in Britain with the superlative novel – and this was an achievement based firmly on his skills as a writer rather than his personality, as he showed a noted reluctance to be accommodating to British journalists interviewing him on the strength of the word of mouth concerning his work. But it is the work that counts rather than keeping one's publicist happy, and Jungersen's novel gleaned the kind of popularity that its recalcitrant creator showed little inclination to finesse. *The Exception* is set in an institution known as the Danish Centre for Genocide studies. Women working here are receiving death threats, and come to believe that they will become the victims of a Bosnian war criminal with a taste for torture. But there is a chance that the danger actually comes from within their own organisation. As the unnerving psychological games continue, the women find themselves in conflict with each other – a situation almost as dangerous as the external threat. Christian Jungersen's disturbing and strongly written novel has an interesting structure: as the narrative progresses, a variety of articles appear treating of major crimes such as genocide, and the reader is given the strong impression that there is much more at work here than the straightforward mechanics of the psychological suspense novel. The author is dealing with our mutual responsibility (and culpability) when it comes to confronting each other – and this is never done at the expense of keeping the tension strikingly orchestrated. Jungersen is adept at characterising his individual protagonists, and makes sure that we are thoroughly involved in a dangerous situation. In some ways, this is a version of the Christie-style plot in which a group of individuals are destroyed by an external threat, but the spin here is very modern indeed; the zeitgeist of the novel, however, seems to inhabit an international mindset rather than a peculiarly Danish one.

14
Danish Uncertainties

The work of the Dane Jussi Adler-Olsen arrived (translated by Tiina Nunnally) in non-Scandinavian countries with a pre-sold reputation, and the author himself arrived with a cluster of awards under his belt: the Glass Key Award for best Nordic Crime Thriller, the Danish Reader's Book Award and the Danish Thriller of the Year (all for the year 2010). The first novel to be translated, *Mercy*, sports a dramatis personae of well-rounded characters (including an on-the-ropes copper) and a striking premise. The book is about second chances. Carl Mørck once enjoyed the reputation of a good homicide detective – one of Copenhagen's finest, in fact. Then a bullet nearly puts an end to his career and his life. He survives, but two of his colleagues are less fortunate, and Carl, as his gun remained in his holster, lays the blame at his own door. As he begins to go off the rails, the imminent termination of his job is clearly in the offing. But to his surprise he is suddenly promoted to the newly created Department Q, designed to deal with 'cases of special focus'. His ex-colleagues are sarcastic, dismissing the new department as a repository for hopeless cases. It is felt that the erratic Carl is the right man for this non-job. But his first assignment concerns missing politician Merete Lynggaard, who disappeared five years ago, and is believed to be dead. Needless to say, she isn't – at least not yet. And Carl, in his new job, may have found his way back to self-respect.

Jussi Adler-Olsen (named after the great Swedish tenor Jussi Björling) was born in Copenhagen and studied medicine, sociology, politics and film, working as a magazine editor and publisher before starting to write fiction. He made his literary debut in 1997 with the novel *Alfabethuset/ The Alphabet House*, which was a bestseller throughout Europe, and in 2007 wrote the first title in the *Department Q* series, *Mercy*. He has written four books in the *Department Q* series, all of which hit the Danish bestseller lists on publication and have remained there. He is a winner of the prestigious Glass Key Award, given annually for a crime novel written by a Scandinavian author, for his novel *Flaskepost fra P/Redemption* (2009), the third in the *Department Q* series. He is also a recipient, in 2011, of the Golden Laurels, Denmark's highest literary accolade, which is awarded by the Danish book trade. The novels are being adapted for international screen distribution.

Adler-Olsen, though Danish, considers himself a child of the world. He appreciates that readers of his *Department Q* novels are taking a vicarious trip to Denmark to soak up the atmosphere and savour the locations (to that end, he is particularly punctilious in his research). Despite this, however, Adler-Olsen never allows the surroundings to take the focus from the key elements in a good thriller: the empathy with the characters, a close attention to the plot lines.

Politically, Adler-Olsen is engaged. As he said to me:

'Am I critical of my country's political system? Certainly. If you ask me whether I'd be prepared to espouse particular party-political agendas, the answer is unequivocally no. My own agenda is primarily to remain constantly critical, regardless of individual political viewpoints, that's to say, to make it clear to the politicians in power that they should understand that they are our servants and not our masters.

'My books are principally motivated by my desire to create and maintain empathy for the protagonists. If you approach your writing with this imperative, it will never be (for instance) corruption in itself that is the narrative's plot engine.

'There is no doubt about that in Scandinavia – and particularly here in Denmark – we have become attached to specific global tendencies, to value highly (for instance) the individual instead of society itself.

'But leaving aside negativity, the right to criticise and reject bad ideas and notions still, thankfully, holds firm. And there is no other place on earth, in my opinion, that embraces this right as frequently and thoughtfully – which makes me proud. This was undoubtedly a characteristic of the writers I admire, such as John Steinbeck, Charles Dickens, Victor Hugo, Jerzy Kosinsky and even the strange Norwegian writer Erlend Loe.

'My overriding themes remain revenge, the striving for justice, and – I realise – insanity. My latest book to be published in Denmark is about a very dark chapter in Danish history; it concerns the island known as "Hell's Forecourt", to which so-called "promiscuous" women were forcefully deported and subjected to abuse of the crudest kind.

Carl Mørck's assistant in Department Q, Rose, gets wind of a scary story that stems from the place, with modern-day murder a result.'

One of Adler-Olsen's predecessors (and contemporaries), Leif Davidsen, is something of an institution among Danish writers, with an imposing gravitas to match his impressive sales. A key book for the author is *The Serbian Dane* (2007). The setting is Zagreb in 1995. A writer and intellectual, crucial to the recently triumphant Croatian independence movement, is assassinated. His killer is Vuk, a Serb who learned his trade in the Yugoslavian Army's Special Forces school, his talents now utilised by rogue elements of the disintegrating Serbian nationalists. Chapter 1, and already Leif Davidsen (Steel Dagger-nominated for *Lime's Photograph* in 2002) is likely to wrong-foot many of his readers in terms of their responses to the characters and plot. The Croat is arrogant and self-serving, the Serb cold but resourceful, and he returns after the hit to a partner traumatised by events in the Balkan conflict. Later it transpires that Vuk was brought up in Denmark, and speaks Danish. Which makes him the ideal candidate for the ensuing job: the murder of Sara Santanda, a Rushdie/Hirsi-like Muslim dissident, visiting Denmark in pursuit of her reformist agenda. Vuk is incredulous. He has, we learn, no reason to support a fundamentalist agenda. But Muslims will be blamed, so he agrees. A timely premise then, especially when the reader bears in mind that this book appeared in Denmark in 1996, a time when British thriller writers (John Fullerton an honourable exception) – if they dared to dip a toe in contemporary events at all – were more concerned with Northern Ireland than with the fallout from the Balkans. Other key protagonists (in what is basically a three-hander) include Lise Carlsen, chair of the Danish branch of the international writer's organisation PEN, and a well-known arts journalist set to interview Santanda, whilst Detective Inspector Per Toftlund has the job of ensuring maximum security for an exercise that will attract worldwide publicity. Lise's marriage is at crisis point; Per is a loner and a workaholic, but an attractive figure. No prizes, then, for guessing just how that relationship works out, as the three key players converge for Davidsen's final exhilarating shoot-out. Davidsen's considerable ability as a writer shines through. The author brings an expert but sceptical eye (sharpened through twenty-five years at Denmark's Broadcasting Corporation) to the background of the novel, whether it be journalistic, social or political. The reader can pick up a tip or two as Vuk slips unnoticed from country to country; note his observations of the changes in Danish society as he reacquaints himself on arrival in the target country. There are echoes of the Danish cartoons affair (which so upset theocrats), for instance, in the government's reaction to Santanda's arrival. An unusually intelligent and thoughtful political thriller – and sensitively translated by Barbara J. Haveland, with nary a false note. Davidsen has clear views of his place in a Danish tradition.

'I am not a nationalist writer, but a writer who happens to live in Denmark,' he says. 'But of course, being Danish and writing in my mother tongue I am indebted to the storytelling tradition of my country. If the truth be told, however, I think I owe more to the inspiration of writers such as Graham Greene and Ernest Hemingway than to any Scandinavian writers.

'I find it important to be precise in details when writing about specific places. Place and setting are crucial elements for me and I spend a great deal of time on research. Atmosphere, also, is everything in the kind of novels I write. Denmark is such a small country that regional differences are minimal, but, again, I try very hard to be precise. I don't want to cheat, just to make the story move.

'Denmark, being a compact country, sports regional differences which are essentially nuances. I live outside Copenhagen, which is really a small town by the sea compared to many other important cities. It is, however, our capital and that distinguishes it from the rest of the country.'

Davidsen keeps his work fresh with a variety of strategies.

'To keep myself up to scratch, I try to maintain a dynamic quality through research and the freshness of language. And – of course – by exercising my imagination. It's also essential for me to keep a close watch on the politics of the world. Also, it's a temptation – to be resisted – that one doesn't strive solely for crime fiction imperatives, but for good quality of writing. Good writing, it seems to me, is as important in a crime novel as in any other work of fiction.

'The Scandinavian countries have notably discrete identities, which is very much the case with the politics too. It is my strong impression – when I follow discussions about the Nordic crime-wave outside Scandinavia – that what is really being talked about, again and again, are Swedish writers, who reign supreme. They are a very strong presence, and they write in a pronounced Social Democratic tradition. The notion of Social Democracy is strongest in Sweden, where there is a deep and abiding belief in the virtues of order, as supplied by the state. You also see this syndrome in the country's crime novels. Readers are presented with a situation where chaos reigns, and then the protagonist arrives and conjures order out of chaos, until – inevitably – the cycle begins again. The welfare state is perceived as the modern version of heaven, but at the same time it can be fraught with ever-present unhappiness and *angst*. So we need the Good Detective, who is often unhappy and discontented with his own dysfunctional life, but whose real function is to discern and re-establish order and meaning in this disorderly life. It is a piquant contradiction, I know – but it seems to me that many Scandinavian writers have a strong hankering for the orderly social democratic welfare state. However, the boredom of life in this society creates the monsters which these writers extirpate in their novels. Sort of like modern-day social democratic King Arthurs cutting off the heads of the disorderly dragons.

'Personally, I am not inspired by Scandinavian writers. My inspiration comes from great British writers such as Eric Ambler, Graham Greene and John le Carré. I am happy to admit that I am much more indebted to the Anglo-American tradition than that of my own region. Gerald Seymour is another great English writer who I much admire – truly a master of character.

'Hopefully, such influences have been absorbed, and I have gotten better and surer of myself from book to book. I know I am willing to take more chances in recent novels. I make a point (despite pressure) of not writing in the commercial, publisher-friendly form of a series of novels with the same protagonist – so every book is different. I try to ensure – every time – that each book is a distinct entity. I used to be a foreign correspondent; the world, both then and now, is my inspiration and feeds and replenishes my creative impulses.

'Key books of my own for me include *Lime's Photograph* – this was the novel which set me on the path of being translated into many languages, and I'm very fond of the main character, Peter Lime. He was fun to write about; as it was fun to write about the Madrid I used to live in.

'*The Woman from Bratislava* is also a book of which I'm particularly proud – because it seems to me that (for the most part) I achieved what I set out to do: create something complex, nuanced and different.'

Barbara Haveland, translator of Leif Davidsen's *The Serbian Dane* and *The Woman from Bratislava*, is conscious of the need to be familiar with the settings of the novels she is translating.

'It can be very important to be conversant with the setting,' she has said. 'It can be difficult to translate a piece – be it a brief passage or a whole work – unless you can visualise the locations. Not least because with many crime writers the physical setting is absolutely vital to the narrative, and in the case of Jo Nesbø's Oslo, for example, (as with Ian Rankin's Edinburgh), the city is almost a character in its own right. In my experience, the translator needs to know how things lie topographically in relation to one another. In my own case, I know the city of Oslo very well and I know certain other parts of Norway and the general geography of the country pretty well, but in working on certain Norwegian novels, I have had an Oslo A–Z and a good road atlas for the whole of Norway right at my elbow – and I've referred to them continually. The same goes for Copenhagen and Denmark: when translating Leif Davidsen's *The Serbian Dane* I had to do a lot of research into Copenhagen Harbour, to make sure that I interpreted Leif's descriptions correctly.

'Knowledge of the location is vital also at the most basic level – for example when translating prepositions. What does a Norwegian writer mean, for instance, when he/she says that someone goes "nedover veien" or "op mod..." to a particular place. In English it may not be "down the road" or "up towards" – you really have to check.'

Haveland believes that similar knowledge is required of all aspects of the country discussed in any given narrative.

'This kind of total knowledge is, of course, vital. And not just in terms of the standard customs, celebrations and so on. It's as much about understanding the mindset of a country and its people. Take, for example, the 17th of May in Norway – their Constitution Day. You can read all you want about that, but unless you actually experience it you'll have no understanding of the place this occupies in the hearts and minds of all Norwegians – and you learn a lot about the Norwegians themselves by seeing them celebrate "17. Maj".

'I would never have dared to start translating from Norwegian before I actually lived in the country. There are so many concepts which are impossible to grasp – and, therefore, to describe in translation – unless you have experienced them from the inside, as it were. I'm living in Denmark and so obviously am very conscious of what is going on in politics here, and through newspapers and television I am kept au fait with current affairs. I have access to two Norwegian television channels so I also get regular updates on political events etc. in Norway. And there are the things you learn from the authors you deal with regarding all sorts of subjects – depending on the writers and their works. In broad terms, the more Scandinavian fiction one translates, the more insight one gains into the historical, cultural and social background of Scandinavia as a whole and of the individual countries. And this is also very important when it comes to understanding the way Danes, Norwegians, Swedes see themselves (not least in relation to one another!).

'This historical, cultural, social knowledge is also a crucial key to the language. The more you translate (in my case, Danish and Norwegian writers), the deeper your own understanding and feel for the language and the better equipped you are to understand and interpret not only the words on the page, but also everything that lies between the lines.'

But Haveland is wary of identifying crime novels as indexes of social conditions in Nordic countries.

'The images presented in each crime novel have first passed through the author's own "filter", if you like – and Scandinavian crime writers often seem anxious to make some sort of political or social statement in their works. To be honest I think there's too much of this, particularly among female crime writers in Scandinavia, many of whom seem to feel that it's almost obligatory to describe the seemingly appalling social conditions in what are some of the most prosperous democratic countries in the world.'

Different concerns energise Michael Larsen's debut novel in English (1996, his second in his native land of Denmark). *Uncertainty* is an accelerando-paced thriller, the uncertainty mooted in the title resulting from the idea that in the new digital age no image we encounter can be guaranteed to have a precise basis in reality. His ambitious and apocalyptic novel *The Snake in Sydney* (2000), like *Uncertainty* a best-seller in Denmark, extends that principle to embrace a good deal of scientific thought. 'I don't know what to believe any more,' confesses Larsen's heroine Annika Niebuhr, in the concluding pages of this novel. The cool, rational Annika is a Danish doctor working in Sydney, Australia, an expert in snakes and a distant, less sympathetic relative to Peter Høeg's Smilla Jaspersen. The reader, engaged in a notably labyrinthine plot, may well sympathise. Perhaps the only certainties in the book are that Australia is home to seven of the world's ten most dangerous snakes, that in high season few gardens in Sydney are complete without its snake (does the Australian Tourist Board know about this?) and that the venom of the taipan, Australia's (and the world's) most poisonous snake, is 850 times stronger than that of the American rattlesnake. Even that latter fact is not certain because an apparently dead young woman, bitten by a taipan concealed in her car, and under examination by Annika in the novel's opening scene, suddenly sits up, pulls out a gun and bolts from the room. Nor, as Annika knows, is the taipan native to Sydney. The girl reappears later in Annika's car as she leaves for home, and warns her against anything or anyone to do with 'Atlas X'. The ultimately implausible plot is the least satisfactory element of the book, smoothly written, translated and readable though it is. Many of its ingredients, though given an extra fascination by the background and training of its key protagonist, are perhaps over-familiar: an apparent suicide, a sympathetic policeman, mysterious photographs, an attempt on Annika's life, hints of stygian secrets at the heart of government.

What marks the book out are the means by which Larsen orchestrates tension. For the expository passages that are the integuments between each plot development, normally descriptive or mood-building, here constitute, more often than not, a debate about the nature of knowledge itself. 'Lack of knowledge is for the lazy' comments Annika at one point. At first we learn about snakes, and how to deal with them, then about the snake and its role in mythology and early religion. Later the argument (and there is one) embraces many different kinds of knowledge, scientific, medical and philosophical. That, for instance, even now, most knowledge is inexact, often based on flaws in the knowledge that came before – and that some knowledge (for the plot is never far away) is deadly. Throughout our respect for Annika grows. In the final analysis, Michael Larsen pulls together the various disparate elements, and revelling in its own complexity, this is hardly an effortless read. But it is, finally, rewarding.

More waves from Scandinavia look set to break on British shores. Sara Blaedel's extremely popular crime series is written in a distinctive 'Copenhagen Noir' style which makes her books both unlike those of her contemporaries as well as highly accessible (she enjoys the sobriquet of 'Danish Crime Queen'). Her novels have been favourably compared to Camilla Läckberg's *Fjällbacka* series but incorporate more pronounced elements of edgy social awareness into the narratives. As a publisher, she made available (and revived) many important Nordic Crime fiction talents, while all of her own books have achieved the status of number one bestsellers in Denmark, and Blaedel has earned the title 'Most Popular Danish Author' on two occasions. She also won the Danish Crime Academy Award for best debut in 2004 with her novel *Green Dust*. In 2010, the influential Nordin Agency concluded the largest publishing deal ever made in Denmark for two new titles in her ongoing series focusing on her protagonist, Detective Inspector Louise Rick. An English translation of the author's *Call Me Princess* is imminent, and a non-Danish breakthrough may be in the offing.

The Boy in the Suitcase is the much-trumpeted Danish thriller (the first in a series) that has been taken up in America before it was in Britain, though it has now found a British home. The highly individual authors are Lene Kaaberbøl and Agnete Friis, who before this criminous collaboration were celebrated for fantasy and children's books, respectively. (The transition to adult thriller is not, of course, unprecedented – the Icelandic Yrsa Sigurðardóttir moved from children's books to highly uncompromising adult fare.) The unusual heroine of the Kaaberbøl/ Friis series is Nina Borg, a dedicated Red Cross nurse who is also a compulsive do-gooder, and The Boy in the Suitcase instantly distinguishes itself in an overcrowded field in terms of crisp pacing and execution. Unusually, for books inaugurating a new series, it does not appear to be possible to encounter a range of opinions on this one – complete surrender to its unusual strategies seems to be the only option for those who have read it. One of several duos making a mark in the Nordic Noir field, Kaaberbøl and Friis have produced in their first joint novel a trenchantly written crime piece that is subtly different from the work of most of their confrères. Individually, the women have enjoyed great acclaim: Lene Kaaberbøl has sold more than two million books worldwide as a fantasy writer, while her teammate Agnete Friis is also a successful children's writer. Their collaboration represented the first time either of them had written adult fiction, but there is no sign of inexperience in this field.

This first volume in their *Nina Borg* series was published in Denmark in November 2008 and quickly became a bestseller, praised for its lean but tautly effective prose. It won a prestigious award for its status as the best thriller in Denmark in 2008 and was nominated for the Glass Key (the much-coveted Scandinavian crime prize). Buoyed by this acclaim, the duo produced *A Quiet, Unfelt Killing* in 2010, and a third Nina Borg novel will be soon forthcoming. Unsurprisingly (after this attention), the trilogy has sold to Britain and America as well as countries from Norway to Lithuania. Film rights are currently being negotiated. Unusually, Lene Kaaberbøl has translated her own work for English-speaking readers in the US edition.

Juliet Grames, the US publisher of *The Boy in the Suitcase* has said that she is not sure how long this hyperactive bubble of attention for 'Scandinavian crime' as a genre will last, but, as she told me:

'Crime as a genre is immortal, and the Scandinavian countries all offer extraordinary literary traditions and a rather high per capita wealth of authors. I'm just glad that the recent bubble of attention has helped publishing companies realise they can afford to translate, and that translations can also be commercial projects. It's been a transformative learning experience for the industry.

'I tend to buy translations from samples. After all, the recipe for a great piece of literature in translation is a great piece of literature plus a great translation, two rather different components. Usually samples come from either agents or foreign publishers. And since Soho Press's core mission with its crime list is celebrating and exploring crime literature traditions around the world, translations fit in very nicely. Translations sometimes require different publicity tactics, since the authors involved are often not as accessible (living abroad, and/or possibly not conversant in English), but we're working on innovative ways to excite readers besides traditional avenues for publicity. Personally, I love the editorial process and engaging with texts – it's my favourite part of being an editor. And translation offers a new and challenging way of engaging with a text. There's also a very interesting dialogue in translation and publishing circles on whether it is better to stay closer to the author's words or closer to the reader's comfort zone – accuracy, that is, versus accessibility. I find this spectrum of opinions fascinating, and it's great fun to be part of that dialogue.'

Lene Kaaberbøl and Agnete Friis are aware (regarding the scabrous picture they paint of their region) that the Danish tourist board will not be dispatching encomiums in their direction in any kind of a hurry. Writing about crime makes it hard, they have noted, to avoid politics entirely:

'Unless one sets one's murders exclusively on archaeological expeditions or on the Orient Express. And in creating Nina Borg, we did quite deliberately pick as our main character someone who is constantly driven to try to "save the world" both through legitimate – and slightly less legitimate – means. As a Red Cross nurse, Nina has long since had any complacency about her society and the way it treats its outcasts stripped away.

'Crime by its nature is that element which society does not accept, and this makes for a sort of negative outline that focuses mainly on that which is *outside* – that which is illegal, unacceptable and inadmissible. A crime novel can of course only paint a very partial and piecemeal picture, but then again, few mainstream novels can claim to do more. But if various studies are to be believed, Denmark is one of the least corrupt countries in the world. And actually, corruption is not a major theme for us – we aim our guns more at complacency and plain incompetence.'

Crime novels, note the duo, are not the most accurate source of information concerning society, particularly where crime statistics are concerned.

'Iceland is a perfect example – the country averages about 2.5 murders a year in real life, but Icelandic crime writers insouciantly kill off four or five hapless victims in every single novel. Happy, contented characters, it has to be said, tend to make for boring stories, so we focus on discontent, crises and disasters.

'The ideals of our society are resilient, but they are under siege. Thirty or forty years ago, it was a much simpler matter to offer such benefits as free hospital treatment, free education and affordable child care to all comers. With globalisation has come new challenges, and we struggle to meet them.

'There are several Scandinavian writers whose works we both enjoy – Arnaldur Indriðason, Åsa Larsson and Johan Theorin, to name just a few – but we don't necessarily feel that we could or should try to write *like* them. As for non-Scandinavians, we both particularly respond to the novelists Ruth Rendell and P.D. James for their penetrating powers of characterisation. These writers certainly represent an example we would like to emulate.'

The duo has a clear view of their principal preoccupations as writers.

'We try to tackle the challenging question of *inside* and *outside*. There is a sort of charmed circle within which "people like us" are protected and cushioned to the best of society's ability, whereas those outside the circle have no such protection. We accept or ignore considerable abuse and misery as long as it does not strike within the circle. During our research for *The Boy in the Suitcase*, we learned that more than 600 children had disappeared from Danish refugee centres over a period of seven years. Granted, some of those so-called "unaccompanied minors" probably absented themselves voluntarily and may have gone to join relatives elsewhere. But some did not. And some, we are fairly sure, were bought and paid for. We have no idea how many, and the point is, we don't seem to care. Had they been Danish children vanishing from Danish institutions there would have been uproar, there would have been searches and enquiries, debates and appeals – no stone left unturned. As it is, it barely rated a mention. If we do have a mission beyond that, it is to lure the reader into identifying with those outside the circle – to imagine, for the duration of the narrative at least, what it is like to *be* someone like that, with no protection, no charm against callousness, exploitation and deliberate malice.

'Currently, we are writing the third Nina Borg novel. It is set partly in Denmark, partly in the Ukraine, and has more historical background than the first two – the roots of the central mystery reach back to the early days of Stalin's rule and the *Holodomor*, the massive famine induced by his policies of collectivisation and "dekulakisation".'

15
Film and TV Adaptations

Comparisons between the three televised versions of Henning Mankell's signature character, the troubled inspector Kurt Wallander, are deeply instructive: apart from the fact that a triple TV incarnation of the same character (from 1995 to the present) is a measure of the character's considerable hold on the popular imagination, there are also intriguing elements freighted into the various adaptations (whether conscious or otherwise) which make salient points about everything from the societal to the geopolitical aspects of Swedish society – but always within the context of smoothly executed popular television drama.

The first actor to play Mankell's dour character for Swedish television was Rolf Lassgård, and it was not to the advantage of the actor's performance in Britain that his appearances were shown out of sequence in the UK. By the time his first Wallander adaptation was shown (*The Man Who Smiled*, filmed in 2003, and capably directed by Leif Lindblom), British viewers had been able to choose between the later episodes in the authentic-seeming, low-key series starring Krister Henriksson (2005 and 2008), and the glossier, more cinema-style British adaptations with Kenneth Branagh (2008 and 2010), shot in high-definition and filmed on location in Ystad. In the debut episode, the distinctly fleshy Rolf Lassgård (who is given a line comparing himself to the heavyweight TV detective Cannon played by William Conrad) suffered in comparison with the two very different versions that British audiences had been exposed to, and there was some resistance to the actor despite the undoubted persuasiveness of his performance.

However, few would deny that the Krister Henriksson and Kenneth Branagh versions, for all the disputes over their respective merits, quickly assumed the status of yardsticks when it came to physical embodiments of Mankell's detective. Henriksson opted for an understated, subtle approach to the character's variety of *crises de conscience* and the various traumas of his private life, while Branagh (as befitting his image as a highly capable stage performer) opted for a more actorly performance: intelligent, full of truth and psychological veracity, but nevertheless a performance in which the mechanics of the actor's art might clearly be discerned. The tighter knit ensemble of the Swedish police team is here somewhat subsumed in Branagh's central turn, though the British supporting players are very capable. Also notable was Branagh's concentration on the more neurotic elements of the character's persona; as opposed to the reined-in, tightly wound (but still outwardly in control) Henriksson, Branagh's Wallander seemed frequently on the point of breakdown, sometimes barely able to articulate a response to the comments of his worried colleagues.

But it was not just the central character that provided an index of the difference between the British and Swedish series. The presentation of Sweden itself (and, more specifically, the detective's designated stamping ground of Ystad) was conceived very differently by the British and Swedish film-makers, leaving aside the problems caused by placing British actors (speaking English) in authentic Swedish settings, while the Swedish series, of course, automatically avoided any inconsistencies in this area. The intersection of the British actors and crew with the Ystad locale threw up some intriguing dislocations, probably noticeable only to inhabitants of the town: the swimming bath, for instance, becomes the TV programme's police station, while (according to the local film council) at least 20 per cent of the local population may be seen in various episodes as extras.

The most notable difference between the two shows was, in some ways, the presentation of the country itself. In the Swedish series, we are shown flat, characterless cities in which the anonymous factories and unwelcoming housing estates present a picture of a country in which the dream of comfortable working class environments has disappeared. While the endemic corruption of business and politics is imported from the novels in a fashion which (in general) pleased Mankell, there was much critical acclaim for the fashion in which the film-makers had resisted the urge to offer a tourists' view of Sweden. We are shown, unvarnished, the quotidian workings of the current version of the social democratic ideal, but never in any tendentious fashion.

The Kenneth Branagh BBC series, by contrast, unfolds (as perhaps befits its status as an outsider's view) an often ravishing, somewhat romanticised picture of the countryside: waving fields of rapeseed, exquisite glowing sunsets straight out of J.M.W. Turner. There is also an acute attention to the aesthetics of Swedish contemporary architecture; in this respect the cinematography of the Swedish show is more direct and functional. However, the closest parallels between the two series, these elements apart, is the direction given to the actors: both the British and the Swedish performances render the characters economically with an almost complete absence of larger-than-life 'indicating' mannerisms (even Branagh's central turn, though more indulgent); the audience is (to a large extent) allowed to make up its own mind about the motivations and inner lives of the characters.

At a Nordic Noir book club evening in London organised by University College London, the producer Francis Hopkinson of Left Bank Productions talked about the choice of locations. Hopkinson noted intriguingly that it was a deliberate choice to go for the programme's 1960s and 70s look because that was when (it was considered) the Swedish welfare state dream entered British consciousness. However, a question about the dumbed-down, anglicised pronunciation of the hero's name (with a 'W' as opposed to a 'V' and the stress on the wrong syllable) received a somewhat unconvincing answer. It was a matter of practicality, Hopkinson remarked, because there were new British actors arriving on set all the time and there had to be a firm guideline on pronunciation, so the producers went for the 'easy' one. Regarding language, there had been a conscious decision that everyone would speak in received pronunciation so as not to draw attention to accents – cf. the approach in the short-lived TV series adapting Michael Dibdin's Italian Inspector Zen, in which Hopkinson was also involved. Anthony Dogmantle, who is British but lives in Copenhagen (and who worked on the film *Slumdog Millionaire*), created the look that defines the Branagh Wallander, specifically the beautiful cultivated fields and exquisite blue sky. It is no coincidence that this imagery mimics the Swedish flag, according to Francis Hopkinson. As a snowbound contrast to the summery setting, two episodes in a later series are set in winter, with *Dogs of Riga* filmed in Latvia.

Interestingly, there has been a recent readjustment (on the part of British audiences at least) of judgements regarding the two series. After British audiences had seen both the Swedish and British shows (both achieved – respectively – impressive viewing figures, though the Branagh, shown on a more popular mainstream BBC channel than its rival, was the winner in this area), received wisdom quickly became that the Krister Henriksson series had, with its understated approach and nuanced psychology, captured more of the feel of Mankell's novels (perhaps the aforementioned 'dumbing down' of the pronunciation of the hero's surname in the BBC series was emblematic here). Henriksson, too, appeared to comprehensively win the Battle of the Wallanders, and his performance was routinely used as a stick with which to beat the more 'method'-oriented assumption of Kenneth Branagh. But then a curious thing happened; by the time of the second series of the British show, commentators were being conspicuously more generous towards it than previously, rightly recognising that its virtues (including the subtle and allusive narrative approach) were considerable when not judged in a beauty contest against the original Swedish series.

There is, however, one element which remains more persuasive in the Swedish series, and that is the political agenda. Without ever labouring any points or freighting in a conspicuous 'seriousness', the social critique of Mankell's novels is refracted more consistently through the SVT shows, while the British series places little emphasis on such factors.

A demonstration of this may be illuminated by a comparison of the Swedish and British adaptations of Mankell's novel *The Man Who Smiled*, dealing with illegal organ sales. The corrupt industrialist in the former series is contextualised in terms of his meetings with foreign colleagues and his importance to the Swedish economy (however suspect his activities), while the British adaptation renders him as something of a maverick figure, with less political clout. The suggestion, somehow, is that the makers of the British show (which was directed by Andy Wilson) have opted not to be too critical of the host country that has allowed them to film there, and this different, softer emphasis is made even more marked by a character who appears in the Swedish adaptation but not at all in the British one: the sinister (and adopted) daughter of the industrialist, up to her elbows in his crooked dealings and even inseminated by him in a gesture designed to underline his malign character.

But this is not to say that the British series sidelines the author's social critique; it is, if anything, more a matter of emphasis, with Kenneth Branagh's existential crises and difficulties with colleagues and lovers moved centre stage in order to play to the actor's strengths; these elements are, of course, to be found in the Swedish series, but there, a subtle graduation of tonality is all: at times, the twitchy, alienated Branagh seemed barely able to function within the context of a busy station (his colleagues are constantly gazing at him in horror or pity), while Krister Henriksson's Wallander conceals his turmoil somewhat more adroitly. In the final analysis, aficionados of the best crime fiction adaptations should perhaps be grateful that two admirable series were made, and that there is absolutely no necessity to choose between them – the differences of approach are so marked that both are equally rewarding after their own fashion.

The film of *Jar City* – which enjoyed particularly enthusiastic reviews in the English press – is an adeptly directed, visually striking thriller, which does considerable justice to Arnaldur Indriðason's much-acclaimed novel. Utilising elements of the police procedural in an unorthodox fashion in the context of a powerful family drama, the film is simultaneously provocative in its evocations of Iceland and Icelandic culture. The connections between an unusual genetic disease, the death of a young woman, a decades-old crime and a missing person are choreographed with understated but impressive skill by the director. Indriðason's hero, the laconic Inspector Erlendur Sveinsson, is expertly incarnated by Ingvar E. Sigurdsson, who conveys the philosophical character of Sveinsson in a performance some distance from the actorly portrayals of most screen detectives. The director also draws subtle and truthful performances from Atli Rafn Sigurdarson (as Örn) and Elma Lisa Gunnarsdóttir (as Gunnur), and the narrative is delivered in a cool, measured but hypnotic fashion.

To some degree, the Swedish trilogy of films made from the novels of Stieg Larsson were an essential part of a battering ram that pushed the author's astonishing posthumous fame to such giddy heights. Although American remakes are in the offing (with Daniel Craig as the journalist Blomkvist, Rooney Mara as Lisbeth Salander and the cult director David Fincher in charge of the projects), it was the Swedish film company Yellow Bird which commissioned and created the original films, enjoying in the process immense commercial and critical acclaim. The company was originally created by the crime writer Henning Mankell and producers Ole Søndberg and Lars Björkman to film the Kurt Wallander novels of Sweden's (then) most celebrated writer. Yellow Bird showed an unerring grasp of commercial realities, and was also involved in the production of the British series adapted from the Wallander novels with the actor Kenneth Branagh. But the ambitions of Yellow Bird extended beyond this enterprise, and a film of Stieg Larsson's *The Girl with the Dragon Tattoo* in 2009 did more justice than was expected to the late writer's original concept through a combination of pared-down writing (by Nikolai Arcel and Rasmus Heisterberg) and effectively utilitarian directing by Niels Arden Oplev. But perhaps the key factor in the success of the film was the canny casting, with Noomi Rapace proving to be the perfect visual equivalent of Larsson's tattooed and pierced sociopathic anti-heroine Lisbeth Salander. Utilising methods derived from the approach of the Russian acting teacher Stanislavsky (and the later New York Method school of Lee Strasberg) the dedicated Rapace was able to find a truthfulness and verisimilitude within what is essentially an impossible character (even more so when rendered on film): a woman who was barely able to function on any kind of social level, but shows a variety of nigh-superhuman skills when situations put her *in extremis*. The casting of Michael Nyqvist as the compromised journo Blomkvist who becomes the unlikely partner and lover of the massively taciturn heroine was more controversial, but Nyqvist was able to maintain a through-line between the resilience and vulnerability of the character (as in the books, the dynamic of Larsson's gender role-reversals was rigorously maintained, with Rapace demonstrating the conventionally masculine traits of violence and retribution while Nyqvist was placed in the traditionally feminine role, being rescued from torture and certain death in the first film).

To some degree, director and actress inevitably failed to render Salander a truly convincing three-dimensional human figure, but this may be laid at the door of the literary original – and there is no question that actress and director made the best possible case for their uncompromising vision of the character, managing to retain our sympathy, despite the character's intransigent behaviour. The film cleverly utilises a variety of Lisbeth's elements: the teased-out solving of a mystery; the unleashing of terrifying violence; the psychotic monster at the heart of the narrative – and charismatic performances to nail the material for cinema audiences. Generally speaking, the second film in the sequence, *The Girl Who Played with Fire*, was less successful, adopting a somewhat different, less understated tone, with a new director (Daniel Alfredson) seemingly less prepared to wrestle the intractable original material into a more appropriate cinematic equivalent. The approach in the second film was more straightforward and action-driven, with the novel's larger-than-life Roger-Moore-era Bond villains undergoing a less happy transition to the screen. The monstrously scarred, evil father figure and the hulking, murderous heavy who is unable to feel pain who had worked on the printed page, but when physically incarnated made their prototypes all too clear (Larsson was an avid consumer of popular culture, and was happy to borrow and transform).

Daniel Alfredson was also the director of the third film in the sequence, *The Girl Who Kicked the Hornet's Nest*, and to some degree was constrained by the structure of the novel in which the fascinating heroine is *hors de combat* for much of the action, confined to a hospital bed after the terrible violence visited upon her by her hideous relatives. But Alfredson nevertheless maintains a rigorous level of narrative coherence, and successfully brings off the climactic courtroom sequence, the latter distinguished by a particular visual coup in which Salander, on a murder charge, strides into court in full Goth makeup and apparel – an alienating appearance that she knows will do her no favours with the judges, but which draws a parallel with her Boudicca-like warrior woman status.

For the Hollywood movie remakes, David Fincher controversially announced that he intended to make some radical changes to the original narratives; to some degree, the directors of the original Swedish trilogy had been similarly cavalier but to positive effect (reducing, for instance, the tedious detail of the financial scam detailed at such length in the first book, and thankfully missing from the film). That first film in fact, quickly attained the status of the most successful Swedish film of all time.

Since the days when F. Scott Fitzgerald and Ernest Hemingway bemoaned the traducing of their work by the film industry, it has been a long and honourable tradition for authors to lament the treatment of their books on screen, and crime writers have no reason to take exception to this tradition. But occasionally, a novelist will feel that some justice has been done to their work – and among that select number, the Norwegian Gunnar Staalesen has pointed out that he is (generally speaking) pleased with the adaptations of novels featuring his resourceful private eye Varg Veum. And it is certainly true that with some attention paid to both writing and direction, Staalesen's signature character has been lucky on film. In 2005, an announcement was made by the film company SF Norge (located in Norway) that they had finalised plans to produce a series of films based on the author's books. The inaugural effort, *Bitter Flowers/Bitre Blomster* enjoyed a successful cinema release in Norway. It was directed by Ulrik Imtiaz Rolfsen, who utilised an economical, stripped-down filmic language. Two years later, and (as directed by Erik Richter Strand) two more serviceable versions were made of Staalesen's original novels, capturing a great deal of the flavour and establishing the detective as a fully rounded and intriguing figure, though most of these films have been (to some extent) compromised by miscasting in certain key roles (though not Veum himself). The films were *Sleeping Beauty/Tornerose* and *Yours until Death/Din Til Døden*. Once again, the decision by the production company to employ a director with a genuinely cinematic vision paid dividends, and the capable blond Norwegian actor Trond Espen Seim managed to suggest quirky facets of the central character's tenacious mindset (though perhaps being a tad too pretty for Staalesen's gritty character). The year 2007 saw another adaptation of the writer's work, and if *Buried Dogs Don't Bite/Begravde Hunder Biter Ikke* lacked some of the panache of the earlier efforts, it was still a more than acceptable take on the original novel, one of the author's most accomplished. To some degree, the reduced ambition for the later films of the sequence were reflected in the fact that the first two adaptations were released in cinemas, while their successors made their way directly to DVD. But Gunnar Staalesen, while perfectly willing to admit that the films were not masterpieces of filmic art, remains generous in his appraisal of them. It's to be hoped that as the popularity of Scandinavian crime fiction grows it will facilitate the films (in subtitled form) acquiring a greater currency in the non-Norwegian speaking markets.

Positive word-of-mouth on a television crime series is something that all producers crave – and even if the series is not a conspicuous success on its first showing, it can glean massive cult status retrospectively, along with impressive kudos for its creators; David Simon's *The Wire* is the *locus classicus* here. And *The Wire* was almost certainly an influence on the remarkable Danish series *The Killing*, which on its British showing in 2011 quickly acquired a reputation of being the kind of show that admirers of crime series like nothing better than to proselytise about (the corollary of that, of course, is the endless apologies necessary from those who have not committed to its considerable length). And the series undoubtedly takes its time: twenty steadily paced hour-long episodes (written by Søren Sveistrup), which the arts channel BBC4 opted to show in two-episode clusters – but even this attempt at telescoping the amount of transmission time would not alter the fact that a certain degree of commitment was necessary on the part of viewers of the show. Ironically, this commitment was to become a badge of honour for those devotees boring non-initiates with the multiple reasons they should see the show, which was perhaps the most talked-about TV drama in years.

The basic premise is straightforward: the methodical investigation of the brutal killing of a young girl in a forest (shown in disturbing detail in the premier episode). Familiar territory, of course, as are the frequent personality clashes between the ill-matched duo of coppers on the case, the shortly-to-relocate Sarah Lund, who has the traditional male policeman's inability to sustain and nourish a normal family life (Sarah is played by Sofie Gråbøl in a markedly understated but commanding fashion) and her ambitious, no-nonsense successor Jan Meyer (played by Søren Malling); the former on the point of leaving her job to move to Sweden with her son to live with her inamorato, her fellow detective an abrasive and impulsive young man, anxious to take over her job and prove himself – and singularly impatient for her to leave. The dynamic between the two is played out along all-too-familiar lines, with, perhaps another overt influence apart from *The Wire* showing itself: the British writer Lynda La Plante's *Prime Suspect*, in which a highly intelligent, conflicted female detective demonstrates again and again the superiority of her instincts over those of her sexist, incompetent male colleagues (the writer is familiar with the British crime fiction field). For the first time in TV crime drama, a tongue-in-cheek cult has grown up around an item of clothing, Sarah's rarely discarded Gudrun & Gudrun knitted sweater, which resulted in massive sales for the company. But, largely speaking, the series is able to avoid the now standard politically correct setup: female = good; male = bad, though a superficial reading of the show would certainly conform to this now-embedded cliché. But it is the multiple layers of character building and the unsparing (but highly economical) evocation of Danish society that more than compensates for the relatively straightforward police procedural aspects. Danish xenophobia is also reflected in a sub-plot involving a non-Danish teacher who comes under suspicion; a character who encourages violent vigilante action in his indecisive boss stands in for many Danes here in his hostility to immigrants. There is, as in *The Wire* blueprint, a crucial political aspect represented in the character of charismatic Councillor Troels Hartmann, mesmerisingly played by Lars Mikkelsen, somehow involved in the murder investigation. This local government element is no mere window-dressing but a crucially integrated plot strand with a degree of political sophistication that leaves many a mainstream series looking thin and etiolated. And the principal theme of this plot strand – the difficulties of maintaining a fraught political coalition – had a timely resonance for Britain, experiencing just such a fractious relationship between two ill-matched parties in 2011.

The other principal factor in the low-key strategy of the series involves the murdered girl's grieving parents, notably the heavyset, terminally taciturn husband (Bjarne Henriksen), who is revealed to have a violent past, and who for some considerable time (over four hour-long episodes, in fact) appears to be inexorably moving towards vigilante action when he has identified who he thinks is the murderer and rapist of his daughter. It is possibly in this plot strand that the extremely leisurely development might be noted: for some considerable time, the viewer is presented with scene after scene of the disconsolate parents grieving for their daughter, and although all of the scenes are impeccably written and acted, they are not for the impatient, with their circumscribed advancement of the plot – it is only at the end of the fourth episode that the silently wrathful father is driving a van which contains the man he now believes to be principal suspect (what's more, the succeeding episode demonstrates that the expected violent consequences are not to happen for a time at least – the suspect is released). Of course, this readiness to test the patience of the viewer is no accident, and is absolutely integral to the strategy of the writer, which is to explode and reconstruct the short attention span dynamic of the standard police procedural with its regulation bursts of action in order to introduce something more reflective and character-driven. Few viewers who show the requisite patience will have cause for complaint, and the incidental detail (such as the sardonic attitude some of the Danes demonstrate towards their Swedish neighbours) is quietly rewarding. And the acting, too, is nonpareil, with Sofie Gråbøl in particular building the character of the nigh-obsessive Inspector Sarah Lund with the most carefully chosen, economical and subtle of means. As with Bjarne Henriksen's uncommunicative father of the dead girl, we watch closely for reactions to events and questions – and are rarely vouchsafed such easy satisfactions.

A final word on the all-conquering Scandinavian literary invasion. With such a cornucopia of writing talent (as celebrated in this volume) currently producing provocative crime fiction in the Nordic countries, the continuing rude health of the field seems guaranteed. Or does it? As this new wave gradually becomes a quotidian experience for readers from other countries, there is clearly the possibility that its current popularity will become less pronounced. However, the Nordic crime fiction phenomenon is much more than a passing literary fashion – it is based on solid, quantifiable literary achievement. The great majority of strong, authentic writing from the Nordic countries will continue to be read, long after any cachet of novelty is forgotten.

Bibliography

[Titles in brackets are alternative titles or English translations of the original titles; books listed are those mentioned in the text.]

Adler-Olsen, Jussi (1997) *Alfabethuset* (Copenhagen: Forlaget Cicero). [*The Alphabet House*]

Adler-Olsen, Jussi (2009) *Flaskepost fra P* (Copenhagen: Politikens Forlag). [*Redemption*]

Adler-Olsen, Jussi (2011) *Mercy* (London: Michael Joseph [2008]).

Alvtegen, Karin (2010) *En sannolik historia* (Stockholm: Brombergs Bokförlag). [*A Probable Story*]

Alvtegen, Karin (2003) *Missing* (Edinburgh: Canongate).

Alvtegen, Karin (2009) *Shadow* (Edinburgh: Canongate).

Auden, W.H. and Louis MacNeice (1937) *Letters from Iceland* (London: Faber and Faber).

Baksi, Kurdo (2010) *Stieg Larsson, My Friend* (London: MacLehose Press).

Bates, Quentin (2011) *Frozen Out* (London: Robinson Publishing).

Birkegaard, Mikkel (2011) *Death Sentence* (London: Black Swan).

Birkegaard, Mikkel (2009) *The Library of Shadows* (London: Black Swan).

Blaedel, Sara (2011) *Call Me Princess* (New York: Pegasus Crime).

Blaedel, Sara (2004) *Grønt støv* (Copenhagen: Lindhardt og Ringhof). [*Green Dust*]

Bondeson, Jan (2005) *Blood on the Snow: The Killing of Olof Palme* (Ithaca: Cornell University Press).

Brown, Andrew (2008) *Fishing in Utopia: Sweden and the Future that Disappeared* (London: Granta Books).

Brown, Dan (2003) *The Da Vinci Code* (London: Bantam Press).

Buchan, John (1916) *The Power-House* (Edinburgh: William Blackwood).

Bush, Peter and Kirsten Malmkjaer (eds) (1998) *Rimbaud's Rainbow: Literary Translation in Higher Education* (Amsterdam: John Benjamins Publishing Company).

Ceder, Camilla (2012) *Babylon* (London: Weidenfeld and Nicolson [2010]).

Ceder, Camilla (2010) *Frozen Moment* (London: Weidenfeld and Nicolson).

Craig, Patricia (ed) (2002) *The Oxford Book of Detective Stories* (Oxford: Oxford University Press).

Dahl, Arne (2011) *Misterioso* (New York: Pantheon Books [1999]).

Dahl, K.O. (2007) *The Fourth Man* (London: Faber and Faber [2005]).

Dahl, K.O. (2009) *The Last Fix* (London: Faber and Faber [2000]).

Dahl, K.O. (2011) *Lethal Investments* (London: Faber and Faber).

Dahl, K.O. (2008) *The Man in the Window* (London: Faber and Faber [2001]).

Davidsen, Leif (2002) *Lime's Photograph* (London: Vintage Books).

Davidsen, Leif (2007) *The Serbian Dane* (London: Arcadia Books/EuroCrime).

Davidsen, Leif (2009) *The Woman from Bratislava* (London: Arcadia Books/ EuroCrime).

Drvenkar, Zoran (2011) *Sorry* (London: Blue Door).

Dürrenmatt, Friedrich (1959) *The Pledge: Requiem for the Detective Novel* (London: Jonathan Cape).

Edwardson, Åke (2008) *Den sista vintern* (Stockholm: Norstedts förlag). [*The Final Winter*]

Edwardson, Åke (2007) *Frozen Tracks* (London: Vintage Books [2001]).

Edwardson, Åke (2006) *Never End* (London: Harvill Secker [2000]).

Edwardson, Åke (2005) *Sun and Shadow* (London: Vintage Books).

Ekman, Kerstin (1995) *Blackwater* (London: Chatto and Windus).

Ekman, Kerstin (1993) *Händelser vid vatten* (Stockholm: Albert Bonniers Förlag). [*Blackwater*]

Engelstad, Audun (2006) *Losing Streak Stories: Mapping Norwegian Film Noir* [doctoral thesis].

Enger, Thomas (2011) *Burned* (London: Faber and Faber [2010]).

Enquist, Per Olov (2002) *The Royal Physician's Visit* (London: Harvill Press).

Fossum, Karin (2010) *Bad Intentions* (London: Harvill Secker).

Fossum, Karin (2005) *Calling Out for You* (London: Harvill Press). [Original title: *The Indian Bride*]

Fossum, Karin (2002) *Don't Look Back* (London: Harvill Press [1996]).

Fossum, Karin (1995) *Evas øye* (Oslo: Cappelen Damm). [*Eve's Eye*]

Fossum, Karin (2003) *He Who Fears the Wolf* (London: Harvill Press [1997]).

Fossum, Karin (2004) *When the Devil Holds the Candle* (London: Harvill Press [1998]).

Gazan, Sissel-Jo (2011) *Dinosaur Feather* (London: Quercus).

Gerhardsen, Carin (2009) *Mamma, pappa, barn* (Stockholm: Ordfront Förlag). [*Cinderella*, Hammarby series]

Gerhardsen, Carin (2008) *Pepparkakshuset* (Stockholm: Ordfront Förlag). [*The Gingerbread House*, Hammarby series]

Gerhardsen, Carin (2010) *Vyssan lull* (Stockholm: Ordfront Förlag). [*Snips and Snails*, Hammarby series]

Gustafsson, Lars (1998) *The Tale of a Dog* (London: Harvill Press [1993]).

Highsmith, Patricia (1950) *Strangers on a Train* (London: Cresset Press).

Høeg, Peter (1993) *Miss Smilla's Feeling for Snow* (London: Collins Harvill).

Holt, Anne (2010) *1222* (London: Corvus).

Holt, Anne (1995) *Demonens død* (Oslo: Cappelen Damm). [*Death of the Demon*]

Holt, Anne (2011) *Fear Not* (London: Corvus).

Holt, Anne (2007) *The Final Murder* (London: Sphere).

Horst, Jørn Lier (2007) *Den eneste ene* (Oslo: Gyldendal Norsk Forlag). [*The Only One*]

Horst, Jørn Lier (2011) *Dregs* (Dingwall, Ross-shire: Sandstone Press).

Horst, Jørn Lier (2005) *Felicia forsvant* (Oslo: Gyldendal Norsk Forlag). [*Goodbye, Felicia*]

Horst, Jørn Lier (2006) *Når havet stilner* (Oslo: Gyldendal Norsk Forlag). [*When the Sea Calms*]

Horst, Jørn Lier (2009) *Nattmannen* (Oslo: Gyldendal Norsk Forlag). [*The Night Man*]

Horst, Jørn Lier (2004) *Nøkkelvitnet* (Oslo: Gyldendal Norsk Forlag). [*Key Witness*]

Horst, Jørn Lier and Jarl Emsell Larsen (2008) *Kodenavn Hunter* (Oslo: NRK). [*Codename Hunter*]

Indriðason, Arnaldur (2008) *Arctic Chill* (London: Harvill Secker [2005]).

Indriðason, Arnaldur (2007) *The Draining Lake* (London: Harvill Secker [2004]).

Indriðason, Arnaldur (2004) *Jar City* (London: Harvill Press [2000]). [*Tainted Blood*]

Indriðason, Arnaldur (2006) *Konungsbók* (Reykjavík: Forlagið). [*The King's Book*]

Indriðason, Arnaldur (2010) *Operation Napoleon* (London: Harvill Secker [1999]).

Indriðason, Arnaldur (2011) *Outrage* (London: Harvill Secker).

Indriðason, Arnaldur (2005) *Silence of the Grave* (London: Harvill Press [2001]).

Indriðason, Arnaldur (1997) *Synir duftsins* (Reykjavík: Forlagið). [*Sons of the Dust/ Sons of the Powder*]

Indriðason, Arnaldur (2006) *Voices* (London: Harvill Secker [2003]).

Joensuu, Matti (1986) *Harjunpää and the Stone Murders* (London: Victor Gollancz [1983]).

Joensuu, Matti (2003) *Harjunpää ja pahan pappi* (Helsinki: Kustannusosakeyhtiö Otava). [*Harjunpää and the Priest of Evil*]

Joensuu, Matti (2010) *Harjunpää ja rautahuone* (Helsinki: Kustannusosakeyhtiö Otava). [*Harjunpää and the Iron Chamber*]

Joensuu, Matti (2006) *The Priest of Evil* (London: Arcadia Books/EuroCrime).

Joensuu, Matti (2008) *To Steal her Love* (London: Arcadia Books/EuroCrime).

Joyce, James (1922) *Ulysses* (Paris: Shakespeare and Co.).

Jungersen, Christian (2006) *The Exception* (London: Weidenfeld and Nicolson).

Jungstedt, Mari (2010) *Den farliga leken* (Stockholm: Albert Bonniers Förlag). [*The Dangerous Game*]

Jungstedt, Mari (2010) *The Killer's Art* (London: Doubleday).

Kaaberbøl, Lene and Agnete Friis (2011) *The Boy in the Suitcase* (New York: Soho Crime).

Kaaberbøl, Lene and Agnete Friis (2010) *Et stille umærkeligt drab* (Copenhagen: People's Press). [*A Quiet, Unfelt Killing*]

Kallentoft, Mons (2004) *Food Noir* (Stockholm: Natur och Kultur).

Kallentoft, Mons (2011) *Midwinter Sacrifice* (London: Hodder and Stoughton).

Kallentoft, Mons (2000) *Pesetas* (Stockholm: Natur och Kultur).

Kallentoft, Mons (2008) *Sommardöden* (Stockholm: Natur och Kultur). [*Summertime Death*]

Källström, Johannes (2010) *Offerrit* (Stockholm: Massolit Förlag). [*The Irrevocable Contract*]

Kepler, Lars [Alexandra and Alexander Ahndoril] (2012) *The Executioner* (London: Blue Door). [Provisional British title; alternative title: *The Paganini Contract*]

Kepler, Lars [Alexandra and Alexander Ahndoril] (2011) *The Hypnotist* (London: Blue Door).

Kepler, Lars [Alexandra and Alexander Ahndoril] (2010) *Paganinikontraktet* (Stockholm: Albert Bonniers Förlag). [*The Executioner/The Paganini Contract*]

Kivi, Aleksis (1929) *Seven Brothers* (New York: Coward-McCann).

Koppel, Hans [(Karl) Petter Lidbeck] (2011) *Kommer aldrig mer igen* (Stockholm: Telegram Bokförlag). [*She's Never Coming Back*]

Koppel, Hans [(Karl) Petter Lidbeck] (2008) *Vi i villa* (Stockholm: Wahlström & Widstrand). [*Homemaking*]

Kristensen, Tom (2010) *Dypet* (Oslo: Aschehoug). [*The Deep*]

Läckberg, Camilla (2011) *The Gallows Bird* (London: HarperCollins [2006]).

Läckberg, Camilla (2008) *The Ice Princess* (London: HarperCollins [2002]).

Läckberg, Camilla (2009) *The Preacher* (London: HarperCollins).

Läckberg, Camilla (2010) *The Stonecutter* (London: HarperCollins [2005]).

Läckberg, Camilla (2007) *Tyskungen* (Stockholm: Bokförlaget Forum). [*The Hidden Child*]

Lang, Maria [Dagmar Lange] (1949) *Mördaren ljuger inte ensam* (Stockholm: Norstedts Förlag). [*The Murderer Does Not Tell Lies Alone*]

Lapidus, Jens (2008) *Aldrig fucka upp* (Stockholm: Wahlström & Widstrand). [*Never Fuck Up*, Stockholm Noir trilogy]

Lapidus, Jens (2011) *Easy Money* (New York: Pantheon Books). [Stockholm Noir trilogy]

Lapidus, Jens (2011) *Livet deluxe* (Stockholm: Wahlström & Widstrand). [*Life Deluxe*, Stockholm Noir trilogy]

Lapidus, Jens (2006) *Snabba Cash* (Stockholm: Wahlström & Widstrand). [*Easy Money*, Stockholm Noir trilogy]

Larsen, Michael (2000) *The Snake in Sydney* (London: Sceptre).

Larsen, Michael (1996) *Uncertainty* (London: Sceptre).

Larsson, Åsa (2008) *The Blood Spilt* (London: Penguin). [*The Blood that Was Shed*]

Larsson, Åsa (2004) *Det blod som spillts* (Stockholm: Albert Bonniers Förlag). [*The Blood Spilt/The Blood that Was Shed*]

Larsson, Åsa (2008) *The Savage Altar* (London: Penguin).

Larsson, Åsa (2003) *Solstorm* (Stockholm: Albert Bonniers Förlag). [*The Savage Altar/Sun Storm*]

Larsson, Åsa (2006) *Sun Storm* (New York: Delacorte Press). [*The Savage Altar*]

Larsson, Åsa (2011) *Until Thy Wrath Be Past* (London: MacLehose Press).

Larsson, Stieg (2009) *The Girl Who Kicked the Hornet's Nest* (London: MacLehose Press [2007]).

Larsson, Stieg (2009) *The Girl Who Played with Fire* (London: MacLehose Press [2006]).

Larsson, Stieg (2008) *The Girl with the Dragon Tattoo* (London: Quercus [2005]).

Linna, Väinö (1957) *The Unknown Soldier* (London: Collins).

Mankell, Henning (2004) *Before the Frost* (London: Harvill Press).

Mankell, Henning (2010) *Daniel* (London: Harvill Secker).

Mankell, Henning (2006) *Depths* (London: Harvill Secker [2004]).

Mankell, Henning (2001) *The Dogs of Riga* (London: Harvill Press).

Mankell, Henning (2008) *The Eye of the Leopard* (London: Harvill Secker [1990]).

Mankell, Henning (2000) *Faceless Killers* (London: Harvill Press [1991]).

Mankell, Henning (2004) *Firewall* (London: Harvill Press [1998]).

Mankell, Henning (2009) *Italian Shoes* (London: Harvill Secker).

Mankell, Henning (2007) *Kennedy's Brain* (London: Harvill Secker).

Mankell, Henning (2010) *The Man from Beijing* (London: Harvill Secker).

Mankell, Henning (2005) *The Man Who Smiled* (London: Harvill Press).

Mankell, Henning (2008) *The Pyramid* (London: Harvill Secker).

Mankell, Henning (2000) *Sidetracked* (London: Harvill Press [1995]).

Mankell, Henning (2011) *The Troubled Man* (London: Harvill Secker).

Marklund, Liza (2002) *The Bomber* (London: Pocket Books).

Marklund, Liza (2011) *Exposed* (London: Corgi).

Marklund, Liza (1995) *Gömda* (Stockholm: Bonnier Albas Förlag). [*On the Run*]

Marklund, Liza (2004) *Paradise* (London: Pocket Books).

Marklund, Liza (2006) *Prime Time* (London: Pocket Books [2002]).

Marklund, Liza (2010) *Red Wolf* (London: Corgi [2003]).

Marklund, Liza (1998) *Sprängaren* (Stockholm: Ordupplaget). [*The Bomber*]

Marklund, Liza (2002) *Studio Sex* (New York: Simon and Schuster [1999]).
Nesbø, Jo (2012) *The Bat Man* (London: Harvill Secker [1997]).
Nesbø, Jo (2005) *The Devil's Star* (London: Harvill Secker [2003]).
Nesbø, Jo (1997) *Flaggermusmannen* (Oslo: Aschehoug). [The Bat Man]
Nesbø, Jo (2011) *The Leopard* (London: Harvill Secker).
Nesbø, Jo (2008) *Nemesis* (London: Harvill Secker).
Nesbø, Jo (2006) *The Redbreast* (London: Harvill Secker [2000]).
Nesbø, Jo (2009) *The Redeemer* (London: Harvill Secker [2005]).
Nesbø, Jo (2010) *The Snowman* (London: Harvill Secker).
Nesbø, Jo (2002) *Sorgenfri* (Oslo: Aschehoug). [*Nemesis*]
Nesser, Håkan (2006) *Borkmann's Point* (London: Macmillan [1994]).
Nesser, Håkan (2010) *The Inspector and Silence* (London: Mantle).
Nesser, Håkan (2002) *Kära Agnes!* (Stockholm: Månpocket). [*Dear Agnes*]
Nesser, Håkan (2009) *Maskarna på Carmine Street* (Stockholm: Albert Bonniers Förlag). [*The Worms on Carmine Street*]
Nesser, Håkan (2008) *The Mind's Eye* (London: Macmillan).
Nesser, Håkan (2007) *The Return* (London: Macmillan [1995]).
Nesser, Håkan (2009) *Woman with Birthmark* (London: Macmillan [1996]).
Nestingen, Andrew (2008) *Crime and Fantasy in Scandinavia: Fiction, Film, and Social Change* (Seattle: University of Washington Press).
Ohlsson, Kristina (2011) *Änglavakter* (Stockholm: Piratförlaget). [*Guarded by Angels*]
Ohlsson, Kristina (2009) *Askungar* (Stockholm: Piratförlaget). [*Unwanted*]
Ohlsson, Kristina (2012) *The Daisy* (London: Simon and Schuster).
Ohlsson, Kristina (2010) *Tusenskönor* (Stockholm: Piratförlaget). [*The Daisy*]
Ohlsson, Kristina (2011) *Unwanted* (London: Simon and Schuster).
Patterson, James and Liza Marklund (2010) *Postcard Killers* (London: Century).
Persson, Leif (2011) *Between Summer's Longing and Winter's End* (London: Doubleday [2010]).
Proust, Marcel (1913–1927) *À la Recherche du Temps Perdu* (Paris: Bernard Grasset).
Ridpath, Michael (2010) *Where the Shadows Lie* (London: Corvus).
Roslund, Anders and Borge Hellström (2005) *The Beast: A Novel* (London: Little, Brown and Company).
Roslund, Anders and Borge Hellström (2008) *Box 21* (London: Abacus). [*The Vault*]
Roslund, Anders and Borge Hellström (2011) *Cell 8* (London: Quercus).
Roslund, Anders and Borge Hellström (2007) *Edward Finnigans upprättelse* (Stockholm: Pocketförlaget). [*Cell 8*]
Roslund, Anders and Borge Hellström (2010) *Three Seconds* (London: Quercus).
Rygg, Pernille (2004) *The Butterfly Effect* (London: Vintage Books [1995]).
Rygg, Pernille (2003) *The Golden Section* (London: Harvill Press [1997]).
Salama, Hannu (1964) *Juhannustanssit* (Helsinki: Kustannusosakeyhtiö Otava). [*Midsummer Dances*]
Scheen, Kjersti (2002) *Final Curtain* (London: Arcadia Books/EuroCrime).
Selmer-Geeth, Harald (1904) *Min första bragd* (Helsingfors: Söderströms Förlag). [*My First Case*]
Sigurðardóttir, Yrsa (2010) *Ashes to Dust* (London: Hodder and Stoughton).
Sigurðardóttir, Yrsa (2011) *The Day is Dark* (London: Hodder and Stoughton).
Sigurðardóttir, Yrsa (2008) *Last Rituals* (London: Hodder and Stoughton [2005]).
Sigurðardóttir, Yrsa (2009) *My Soul to Take* (London: Hodder and Stoughton [2006]).

Sjöwall, Maj and Per Wahlöö (1973) *The Abominable Man* (London: Gollancz [1971]).

Sjöwall, Maj and Per Wahlöö (1971) *The Laughing Policeman* (London: Gollancz [1968]).

Sjöwall, Maj and Per Wahlöö (1970) *The Man Who Went Up in Smoke* (London: Gollancz [1966]).

Staalesen, Gunnar (1986) *At Night All Wolves Are Grey* (London: Quartet Books [1983]).

Staalesen, Gunnar (1993) *Begravde hunder biter ikke* (Oslo: Gyldendal Norsk Forlag). [*Buried Dogs Don't Bite*]

Staalesen, Gunnar (1991) *Bitre blomster* (Oslo: Gyldendal Norsk Forlag). [*Bitter Flowers*]

Staalesen, Gunnar (2009) *The Consorts of Death* (London: Arcadia Books/ EuroCrime).

Staalesen, Gunnar (1979) *Din til døden* (Oslo: Gyldendal Norsk Forlag). [*Yours until Death*]

Staalesen, Gunnar (1980) *Tornerose sov i hundre år* (Oslo: Gyldendal Norsk Forlag). [*Sleeping Beauty*]

Staalesen, Gunnar (2010) *Vi skal arve vinden* (Oslo: Gyldendal Norsk Forlag). [*We Shall Inherit the Wind*]

Staalesen, Gunnar (2004) *The Writing on the Wall* (London: Arcadia Books/ EuroCrime [1995]).

Staalesen, Gunnar (2009) *Yours until Death* (London: Arcadia Books/EuroCrime).

Tegenfalk, Stefan (2009) *Vredens Tid* (Stockholm: Massolit Förlag). [*Anger Mode*]

Theorin, Johan (2009) *The Darkest Room* (London: Doubleday).

Theorin, Johan (2008) *Echoes from the Dead* (London: Doubleday [2007]).

Theorin, Johan (2011) *The Quarry* (London: Doubleday).

Theorin, Johan (2007) *Skumtimmen* (Stockholm: Wahlström & Widstrand). [*Echoes from the Dead/In the Twilight Hour*]

Tolkien, J.R.R. (1954) *The Lord of the Rings* (London: Allen and Unwin).

Tursten, Helene (1998) *Den krossade tanghästen* (Gothenburg: Anamma).

Tursten, Helene (2010) *Den som vakar i mörkret* (Stockholm: Piratförlaget). [*The One Who Watches in the Dark*]

Tursten, Helene (2003) *Detective Inspector Huss* (New York: Soho Crime).

Tursten, Helene (1999) *Tatuerad torso* (Gothenburg: Anamma). [*Tattooed Torso/ The Torso*]

Tursten, Helene (2007) *The Torso* (New York: Soho Crime).

Venuti, Lawrence (1994) *The Translator's Invisibility: The History of Translation* (Abingdon: Routledge).

Wagner, Jan Costin (2006) *Ice Moon* (London: Harvill Secker).

Wagner, Jan Costin (2002) *Nachtfahrt* (Frankfurt: Eichborn). [*Night Trip*]

Wagner, Jan Costin (2010) *Silence* (London: Harvill Secker).

Wagner, Jan Costin (2011) *The Winter of the Lions* (London: Harvill Secker).

Waltari, Mika (1949) *The Egyptian* (New York: G.P. Putnam's Sons).

Waltari, Mika (1956) *The Etruscan* (New York: G.P. Putnam's Sons).

Waltari, Mika (1951) *The Wanderer* (New York: G.P. Putnam's Sons).

Wambaugh, Joseph (1975) *The Choirboys* (New York: Delacorte Press).

Westö, Kjell (2005) *Lang* (London: Harvill Press).

Index